One of *Esquire*'s Best H

One of *Vulture*'s Best H

One of Tor Nightfire's Horror Books
We're Excited About in 2022

One of *Den of Geek*'s Best New Horror Books
in September 2022

A September 2022 LibraryReads Pick

An October 2022 Indie Next Pick

"A Gothic-punk graveyard tale . . . an addicting read that
draws you into its descent from the first page." —CHUCK WENDIG,
New York Times best-selling author of *The Book of Accidents*

"Reads like a scared straight program that horrifies you into
choosing life." —GRADY HENDRIX, *New York Times* best-selling author
of *How to Sell a Haunted House*

"A terrifying meditation of the horrors of modern life and
our collective fixation with death. . . . But be warned: follow
Chapman down this rabbit hole and you will see dead people."
—ALMA KATSU, author of *The Fervor*

"Chapman weaves hair-raising, goosebump-inducing horror
through a sharp exploration of loss, addiction, and grim
history. Haunting guaranteed."
—RACHEL HARRISON, author of *Such Sharp Teeth*

"A dark, gripping tale that is by turns snarky, horrifying,
and brutal—this book is as good as modern horror gets."
—JOHN HORNOR JACOBS, author of *A Lush and Seething Hell*

"A legitimately terrifying ghost story. . . . Should make Clay McLeod Chapman a star." —*VULTURE*

Erin hasn't been able to set a single boundary with her charismatic but reckless college ex-boyfriend, Silas. When he asks her to bail him out of rehab—again—she knows she needs to cut him off. But days after he gets out, Silas turns up dead of an overdose in their hometown of Richmond, Virginia, and Erin's world falls apart.

Then a friend tells her about Ghost, a new drug that allows users to see the dead. *Wanna get haunted?* he asks. Grieving and desperate for closure with Silas, Erin agrees to a pill-popping "séance." But the drug has unfathomable side effects—and once you take it, you can never go back.

ghost
eaters

A NOVEL

CLAY McLEOD CHAPMAN

QUIRK BOOKS
PHILADELPHIA

for M

Copyright © 2022 by Clay McLeod Chapman
Excerpt copyright © 2023 by Clay McLeod Chapman
Discussion questions copyright © 2023 by Quirk Productions, Inc.

First paperback edition, Quirk Books 2023
Originally published by Quirk Books in 2022

Library of Congress Cataloging-in-Publication Data
Names: Chapman, Clay McLeod, author.
Title: Ghost eaters : a novel / Clay McLeod Chapman.
Description: Philadelphia : Quirk Books, [2022] | Summary: "Erin and her friends
   from college, now in their mid-twenties, are shaken by the death of Silas, one of their
   own. They are plunged into a waking nightmare when they take a pill Silas learned
   of that allows them to see—and interact with—ghosts"—Provided by publisher.
Identifiers: LCCN 2021062505 (print) | LCCN 2021062506 (ebook) | ISBN
   9781683692171 (hardcover) | ISBN 9781683692188 (ebook)
Classification: LCC PS3603.H36 G46 2022 (print) | LCC PS3603.H36 (ebook) |
   DDC 813/.6—dc23
LC record available at https://lccn.loc.gov/2021062505
LC ebook record available at https://lccn.loc.gov/2021062506

ISBN: 978-1-68369-378-9

Printed in the United States of America

Typeset in Bembo

Designed by Andie Reid
Cover photo by Jakub Krechowicz / Shutterstock
Production management by John J. McGurk

Quirk Books
215 Church Street
Philadelphia, PA 19106
quirkbooks.com

10 9 8 7 6 5 4 3 2

Branches they bore of that enchanted stem,
Laden with flower and fruit, whereof they gave
To each, but whoso did receive of them
And taste, to him the gushing of the wave
Far far away did seem to mourn and rave
On alien shores; and if his fellow spake,
His voice was thin, as voices from the grave. . . .

—ALFRED TENNYSON, "THE LOTOS-EATERS"

Behold, if the plague be spread in the house,
it is a fretting leprosy in the house: it is unclean.

—LEVITICUS 14:44

contents

PROLOGUE

a ghost story

three years ago

Tripping our asses off in the cemetery is Silas's idea. We dose back at his dorm to give the acid a head start. By the time we abandon campus and hop the wrought-iron fence surrounding Hollywood Cemetery, the four of us are all well on our way to peak fry.

"What're we doing what're we doing," Amara keeps repeating under her breath, a giddy litany. "What're we doing what're we—"

"Remember your partners," Silas whispers as he scales the fence first. He just high-jumps those spikes like a grave-robbing Olympian. Now *that's* some gold-medal trespassing.

Poor Tobias can't seem to find a foothold on the fence. His tattered Vans keep slipping, reminding me of that puny kid on the playground who doesn't have the upper body strength to pull himself up the monkey bars on his own. He's too embarrassed to ask for help, shooing Silas's hand away whenever he offers it. "I got it, I got it," he keeps muttering.

Amara and I are the only ones left on the street, so we plant our hands on Tobias's scrawny ass and heave-ho him over. I can literally feel the bone in his butt cheek as we push. From where I'm standing, it looks like he takes flight for a moment, just a beanpole of a bat flapping his wings through the bruised purple sky.

Amara is next. She starts to shriek, practically impaling herself on one of the rusted spears. We all shush her—try to, at least, in between laughing our asses off. She flips over the fence and falls flat on her face. It's far too dark for me to see her land—Silas won't let us use the flashlights on our phones—so there's a hot second where I worry if Amara's cracked her skull open on a tombstone or something. But she's cackling like an absolute candyflipping witch, rolling around in the grass, so we know she's still breathing.

"Come on, Erin." Silas beckons through the bars. He's gripping them with both hands, leaning his face through the gap. He's a convict and I've come to break him out. "Your turn."

I can't help myself. His face is right there. Lips *right there*. I lean in and kiss him through the fence. Flecks of rust dig into my cheeks, smearing my makeup. Here comes the lockjaw.

"Jesus, guys," Amara whispers-but-not-really-whispers. "Get a tomb already."

Suddenly I'm second-guessing myself: *I can't climb over this.* What if I lose my footing and fall on one of those spikes?

"Easy does it," Silas says. "I got you."

Silas and Tobias each grab a foot and hoist me up while I pull on the top rail. Imagine a cheerleader pyramid, where these two strapping young lads lift me over their heads and I perform the most absolutely fucking perfect hip-over-head airborne tumble you've ever seen, both feet landing directly on a headstone, a total *Bring It On* crowd-goes-wild dismount.

You'd be wrong. I land on my ass. Hard.

Silas hovers just above me. "You okay?"

"I think I broke my hip."

"You'll live," Silas says. "Take my hand."

Silas says hop on one foot.

Silas says pat your head.
Touch your nose.
. . . Silas didn't say.

The four of us take in the meandering rows of tombstones tilting like loose teeth. The cemetery's called Hollywood because a few Richmond natives became celebrities way back whenever, returning home only after they kicked the bucket to get buried in their native soil. Everyone returns to Richmond someday. Mostly this place is full of dead Confederates, but there are a few forgotten starlets in the ground. Tourists take photos next to their gaudy graves—but tonight, hours after the cemetery gates close and the only occupants are six feet under, all 135 acres of this place belong to us.

"Follow me," Silas says. "Watch your step."

Tobias trips on cue. Tripping while tripping, *hardy har*. He's practically blind on the best of days, even with his wire-rimmed specs. Swap out the daylight for some liquid sunshine and add a few granite stumbling blocks and it's no wonder he can't stay on his feet.

"Where are we going?" I have to ask.

"You'll see."

Silas never tells us what he's got hidden up his sleeve. That would ruin the surprise, wouldn't it? He has this uncanny ability to rally the troops, enlist the rest of us to do just about whatever he wants—and what he wants most out of life is to *gogogogo*. His lust for life is addictive and thrilling and downright exhausting all at once. Who cares if we have to wake up tomorrow morning for class? Haven't we realized academia is merely for sheep? Silas says we're better than all the other undergrad lemmings, and who are we to argue? Sounds good to me. He can somehow convince us to forget our inhibitions, to lose ourselves in the white heat of the moment. To hop trains in the dead of night. To embark on random road trips with no destination. To take jaunts through haunted plantations that last until the sun rises over the abandoned tobacco fields.

This city is ours, he always says. The Four Musketeers. All for one and one for Silas . . .

We found each other through our mutual admiration for post-modern authors during our freshman fiction writing workshop. Paul Auster cosplay, basically. Silas wants to be David Foster Wallace, bandana and all. Tobias called dibs on DeLillo. Amara has an unhealthy obsession with Pynchon, so she claimed him. Silas said I had a Lethem streak in me, but I've never read him. *L'eggo my Eggers*, I said, hoping to sound pithy. *I'm ready to be the world's first Erin Hill.* The literary world was our oyster and Silas made me feel like I was its black pearl.

"Something bit me." Amara groans as she smacks her palm against her bare shoulder. Figures she didn't dress appropriately for grave robbing. "How much further?"

"Almost there."

"Can you just tell us where we're going? I'm getting eaten alive out here."

"Patience," Silas says. "Good things come to those who wait . . ."

A cherub perched on a pillar twists its neck toward me just as I pass it. I stop to make sure, staring at the chubby naked baby with brittle wings. Its washed-out eyes blink back.

Oh, good, I'm not just imagining it. Glad I cleared that up.

Its chiseled features have been sanded down, all the decades of rain and cold weather erasing its face to a gray plane. But it still has its eyelids, opening and closing over two slopes of stone, a pair of rotten eggs stuffed in its sockets. The headstone is too small for an adult.

Oooh, shit . . . A baby is buried here. Did I just say that out loud? I can't tell for sure. I run my hand across the tomb, tracing every letter with my fingertips like I'm reading braille:

LONNIE NADLER. GOD'S LENT CHILD.

"Erin?" Silas takes hold of my arm, bringing me back. "You okay?"

"Yeah."

"You sure?"

"Uh-huh."

"Stay with me," he says, taking my hand and leading me through the undulating row of graves—and in my head, I think it's in my head, I say *stay with me, stay with me, stay.*

The headstones won't keep still. The marble flexes. Tombstones turn my way as I walk by. They may as well be dancing toadstools, their inscribed umbrella caps bopping along—

BELOVED WIFE. IN LOVING MEMORY. GONE TOO SOON. ABSENT IN BODY, PRESENT IN SPIRIT.

I just have to keep cool. Breathe in deep. Don't freak.

"What're we doing," Amara keeps reciting. "What're we doing what're we doing . . ."

We're pushing our personal boundaries, I imagine Silas might say. *We're living life to its fullest. We're turning this city into our own personal playground and howling at the moon.* But he keeps quiet, silently guiding us through the bopping headstones.

Tobias won't talk. Won't peek out from his shell. The acid isn't helping, I can tell. I don't want to know what personal horror movie is projecting across the inside of his skull right now.

But I don't care. My world is me and Silas. My hand in his. He's leading me along, always my guide. I don't know if my feet are touching the ground anymore. I could be a balloon, for all I know. My arm is a string and Silas is running through the cemetery while I whip in the wind.

"Here we are," he says, stopping before a mausoleum that seems to be some bizarro cross section of Masonic and Egyptian architecture. The concrete is covered in kudzu—nope, scratch that. It's spray paint. I have to squint to make out what's scrawled across the vault. Even then, the warped words don't want to keep still long enough for me to read them. All I can make out is—

RISE, REVENANT OF RICHMOND, RISE!

The gate to the tomb should be locked—shouldn't it?—but Silas pries it open no problem, hinges giving in with a rusted wail that echoes throughout the rest of the cemetery.

"No fucking way," Amara says. "I'm not going in there. There are spiders!"

"Then wait outside," Silas says. "You're on lookout."

The mausoleum swallows Silas right up. Tobias ducks his head in next, as if he's Silas's lost shadow, careful not to clock his noggin against the top of the doorway.

Wait for me, I imagine Silas's shadow saying, *wait for meeeee!*

Amara looks at me. At this point in our friendship, the two of us have perfected our psychic abilities, communicating with one another strictly through brain waves.

Are you really going to do this? she asks with her eyes, her voice coming in loud and clear in my head.

I, uh . . . guess so? We've come this far, you know?

The fuck, Erin? She's not pleased, clearly. *For real?*

Come with me!

No, no way.

Fine. Party pooper. I duck into the mausoleum and immediately feel the drop in temperature. The chill is thick. It seeps through my skin, reaching deep, all the way to the bone.

I have a quick minute to myself while Silas and Tobias plot together and Amara confronts the massive expanse of slumbering corpses just beneath her feet outside.

I do what I always do in moments like these: I pull out my Sharpie from my pocket and find a free spot on the wall. The inhabitant of this mausoleum will forgive me one small indiscretion, considering the countless others who have already thrown up their own graffiti. Couples have scribbled their names: PAUL + HANNA 4-EVA. A few rudimentary pentagrams. Loopy-lettered tags: ZOMBI. LONG LIVE VIDEO FAN. GHOSTBUSTAZ.

My contribution is relatively simple in comparison:

ERIN IS HERE

Present tense. Not past. I'm leaving a little part of myself behind. I'll always be here.

"Jesus, it's freeeezing," Amara squeals behind me. She can never be alone for long. She knows this, I know this. Silas *definitely* knows this. She can't stand being by herself. She slides up next to me and threads her arm through mine, shivering. "Miss me?"

"Always," I say. The two of us hunch together in our ringside seats to Silas's séance.

"Everybody sit in a circle," he says.

He's brought candles. Of course he has. His backpack is like a one-stop shop for all your supernatural needs. He pulls out the appropriate paraphernalia and gets to illuminating.

"I'm not sitting on somebody's grave," Amara snipes—and for once I don't disagree with her. I can hear the chitinous limbs of insects flexing all around us. Some mile-long centipede is winding up my leg and it won't stop, no matter how many times I try swatting at it. *I'm coming for your coooch*, the centipede utters as it rounds the bend. *Coochie-coochie-coooo!*

"Come on," Silas says, snapping me out of it. "Mr. Pool won't mind."

"Who's that?" I ask.

"Ever hear of W. W. Pool? Some call him the Richmond vampire, but that's just bullshit. He's really a revenant."

Amara's snort reverberates through the tight confines of the crypt.

"Sorry," she says. "What's a . . . a reve-whatever . . ."

"Revenant. Someone trapped between the living and dead."

"Poor him," I say, my focus drifting to the liquid-like shadows cast by the candles. I don't feel any wind but they certainly seem to be flickering from some external force, rippling outward.

"Give me a hand," Silas says to Tobias while running his fingers along the crypt's marble shutter.

Tobias hops to it without protest. "Yeah, okay." It's the most I've heard him talk all night.

Silas says help me break into this tomb.

Silas says help me dig up this grave.

Silas says . . .

"Um," Amara starts, "what're you doing?"

"I just need to get his tongue."

"I'm sorry, what? Come the fuck again?"

"They say if you can cut out a revenant's tongue, you can speak to the dead." Silas says it so matter-of-factly, as if this is the most normal thing in the world.

"Nope," Amara says. Her voice bounces off the mausoleum walls. "Goodnight, I'm out."

"A little too late to back out now, don't you think?"

"Are you kidding? You never told us we were gonna be chopping off crusty body parts!"

"Would you have come if I had?"

"Hell no!"

I watch from the sidelines as Amara and Silas continue to bicker.

"And why exactly did we have to drop acid for this?" Amara asks.

"Why not?" is Silas's answer. Always his answer. "It helps with the spiritual connection. There's somebody I want to talk to."

His mother, I think. Silas doesn't say her name out loud. He doesn't have to. We all know she passed away when he was nine years old. He freely shares that she'd been in a car accident, but I'm the only one who knows Silas was buckled in the backseat when a sixteen-wheeler smashed into their Toyota Matrix on the interstate. Silas told me about their vehicle spiraling through the air, how he lost himself in the vertigo of the moment, how he remembered watching his mother's hair whip around, fanning around her face as her neck twisted . . . and twisted. Suddenly they were staring at each other, his mother's bloodshot eyes peering into the backseat through the gap in the headrest, her chin perched between her shoulder blades. Her spinal column had curlicued to the point of near decapitation. The only thing keeping her head physically attached to the rest of her was her corkscrewed skin.

Not that it stopped her from talking. *She looked so confused. She didn't understand what was happening to her. She was already dead by then, but she was still talking to me. Telling me everything was going to be all right. That I was going to be okay. That she loved me.*

Silas walked away from the wreck without a scratch. *A miracle*, he said. That's when he started believing in ghosts. Always chasing after his mother.

The mausoleum wall has crumbled along the corner. All it takes are a few swift kicks administered by Silas's heel for it to give away. The rock disintegrates, exposing a casket inside.

"Fuck this," Amara moans. "Fuuuck this so muuch."

"You take that side," Silas instructs Tobias. "Just help me pull."

The boys are busy busting out some Podunk Dracula or whatever the hell Silas called him, leaving me and Amara to wig out. We both know this is fucked. Amara doesn't need to convince me, but she'll blame me because she can't blame bulletproof Silas, and of course she'd never blame herself.

My attention drifts toward the mausoleum entrance. To the dark pressing in.

". . . Guys?" Nobody pays attention to me. "Guys!"

"What?" Silas asks. "What is it?"

"Ghosts" is all I can say as I point to the doorway. The cemetery is full of them. Orbs of light wash over the graves. They're drawing near. Floating our way.

"You see them too, right?" I whisper. "Please tell me you see them."

"What are they?" Amara asks, awestruck.

"Run," Silas says.

Silas says . . .

Silas says . . .

Silas grabs my wrist and yanks. My arm snaps taut before the rest of my body is whisked out of the tomb. I can't look away from the balls of light bouncing through the rows of graves, the ghosts stretching their spectral bodies out farther and farther.

Wait. Those aren't ghosts.

Flashlights. We're being chased by cemetery security. Well, fuck a duck. We're booking it through the world's most impossible obstacle course. I count three beams behind me. There's more of us than there are of them, which means maybe one of us will be lucky enough to survive the night.

"Go go go!" Silas shouts over his shoulder.

Amara screams. She's done for, I know it. There's no way she's going to make it. I'll bail her out later, I promise myself. My parents will fork over the money to spring her from jail. Can you even bail a pal out on your Amex?

Tobias takes the lead. He doesn't even look back. Fucking long-legged gazelle in drain-pipe jeans. He's leaping over graves like his life depends on it. *Oh shit oh shit oh shit*, he pants between each pump of his legs before banking left and vanishing among the headstones. Good as ghosted.

Silas hasn't let go of my wrist, thank god. I'd be done for without him leading the way, guiding me through the endless maze of graves. I'm thinking far too linearly to be running for my life right now. I want to run straight while the headstones won't stay in a single-file line.

The cherubs cheer us on, clapping their tiny hands. A granite angel solemnly shakes her head. I can't help but think of my mom, how disappointed she'd be in me right now.

"Run faster," Silas says. "Come on, Erin!"

He yanks my arm to the left and it nearly pops out of its socket. Before I can see where I'm falling, we land on the ground. Blades of grass scratch my neck. Silas presses his palm over my mouth and I know I'm supposed to be still, be quiet, but everything inside me is shrieking.

A grave. We're lying on someone's grave, hiding behind their tombstone.

I'm trying so hard to hold my breath as a rent-a-cop waddles right on by, key chain jangling. Silas and I cling to each other and squeeze, compressing our bodies together to fit behind the headstone. Even after the guard passes us, we don't move until we know for certain the coast is clear.

"Think we can make a break for it?" he asks. I inhale Silas's words. I can taste them on my tongue. The sun will be coming up in a couple hours. We could run or we could . . .

"Stay." I kiss him so hard that the back of his head hits marble but he doesn't pull away. I run my fingers through his hair and can feel dead leaves tangled within it. "Stay with me."

I want to keep hidden within the shadow of the tombstone, our heads pressed against it, chests rising and falling with every frantic breath, hearts never settling, inhales tethering together until we've syncopated our exhales, breathing in and out in unison, sharing a pair of lungs.

My hand wanders down his chest and lands on his pants.

"What're you doing?" he asks.

"What do you think?"

"You sure? I don't have any protection on me."

"Yes."

"We have to keep quiet."

"Very quiet," I whisper.

Silas's hand runs down my waist. That's his hand, isn't it? It takes a moment for me to realize those aren't the infinitesimal legs of a centipede lockstepping their way across my skin.

I need to focus on his body. Focus on his flesh. Focus on his hands. I can feel the coarseness of his fingertips as they tunnel beneath my shirt—and for just a moment, I slip out of reality. They're not his fingers anymore but the squiggly insects that call these coffins home, that squirm through the muck and mud and feast on the flesh of every last corpse in this godforsaken cemetery. Long forgotten starlets. The corpses of dead Confederate generals.

And now me. I'm next. I have this stupid poem running through my head from when I was a kid—*the worms crawl in, the worms crawl out, the worms play pinochle on your snout*—and now that I've thought it, I can't un-think it.

The worms crawl in, the worms crawl out—

Silas's fingers burrow their way into my body.

worms crawl in—

I know I'm just buckling under a bad trip, but it doesn't stop the worms from foraging through my skin. I need to stay focused. Follow Silas through.

worms crawl out—

Silas's lips mash into mine, but his lips aren't lips, they're maggots. I feel one slip in and tumble upon my tongue, down my throat.

worms play—

My zipper exhales. Silas has found what he's looking for. What I've offered. I just have to work through the trip. If I keep my eyes closed, it won't be so bad. I just have to hold on to Silas.

Hold on . . .

Hold . . .

Now I hear them. All of them below. The dead. We must have woken them. Agitated their eternal slumber. Now they're moving around, tumbling in their caskets, awake and aware of us writhing above them. I can hear the creaking of their brittle fists and I can't stop myself from picturing them all jacking off just underneath us, hundreds of bones draped in papery husks, buffeting against the tight confines of their coffins.

We've raised the dead. Every last gasp, every slipping sigh that escapes my mouth must send them into a frenzy. They're cheering Silas on with their parched voices, *Go go go!*

They want me.

I can't feel Silas anymore. The second he releases himself inside me, his body loses all of its contours. The entirety of his physical being bursts over me and the thing I'm holding in my arms is no longer flesh but a knot of worms, all of them tangled into one another, writhing against my skin, working their way through me and over me and oh god they won't stop squirming they're feeding on me *crawling in crawling out playing pinochle on my snout.*

losing a friend

datestone

I can't pick up a pulse. There's no responsiveness. No breath. Vitals all point toward a code blue. It's going to take a second for the defibrillator to charge up and that's a second I don't have. I'm losing him. I can launch into CPR, but I usually save that for the end of the night.

"I hear they've got good chicken wings," Tanner says.

I should just call it. Announce the time of death on this blind date, bag it and tag it before happy hour ends—but no, I'm not giving up. No one dies tonight. Not on my watch.

The waiter finally arrives with my G&T, not a moment too soon. Every sip counts here, so I quickly apply the pads—*Clear!*—hoping to jolt some life back into this conversation.

"So," I start.

"So," he echoes, drumming his fingers against the table.

Nothing. Still can't hear a heartbeat. I ask the waiter to prep another round of epinephrine, raising my already half-empty glass, the swirling ice *clink-clink*ing inside.

"How do you know Amara?" I ask.

"Catering."

"You're in catering?"

"No, no. She was catering this thing my company was sponsoring."

"*Your* company? I didn't know you—"

"The company I work for." I think he just blushed. Check out those cheeks! Is Tanner getting sheepish on me? "I spotted her on her smoke break. She got me high in the parking lot."

Sounds about right. "Amara to the rescue!" I lift my glass in a salute.

"She told me she had a friend she thought I'd be a good match for and . . ."

". . . Here we are." I'm surprised that Amara would think Tanner was the right call for me. He's cute but plushie. Not a tattoo on him. Probably gets carded all the time, which no doubt embarrasses him. His clothes are crisp, right off the rack. His cologne competes with the juniper berries in my gin but he bathed, so he's already a step ahead of the dudes in band tees I tend to cycle through. Plus he knows how to make a reservation.

"You know what this building used to be?" I ask.

"Should I?"

"This used to be part of a plantation house. We're sitting in the slave quarters."

I watch Tanner's Adam's apple take the plunge.

"Most of the house burned down way before the Civil War. This is all that's left. The kitchen was on the ground floor. The kitchen slaves slept upstairs, came down to cook for their masters, and then went back upstairs at the end of the day. They hardly ever left the house."

I look out the nearest window onto Foushee Street. The rest of the block was developed into apartments decades back, but nobody knocked this particular building down—this two-story testament to Richmond's illustrious history. You can ignore it without trying too hard. There's a stone engraved with the date 1797 near the entrance, hinting at the building's past but never describing it outright. Tanner walked by without so much as a glance.

My eyes scan the dining room. Limited seating; ten tables, each occupied by posh patrons. All white. We're the youngest customers by far. This place just opened so Tanner must've pulled a few strings to get us a res. He's trying hard to impress me, but from the petrified look on his face I can tell he has no idea of the place's heritage.

That's Richmond for you. Everywhere you step, there's another history lesson just under your feet. This whole city's a graveyard. You're standing on graves no matter where you go.

"Wow . . . I had no idea. Is that on the restaurant's website or . . . ?"

I decide to let him off the hook. "I've always been fascinated with Richmond's history. I took a course in college and just kinda kept at it." I'm not going to go into how enslaved cooks were a point of culinary pride for their masters, that the fried okra appetizer going for fifteen bucks, not to mention the rest of this overpriced menu, has its roots in the esculent traditions of the slaves who cooked for these Richmond dynasties.

"You're a closeted historian? I should be taking notes, shouldn't I?"

This isn't the best blind date banter. I could simply tell Tanner I prefer not to be defined by my career, which is to say I'm currently in between jobs, gunning for a spot at a lauded advertising agency while spending the summer dicking around at my dad's law firm as his most prized social media manager. But I'm not here to brag about my office accomplishments, am I?

"I'm a serial killer, actually."

Tanner locks eyes with me as if this is the first time he sees me.

"Amara and I have this routine"—I continue to fuck with him, now that I have his undivided attention—"she selects rando guys she finds at these catering gigs and gets them stoned, then she'll casually mention she's got this friend who she thinks would make a great fit. Then I wine 'em and dine 'em, get them tipsy enough to lower their guard, lure them back to an undisclosed location where Amara waits, and we chop them into tiny pieces together."

Tanner doesn't blink. "That's . . . not what I was expecting."

"Trust me"—I lean in and whisper—"they never do."

"So . . ." He leans forward, elbows on the table. "What do you do with the bodies?"

I'm warming up to this guy. "Disassemble them, of course. Dump them in the James."

"Makes sense." He smiles. It's a nice smile, I'll give him that. "But you can't just dump them all in one place. You gotta, like, sprinkle them around a bit. Spread them out."

Tanner has joined in the fun, ladies and gents. "You've done this before, haven't you?"

"Me? Nah . . . My brother was butchered by a pair of serial killers."

"Oh no! I had no idea."

"It's all good. I've spent the last year tracking down his murderers. Avenging his death."

"And you found me! This must be fate."

He laughs. A genuine laugh. I see him for the first time, what he must've looked like as a child. "Meant to be, right?"

And there it is. It's faint, but I can feel it now. A heartbeat. The ECG picks up the pulse, just the slightest blip on the monitor.

This date may not be so dead after all. "Okay," I say. "You can live. For now."

"*Whew.*"

My phone vibrates. I assume it's Amara checking in. My ribs seize when I see it's Silas. *Not now.* I flip my phone over and wade back into our conversation. "So. Ever been on a blind date before?"

"Not really. You?"

"No." Richmond is small enough that one's romantic past is public record. You have to leap out of your own social circle to meet someone who doesn't play in a band with an ex.

"So why'd you come?" Tanner asks.

For the pulse. The quickening heartbeat. I'm bored with my taste in men and, at twenty-four, it's high time I break free from my bad habits. I'm that fish crawling out from the primordial ooze of my past relationships, ready to shed these exes and walk on my own two feet.

To breathe. I need to evolve out of my disastrous love life.

"Amara's got a pretty good sixth sense for guys, so I trust her judgment," I lie.

"How's her sixth sense working tonight?"

"Reply hazy," I say, doing my best Magic 8–Ball impression. "Ask again later."

Tanner's got his fair share of charm, but I'm not totally sold on a second date. I won't ghost, though. I'm here to, as Amara pleaded, *expand my horizons.* I need to leave my comfort zone of scruffy drummers and embrace the unknown. No more guitarists. No more suburban revolutionaries in keffiyehs. I never would've agreed to a blind date if Amara hadn't outright begged. She's like a cat who brought me a dead bird, offering up its bleeding corpse in her mouth. *Look, I caught you a tech bro!*

"So." Tanner clears his throat, snapping me back. "Amara says you're a community organizer?"

That's the best she could come up with? Jesus, I'm surprised he agreed to see *me.*

"In college," I manage. "Not so much anymore. I used to do a lot of work with local nonprofits that focused on addressing prejudices within the university system—"

Tanner's eyes cloud over.

"—helped coordinate the social media campaign for—"

I'm losing him again. He's flatlining on me.

"Do you mind if we skip over the job talk? Even *I'm* getting bored listening to myself."

Tanner comes back to life. "You wanna jump straight to the dirty laundry?"

"Yeah. Go for broke, right? Tell me something you'd *never* tell anyone on a first date."

"Sounds too risky for my blood."

"Come on. What've you got to lose?"

"Okay, you're on." Tanner's being a good sport. "Ladies first."

"How chivalrous." It takes a moment to come up with something worthwhile. Something devastatingly honest. "Okay. Here we go. Ready?"

"Ready."

"I was . . ." Deep breath. "A pageant girl."

"Get out."

"Little Miss Confederacy. I was a JonBenét Barbie, complete with the pastel cowgirl hat. Every yearbook picture of me looks like a Glamour Shots spread." I cringe just thinking about it, but Tanner's tickled.

"I don't believe you."

"It's true!"

"I'm sorry, but I call bullshit."

"Why would I lie?"

"I just can't see it. Got any proof? I want photographic evidence."

"Not on your life." I don't tell him I snapped every tiara I ever won on my tenth birthday. Mom discovered the pile of jewel-encrusted bones in the center of my bedroom. She still hasn't forgiven me. All those rhinestone ribs. "That's third date material, if you're lucky."

"Man, I had no idea I was on a date with Southern royalty."

"Don't let it go to your head." I'm not going to let on that I'm a direct descendant of General Ambrose Powell Hill Jr. on my dad's side. I've dated creepy guys who actually get off on that Civil War shit. This city is full of legacy gentility types. "Your turn."

"How can I top that?"

"It's impossible."

"All right, I think I got something—"

My phone vibrates again. I flip it over and glance at the caller ID. *Silas again.*

"You want to answer that?"

"No." I manage to smile. "Just a friend. Nothing important."

"It's no problem, really."

"No, it's fine." I power down my cell and slip it in my purse. "So . . . what's your secret?"

I convince Tanner to abandon his car and take a walking mural tour with me. This is the real test for potential romance, as far as I'm concerned. Let's see what he sees out in the streets.

I remember when I first realized there's a separate, almost parallel account of our city. Everything that's happened in Richmond is scrawled across the walls of nearly every building. I was stumbling back from a bar one night in college, only to stop dead in my tracks at the image of a Black girl staring down at me. Her face was covered in tears the size of my fists, but there was anger in her eyes. I reached out to touch her and felt the brick beneath her skin. In lacelike, looping spray-painted letters above her head were the words:

JUSTICE FOR KENDRA

Who was Kendra?

When I got home, I googled around until I found her: Kendra Thomas. Nineteen. Shot and killed at that very spot. No one knew who pulled the trigger and no one was looking—not anymore. Her murder hadn't even made the local papers, so it was no surprise that I'd never heard her name until now. But Kendra Thomas is still there, hovering over the corner of Grace and North Henry, staring at every car and pedestrian that goes by, insisting that they acknowledge her existence. The mural didn't ensure justice—there would be none— but its existence meant that Kendra hadn't been erased yet.

Kendra is here.

There are more murals like this. They're all around us, waiting for us to bear witness, recording the history no one talks about, enduring even as the city evolves and sheds its skin every few years. The stories behind these murals might not be fully told but the sheer number of them tells me this isn't the city my parents grew up in. The murals multiply, while the statues of Confederate generals along Monument Avenue are just waiting for the day they'll be toppled over.

I want to share this version of Richmond with Tanner. I'm curious how he'll react. Am I feeling, I don't know, hopeful? Optimistic? It's been a while since I've done this with anyone. Not since—

"Where are you taking me? You were kidding about that whole serial killer thing, right?"

"This. This is one of my favorites." We stop before an albino octopus that covers the eastern wall of Fan Thrift. Its pale tentacles branch across the broadside of the brick building, curving around the corner, as if squeezing the building. "What d'you think?"

"Wow. Never noticed it before."

"How could you miss it? It's as big as the whole building."

"Guess I never looked."

"Murals are *everywhere*. All around you. You just have to look up."

"Isn't it illegal? Defacing public property?"

"*That's* where your mind goes?" *Major points taken off for that one, Tanner* . . .

"Shit. That was a dumb thing to say, wasn't it? Can I rewind? Just ten seconds?"

"No take-backs, sorry."

"It's just . . . I've never been on a date with someone like you before," he says.

"Like me?"

"You're . . . cool?"

"*Cool?* What is this? Sixth grade?"

"Most of the girls I date are—I don't know. Not like you. You're different?"

"'You're not like other girls' is not the line you think it is."

He laughs, turning away from the mural to look at me. He leans in like he's thinking about making a move, but instead says, "What should I say to get you to go on a second date with me?"

"How about 'Drinks are on me'?"

We're closing in on my apartment and I realize it's do-or-die time. I've played a full-on mental tennis match with myself—*invite him in, don't invite him in*—when I realize my phone is still off. I turn it on and my phone explodes with texts. Silas. Silas. Silas. I can't read them all.

There is a voicemail. I mouth *just a minute* to Tanner and raise the phone to my ear.

Come save me.

That's the whole message. Less than three seconds. Silas needs someone to rescue him again. Needs *me*.

I play the voicemail again, just to make sure I heard it right. This tactic is certainly new. He's never come out and begged for help before. *Come save me.*

Silas says spring me out of rehab.

Silas says bail me out of jail.

Silas says . . .

"Everything okay?" Tanner asks.

"Fine," I say. *I'm in friendship recovery*, I should tell him. "Just dealing with a friend with some boundary issues." Why does Silas always do this to me? He always expects me to drop everything and come to his fucking rescue.

Does he know I'm on a date? I wonder. Of course not. That's absurd. He never knows what I'm up to, never cares to ask what's going on in my life. *My life.* The thing I'm still trying to get going two years after graduation.

Come save me, he said.

I say goodnight to Tanner in front of my apartment and give him a peck on the cheek. I can tell by his baffled expression that he was hoping for more, but he's a perfect gentleman when it becomes clear this is where our date ends. We make a few hazy promises. Drinks next week?

"There's this new sports bar on Franklin I've been wanting to check out," he says, and I hear myself halfheartedly reply, *Sure, sounds good*. His number is already in my phone, so I tell him I'll text. I watch Tanner awkwardly turn, like he doesn't know what to do with his legs anymore. As he walks down the street, I see him glance up at the surrounding buildings and take them in, like he sees them differently—or he's trying to, anyway.

"Promise you'll call?" he shouts from the end of the block.

"Cross my heart," I holler back, dragging my fingers across my chest in an *X*, even though I can taste the lie across my own tongue. Then he's gone. Swallowed up by the city.

I text Silas as I head to my car parked just down the block:

where

rehab is for quitters

How many times have we been down this road? What is this, the tenth—Christ, the hundredth—time I've bailed his ass out? I've heard all of his excuses. I'm the one who has been there through his darkest stretches. I took care of him during his worst withdrawals. It's my couch he crashes on, my money he borrows, even when it's painfully obvious what he's really using it for.

A faint rain begins to spatter-pattern the windshield. I avoid my reflection in the rearview mirror and focus on the road. If I catch sight of myself I'll regret it—the accusing stare wrapped in eyeshadow. What the hell am I doing? We're not kids anymore. Our college days are done. We're supposed to be adults now, right? Striving to, at least. Only Silas didn't get the memo.

I turn the radio on. None of this bland pop pap sounds right, so I switch it back off and drive in silence.

While my childhood friends were busy landing football-player boyfriends who would become their husbands, I was shedding my J.Crew skin, dyeing my hair, piercing my nose—all the obvious forms of teenage rebellion. But nothing scared my parents quite like Silas.

I first spotted him at the crossroads of All-American Avenue and Vagabond Boy Lane in our freshman year. He had a Rimbaud-quarterback build, strong without being brutish, muscular without being brawny. A real Sal Paradise knockoff. I fell prey to his smile, just like everyone else did. That devilish grin—always looking like he was up to no good. The cat who ate the goddamn canary, smirking with a stray feather still clinging to his bloody lips. He was utterly unlike the boys who manhandled me in high school. Silas possessed a restless spirit, always searching, yearning for *more more more*. He made me feel alive when everything else in my life up till that point had left me for dead.

Our relationship flared up fast and burned out just as quickly. We spent most of freshman year breaking up, making up, and repeating it all over again. Sophomore year, too. Even when our relationship was done for good, our friendship never faded. We became closer, actually, as if we just needed to plow through the romantic BS to finally reach the real core of our kinship. There were always persistent whispers behind our backs about whether or not we were still sleeping with each other. He loved fueling those rumors. *Let them talk*, he'd say. *Our friendship goes deeper than that.*

I wanted to see myself the way Silas saw me. When he laid his eyes on me, nothing else existed. There was just me and him, the here and now and those breaths in between.

Amara and Tobias felt it, too. We were all under his spell.

Then we graduated.

Now we're stranded in that liminal space between childhood and adulthood, which most days feels like being stuck somewhere between the living and the dead. Amara moved back in with her parents so she could shovel her way out of student debt. Tobias has twenty roommates in some dingy apartment I've never been invited to. He's plodding away at some brain-dead temp job while Amara has her soul-sucking waitressing gig. Careers with no consequence, if you can call them careers.

I have chosen survival at whatever cost. Any writerly ambitions I might've had after graduating—which, let's be honest with ourselves here, was never going to happen—have long since faded. I'm just trying to land an entry-level job at the McMartin Agency and buy the independence I've been dreaming of.

That includes letting go of Silas. Living in his orbit has always been exhausting. What burned as bright as the sun all through our undergrad years now feels like a black hole. I keep getting dragged back into the gravitational pull of his bullshit. His nu-beatnik existence always defied the rest of our conventional career paths. At first, I used to think if he could succeed—and by succeed I mean just *be* him, just *live* his life and write—then maybe I could exist vicariously through him. It became my postgrad project to take care of Silas. I took it upon myself to ensure his survival at whatever cost, even if that meant protecting Silas from himself.

But I'm tired. I'm done being his lifeline. I can't keep doing this. By the time I pull off the interstate, closing in on the Wawa, I've made up my mind. This is it. No more bailouts.

I never know what he's on most of the time. I don't want to know. *Don't ask, don't tell* is our policy now. I always spot the paraphernalia falling out of his pockets—a charred spoon, a lighter with REHAB IS FOR QUITTERS printed on its side, burnt asteroids of tinfoil with a gummy black tar clinging to their crumpled cores—the totems of his own decline. His addiction shouldn't have come as a surprise to any of us. Silas always wanted to experience *everything*. That addiction entered the fold was just the natural progression of things.

I know how awful that sounds. That we're all—that I'm—resigned to Silas's fate somehow. But sometimes the best kind of help a friend can offer is to just stop helping. I've tried everything else. Silas keeps contaminating everything he touches, like a bacterial infection spreading throughout our circle.

His younger sister finally convinced him to go to rehab when no one else could. It's just been the two of them ever since their mother died. Silas is the only family Callie has at this point. Somehow she got Silas to enroll in a no-frills twenty-eight-day residential treatment program. A cage with no bars. By my count, he's barely made it through the first three days—a new record for him—before stealing back his phone.

Come save me.

I light a cigarette and roll down my window a crack to let the smoke out. Rain dapples my forearm. There's the Wawa sign up ahead. Better script out what I'm going to say to Silas:

I can't do this anymore . . . I'm sorry. I need to move on with my life.

I spot a gauzy form through the windshield as I pull into the Wawa lot. The wipers sweep over the glass, parting the veil of rain, revealing him.

Silas.

I spring up in my seat, gripping the wheel with both hands. The rush is instantaneous. After all these years, even now, just the sight of him is enough to send a flood of blood straight through me.

He steps into my car's headlights. He's completely drenched. His stringy hair covers his face. He's carrying a plastic shopping bag, a yellow smiley face printed on its side: THANK YOU FOR SHOPPING WITH US. He's barefoot. Wet leaves cling to his feet. He doesn't look like Silas. Doesn't *feel* like him somehow. He's gotten worse, as if he has atrophied in rehab.

"Where are your shoes?" I ask as he opens the door and jumps in.

"You don't see them?"

I glance over my shoulder. ". . . See who?"

"Nothing? Nothing at all?"

"I don't see any—"

"Never mind. Just go. *Go go goooo.*" He punctuates each *go* by smacking the armrest.

I pull out of the parking lot, suddenly worried the police are on his tail—that this is actually some kind of jailbreak and I'm his goddamn getaway driver.

"You wouldn't believe that place. Fucking religious nutjobs sitting in a circle, talking about accepting Christ into their life. Such a con. You realize that, right? They pull you in with these promises of getting better but it's really just a front for converting you. Once you sign in, they don't hide it anymore. They just keep the God talk out of it until you're stranded. Then it's all tambourines and prayers and—"

"Where are we going?"

He glances over his shoulder, checking to see if we're being followed. "Your place?"

"What's wrong with your apartment?"

"Home's in flux. It's safer at your pad."

"*Safer?*"

"Less static. Less interference." He keeps peering into the side mirror. *Objects in mirror are closer than they appear.* The headlights from passing cars streak through our windows.

I can't help but think, *I ditched Tanner for this?* I could still be out, at least striving to have the quasi–time of my life, but instead, I'm stuck carting Silas's soaking-wet ass back to my apartment before he freezes to death. "Callie will be worried if we don't—"

"She's dead to me. Fucking witch. Anyone who would—who would do *that* to their own brother? And call it love? Fuck *that.* That's not love. She doesn't understand what I'm trying—"

"That's not true. She just wants you to be—"

"Look out!" Silas's attention locks onto something outside of the windshield. He braces himself for impact, as if there's something in the middle of the highway, but nothing's there.

"What?" I shout. "What is it?"

Silas spins around to look out the rear window. "Did you . . . ? Did you *see* that?"

"See what? I don't see anything!"

Another car passes us, its high beams illuminating his wild eyes. "Pull over."

"We're on the highway!"

"I need to get out. *Now.*" He's already opening his door as the car clocks in at sixty-five fucking miles an hour on the rain-slicked interstate. I'm in the middle lane of a three-lane highway at eleven at night and he's about to leap.

"Silas! Stop!" I have to veer to the right to reach the shoulder before he jumps. A horn blares behind us as I cut off another car. We swerve onto the far shoulder, gravel shredding the chassis's underbelly before I suddenly skid, dovetailing back onto the interstate.

"Are you crazy?! You're gonna—"

"*Pulloverpulloverpullover!*" Something in his voice—the sudden rush of words, the fury that fills the cabin—frightens me. I course-correct the car and pull over. We barely come to a stop before the door flies open and Silas tumbles onto the gravel. He lands on his hands, then springs to his feet.

"What the hell are you thinking? You could've—"

But he's not listening. He leaves his door open and bolts. The steady rush of traffic flies by, high beams sweeping over his body.

"Silas, where are you—"

I put the car in park and turn the hazards on—orange lights pulsing with a *click-click-click*—then reach over the passenger side seat to close his door.

"Silas!"

By the time I sit up, Silas has climbed over the barrier and is entering the woods that surround the interstate, the happy-faced shopping bag bobbing along behind him. *Where are his shoes? Why isn't he wearing shoes?*

"SILAS!" I scream.

But it's too late. He's gone.

Fuck this, I think. I can't do this anymore. I'm done. Fucking through. No more saving Silas. Let him save himself. Or kill himself. I don't care anymore. *I just don't fucking care.*

Here's the straw, here's the camel's back. Listen to it snap like a goddamn bone.

———

When Callie calls, I pretend I don't know what she's talking about. I lie to her about breaking Silas free and releasing him back into the wilds of Richmond. I feel bad about it but I've been down Relapse Avenue with Silas before. He's always managed to pull himself out, hasn't he? He's stronger than his addiction—or that's what I want to believe.

Silas has to survive himself. No one else can save him.

I can't save him. Not anymore.

When he knocks on my door at three a.m.—*poof*, materializing out of thin air—I still can't get over how little I recognize him. The flesh under his eyes has a sallow tint. His hair is wirier than before. This bag of skin and bones is supposed to be my friend.

He cups my face with both hands and presses his lips to my forehead. "Hey, Li'l Deb." Deb, as in debutante. Funny, right? "Mind if I crash here tonight?"

Before the synapses in my brain fire off—*I don't think that's a good idea, Silas*—he pushes his way into my apartment. He's still got his smiley-faced plastic bag with him.

"I'm fixing myself," he starts right in, giving me the same spiel he always does. "I'm getting my shit together. I just need somewhere to stay . . . Somewhere I'm not alone."

Just say no, I hear Nancy Reagan's voice in my head. *Silas isn't the only addict here, and you need to focus on your own recovery. Go cold turkey. Let Silas go.*

Say it.

Say—

"Okay," I say, opening my home up to him even though he's already inside.

"I swear I'm going to get better. Hand to God. You believe me, right?"

"Yeah," I manage.

He's already passed out by the time I walk into my living room. His shirt has slid up, exposing his prominent ribs against waxen skin.

I can't tell if he's still breathing or not, so I take a step closer. Just waiting for him to inhale. To see his chest rise. *Fuck*, I think as I lean in, *please tell me he didn't OD on my couch—*

His breath catches. I leap back, my heart racing.

Tomorrow, I'll call Amara and Tobias and beg for their help. His friends will be there for him this time. The ol' undergrad gang back in action. Silas needs us.

Needs me.

But this is a ghost story. A ghost is someone caught in a loop, doomed to repeat the same actions over and over again. So who's the real ghost here? Who's haunting who?

Through it all, I still believe—need to believe—he is finally, *finally* turning a corner, even though I know that Silas is long gone now. He's no longer the Silas we all knew.

What's left of our friend is nothing more than a shadow of his former self. A phantom.

Silas was a ghost long before he passed away.

municipal waste

The intervention is Amara's idea. I'm surprised how jealous I am that I hadn't thought of it first. Whether I'm willing to admit it or not, this isn't just for Silas. Not really. It's for us.

We're tired. We want to feel like we gave it our best, the ol' college try, that we've done everything in our strength to help him get better . . . but none of us believe it's going to help. Not really.

"He's walking all over you, you know," Amara shouts over the feedback from the bar's shoddy sound system. "You've enabled a lot of this."

"So this is all my fault?" I shoot back.

"I'm not blaming you . . . but just look at the two of you. Look at *yourself*, Erin."

"What the hell have I done?"

"Um, pretty much *everything* he asks?"

Silas says can I stay the night.

Silas says can I borrow twenty bucks.

Silas says . . .

Poe's, our favorite haunt, is in the basement of an antebellum house that was a storage spot during the rum-running days. There's even an ancient cask in the storeroom that supposedly comes with its own fermented corpse. A moonshiner allegedly double-crossed the wrong boss and now he's been pickling in the backroom for the last century. Poe's offers a cocktail for brave souls called Blood of the Bootlegger, though why they don't capitalize on the cross-promotion and call it the Cask of Amontillado is beyond me. That's why I'm destined for employment at the McMartin Agency—brand synergy shall totally be thine thing. You might not have ever heard of this advertising firm, but you've certainly seen their work. Talking geckos. Free credit scores. You can even blame them for the Virginia Is for Lovers slogan.

Silas used to pick up shifts at Poe's whenever James, the regular bartender, needed a night off to play a gig. That didn't last. The manager caught him pouring beers for his friends and not charging us a dime, so he got the boot. He still hosts their open mic night, setting up foldout chairs and a microphone in the corner every Tuesday. Even if nobody shows, he'll read his own poetry until the bar closes. Sometimes I'm his only audience.

Silas is a no-show tonight, though. I haven't seen him since Tobias swung by earlier this afternoon to pick him up. They wouldn't say where they were going. I didn't ask, relieved that Toby was taking Silas off my hands for a few hours. The Strung-Out Baby-Sitters Club.

Instead of open mic night this Tuesday, Amara and I are treated to the dulcet harmonies of some local thrash band I've never heard of called Municipal Waste. Charming.

"It's no surprise he's not getting better," Amara shouts between sips of her Stoli and soda. She just dyed her hair a superbly sterling silver. It absorbs the light from the neon Pabst sign hanging behind the bar. "*Wait.* You're not *still* sleeping with him, are you?"

"*What?* No! Of course not."

"I'm not judging." She's totally judging.

"No, I am not sleeping with Silas."

"Message received." I can always count on Amara to cut to the bone. She has no issue diagnosing everybody else's problems, even if she can't point that high-powered perception at herself—except in her writing, which edges into personal narrative, chronicling the liminal space of an Iranian Southern belle living in Virginia. Amara is of this world and utterly outside it all at once. She fantasizes about interviewing obscure bands for the *Village Voice*, penning essays for the *Paris Review*, living that good ol' Didion existence. But for now she's slouching her way through the graveyard shift at the 3rd Street Diner, serving coffee to dead-eyed drunks who never tip. She knows exactly how much her life sucks. No matter how much she gripes about it, she insists her waitressing gig *must* suck, that living at home with her family is the only choice, so she can keep her eye on the real prize: getting the hell out of Richmond.

I floated the idea of us being roommates right after graduation, but Amara wouldn't hear it. Every penny she earns goes toward crossing the Mason-Dixon. Her sights are set on New York City, cliché as it is. She swears there's a media internship at some Condé Nast publication waiting for her, the siren song of low-paid labor calling. After applying and getting rejected last year—and the following weeklong blur of a bender—she recalibrated her battle plan: if she can just rent some crappy apartment in Brooklyn and get the lay of the land up north, she'll have a better chance at landing the gig and never returning to Richmond again.

Everybody knows Richmond is quicksand. If you don't move out by graduation, the ennui of the city seeps into your system and you're stranded. Our circle is a grim reminder of how little Amara has actually accomplished since college, and it's becoming painfully obvious that she not-so-secretly feels as if her friends are the ones dragging her down.

Dealing with Silas's addiction is probably the last thing Amara wants to worry about. And yet, here we are, back on our bullshit.

"The only way he comes out the other end of this alive is if we confront him," she says.

"When did you become such an expert?"

"Have you *never* watched *Intervention*? That show literally maps out everything."

"I'm sorry I haven't binged your fave addiction porn."

"If we really want to do this intervention right, we should bring in a specialist. Someone who'll make sure Silas doesn't hijack it."

"Silas would kill us if we hired someone."

Already this is feeling a wee bit too conspiratorial for my tastes: meeting up to discuss how to sneak-attack one of our best friends— *et tu, Erin?*—between happy hour drinks.

"What about his family?" Amara asks. "His sister could help."

"I don't think we should involve her."

"Why not?"

"Callie found out that I sprung him out of rehab. She *hates* me right now."

"Ugh. Fine. Scratch that. The three of us need to make a plan. Like a straight-up outline of everything—who's speaking first, what we're gonna say. We can't let Silas walk all over us."

It's very likely Silas will sabotage this. He can easily turn this entire intervention into an indictment of our friendship if we let him. We can't let him.

"We need to write our own impact statements."

"What are—"

"Just personal statements about how his addiction has harmed us."

"He'll love that."

"Are we just dicking around or what? Because if we're serious about this, then we need to be prepared. We need to treat this like life or death, Erin, 'cause that's *exactly* what it is."

We decide to do it at my apartment. "The sooner, the better," Amara insists.

"How about this weekend?"

"Sooner. Silas could ghost on us again. How about tomorrow?"

"*Tomorrow?* I've got my interview with McMartin on Thursday."

"We need to do this now," Amara says. "For real, Erin—no messing around. You've got to make sure he shows. Give him an exact time, don't let him bail."

"He'll know something's up."

"Then tell him it's—I don't know—your friendiversary or something. Just get him there."

"What about Tobias?" I ask.

"I'll rope him in."

"Good luck with that." Getting Tobias to agree to anything without Silas's approval would be like enlisting your own shadow to stab you in the back.

It's eleven by the time Amara and I have hammered out all the details. It's starting to almost feel like fun, brainstorming together. I half convince myself we're planning a surprise party, decorations and all: *HAPPY INTERVENTION, SILAS!!!*

"I should call it a night," I say. "I'm gonna close out our tab."

"Nooooo! One more drink."

"It's getting late . . ."

"Just one more." Amara pouts. "*Pleeeeease?*"

You know who your true pals are when you Alamo the bar. Whoever's standing by your side at last call is a friend for life. Amara and I have been kicked out of every watering hole in Richmond over the years—how could I say no to her?

"*One* more," I eventually relent. "Sometimes I think you love me just for my credit card."

"As God is my witness," Amara says, doing her best Scarlett O'Hara, "I'll never be sober again." Suddenly her jaw drops. She's clearly had an epiphany, which always spells trouble. "Come to New York with me!"

"Seriously?"

"Yeah, why not? You don't owe Richmond anything. What's keeping you here?"

Silas, I almost say. "Let's see if I land this gig on Thursday."

"There are a million jobs just like it in New York," Amara says. "Run away with me."

I give the daydream a test drive, just to see how the engine purrs.

Let's play house in New York. What kind of life would I have up north? New friends. Out every night. Cramped apartment in Bed-Stuy. Too many roommates. Searching for an entry-level job, any job, settling for being an after-school tutor for some overprivileged kid on the Upper West Side. Is that the kind of life I'm after?

"New York's your dream, not mine," I say. Amara can have the rats, the smell of sweltering garbage, the heat radiating off the asphalt.

"You know what?" She takes a sinister sip. "Deep down, I think what you really want is to get domesticated."

"*Ouch.* Don't hold back, bitch, tell me what you really think!"

"Come on. Admit it. You just wanna get hitched, don't you?"

"Fuck you!"

"Settle down. Pop out some babies. Have a nice house on the hill . . ."

"Just because I don't want to move to New York with you doesn't mean I'm some kind of closeted homemaker."

I know Amara's just fucking with me—she has a special knack for getting everyone's goat—but it still stings. This is not who I am. Or, at least, who I want to be. I could tell her most days I feel like a piece of driftwood that sprouted twiggy limbs and I'm frantically paddling upstream. *I am not driftwood,* I say to myself. *I am a schooner. I'm setting sail. Anchors aweigh.*

"I'm sure your mama's pleased as fucking punch you're sticking so close to home."

"Okay, now *that's* crossing a line . . ." Mom talk is fraught territory between us. Amara knows better.

"Okay, okay—look me in the eye, in front of these witnesses"—Amara's witnesses being Municipal Waste, apparently—"and repeat after me: I, Erin Hill, do solemnly swear . . ."

I hold up my hand. "I, Erin Hill, do solemnly swear . . ."

"That I will never settle down . . ."

"That I . . . uh . . ."

"I will never settle."

"I'll never settle . . ."

"That I believe domestic bliss is as good as death . . ."

"That domestic . . ." I can't do it with a straight face. I burst out laughing.

"I knew it!" Amara shouts over the band. "You are *such* a house-wife!"

"Screw you!"

"You're totally gonna send me some pink pastel invite to your baby shower!"

"That hurts!"

Three rounds later, Amara and I stumble through the streets of Richmond, sandals in hand, serenading the city and its slumbering spirits with our best rendition of blotto Bon Jovi.

"Whooooooooa, we're halfway there—"

We wrap our arms around each other, shoulder to shoulder, laughing and weaving in the middle of the road as we belt out the lyrics as loud as our lungs will allow.

"WHOOOOA-OHH! LIVING ON A PRAYER!"

"Shut the hell up!" a disembodied voice shouts from the sur-rounding shadows.

"Take my hand!" I call out to Amara as melodramatically as I can. "We'll make it!"

Amara strikes her best damsel-in-distress pose, draping one arm drunkenly over her face, the other swinging at her side, still holding her sandals. "Do you swear?"

"Some of us are trying to sleep here!" the immaterial voice yells again, and we lose our shit, cackling our asses off. We pick up our pace, pulling each other through the street.

Amara makes sure I get into my building safely, then calls herself a cab. The hallway wall holds me up as I tumble into my apartment. I'm ready to fall into bed when I discover what appears to be a pillar of marble composition books stacked in the center of my living room.

Silas always carries around a notebook, creased and softened from rolling and binding it with a rubber band that he slips around his wrist whenever he writes. Sometimes he ties his long, dark auburn hair back with it. It's his signature accessory.

"What the fuck," I declare to the empty room, expecting someone, *anyone*, to answer. The apartment smells like a locker room.

I spot a few cardboard boxes shoved against the wall. I flip the lid on the top box and find it full of musty-smelling books. The book on top is so old its leather binding has blistered and bubbled. Is Silas moving all of his shit in? Since when did my living room become his self-storage unit? He's not anywhere to be seen, so I step into the center of the room, standing before the tower of composition books. There have to be three dozen notebooks piled on top of one another, threatening to topple at the slightest exhale. I place my hand on the top notebook and immediately feel the entire column wobble. I gingerly lift the—

"No peeking," Silas says over my shoulder.

My hand retracts and the tower comes Jenga-ing down, black-and-white covers spilling all over the hardwood floor.

"What the hell's this?" I say, dizzy from the alcohol but trying to assert control over the situation.

"I had to get my shit out from my apartment."

". . . And why is it here?"

"You mind?"

"A little." No response from Silas, so I fill in the silence. "You could've at least asked."

Tobias peers over Silas's shoulder, carrying yet another cardboard box to deposit in my living room—more dusty books from the smell of it. "Can I put this down?"

"It's just temporary," Silas says to me, ignoring Tobias.

"Two days? Two weeks? How long is *temporary*?"

"Nothing lasts forever."

"What's that supposed to mean?"

"I'm going to live forever."

He looks so dead serious when he says it, I actually have to take a second to figure out if I heard him correctly. "Not in my apartment, you're not. You want to live here, then pay rent."

"This is really getting heavy," Tobias pipes up, but neither of us are listening to him.

"We need to talk," I say to Silas. "You and me. Tomorrow. Eight o'clock?"

He shoots me down: "I've got plans."

"Nine? Ten? Or should I change the locks?"

"Fine. Ten."

"Promise me you'll be there."

Silas shrugs. "Promise."

"I'm serious."

"Okay, okay, Christ, Erin, cross my heart. Are you satisfied?"

A to B is a bit blurry for me, but the next thing I know, my face is buried in my pillow. I can hear the faintest trace of whispers down the hall as Silas and Tobias conspire in the living room. I can't hear what they're saying. I don't care. I just want his shit out of my apartment, preferably when I wake up. *Poof.* Gone.

I flip onto my back and stare at the ceiling. I'm praying for sleep but it just won't come, so I start listing off my week: *Intervention on Wednesday. Job interview on Thursday. Clean slate on Friday. Brunch with Amara on Saturday* . . .

I check the alarm clock and realize only three minutes have passed. I spot my Sharpie on the nightstand table and pick it up, twirling the marker in my fingers a few times before facing the wall. I bite the cap and pull it off, adding a tag next to my bed:

ERIN IS HERE

I'm here, I think. Something about the permanent marker makes it feel all the more, well, permanent. Let my landlord pitch a hissy fit. I'll paint over it before I move, whenever that might be, but right now I feel content knowing a little part of me will always be here, even if it's buried under layers of Chantilly Lace paint.

intervention

Tonight's the night. Our Big Intervention. I spent the day writing my impact statement, making sure it doesn't sound like a personal attack. I researched different treatment programs in the city, focusing on secular clinics Silas won't completely scoff at. Amara did the hard work of recruiting Tobias, who resisted initially but crumpled under the weight of Amara's emotional blackmail. The three of us even rehearsed, for Christ's sake, as if we were about to stage a high school musical. *Merrily We Arbitrate Along.* Now it's showtime—or supposed to be. We're still missing our leading man. This all has the vibe of a surprise party stalling out. I put out a bowl of chips, which I immediately regret. Who the hell serves snacks at an intervention?

Tobias keeps checking his phone. He texts somebody.

"Hot date?" Amara has this unhealthy tendency to pick apart people's insecurities and Tobias is barely held together by his.

Toby glares at her.

"*Tobyyyyyyyy*," Amara woundedly croons. "Don't be mad at me, I'm just *booored*."

Silas adopted Tobias freshman year. He was an abandoned pup who had yet to talk to a single member of the opposite sex. He became a pet project for Silas—for all of us, actually—teaching li'l Toby how to speak to women without melting into a mealy-mouthed mess.

You know he's got a crush on you, Silas teased me while we were still dating.

Worried he might steal me away? I bit back, trying to keep things light and not sound like I was a little unnerved by the fact that Silas would bring it up in the first place.

I was actually wondering if you'd sleep with him.

I laughed at first, but stopped the second I realized Silas was serious.

You can help him out of his shell, he said. That particular conversation didn't end well.

Tobias finally puts his phone away. "Are we sure about this?"

"A little late to back out now," I say.

"What if he doesn't come?"

"He's got nowhere else to go . . . unless he's hiding at your place?"

"No."

Silas burned all his bridges. He's tapped every friend of a friend. Every mysterious faceless girlfriend I've never met, ex-girlfriends going all the way back to high school. He's borrowed all the money he can borrow, crashed on his last couch. We are it for him. Now it's time for us to draw the line.

Amara glances at her own phone. Tobias's anxiety is infecting the rest of us. "Where the hell is he?"

"He'll be here," I say. Even I can hear the strain in my voice. The uncertainty.

"He's not coming." Tobias cleans his glasses on his shirt for the fifth friggin' time.

"He's coming."

"Maybe he found somebody else to stay with."

"Who?" I ask.

"I don't know! Silas is always making friends. Maybe he met somebody new."

"He'll be here," I say, hoping to convince myself. "Give him another minute."

"It's already eleven thirty," Tobias mutters. "I've got work in the morning."

"We've all got work." Tomorrow is the Most Important Job Interview of My Fucking Adult Life. I'd like to get some sleep beforehand so I can be all bright-eyed and bushy-tailed, but you don't hear me griping. "This is Silas we're talking about. We're doing this for him."

"Yeah," Tobias says, "but he needs *to be here* for us to do anything."

"Just a little longer. Please. We've come this far."

"You ever think that maybe he just needs to go through with it?" Tobias asks. "The only thing that'll actually make any difference is for him to deal with it on his own."

"So we should just let Silas OD?"

Tobias nods, as if that's actually a good idea. "Maybe, yeah."

"I'm not going to just watch him—" We all hear the front door unlock.

I was going to say *die*, but my throat constricts as I listen to the door open and shut. A set of keys—my spare—land in the goldfish bowl on the IKEA table by the door. It's something my parents purchased, a housewarming present to make the apartment look more *respectable*.

"Erin?" Silas calls out. His voice echoes through the hall, reaching for me.

I don't say anything. Why can't I talk? Why do I feel like I'm hiding?

"Anyone home?"

"In the living room," I say, the words almost choking me.

Silas ambles in. If he's caught off guard by the presence of his friends, the expression on his face sure doesn't show it. He looks like he hasn't slept in days—Jesus, *weeks*. He's wearing the same clothes from yesterday. Maybe even the day before. He's still got his plastic shopping bag with the smiley face.

Amara and Tobias both shrink into the couch. Tobias lowers his eyes the moment Silas's land on him. The silence sickens me. He knows. Of course he knows. "What're we celebrating?"

"Silas . . ." I sound so pitiful. So weak. I can't do this—not alone.

Amara picks up the sudden slack. "We need to talk."

"Ah. I see." Silas turns to Tobias. "You wanna talk, too?"

Tobias shrugs. "It was their idea."

I turn to spineless Tobias, furious at him for throwing the whole fucking intervention under the bus in one dismissive flick, but Silas seems to take it all in stride. "Okay. Let's talk."

I'm supposed to speak first. I have my statement in my hands. The sheet of paper feels flimsy between my fingers. I want to ball it up and throw it in the trash. The words on the page feel dirty, somehow. I can't do this. Not to him.

"We're worried about you." Amara sticks to the script when no one else does. We need to be a unified front—*all for one and one for Silas*—no matter how afraid we are of him.

"Worried over *what*?"

Amara glances me, suddenly unsure of herself. She has to say it. Someone has to say it. "We know you're still using."

Silas actually guffaws.

I manage to find my voice. "Please, Silas. We want to help."

"What kind of *help* do you think I *need*, Erin?"

"We won't support your addiction anymore." Do I even believe what I'm saying?

"So you wrote this all down? Have you been practicing? Oh, man." He laughs again, as if he's impressed at the whole undertaking. "You guys . . . This is priceless. Really. Bravo."

"Silas, please. We just want you to get better. I—I think—"

His laughter stops. Silas stares at me, his gaze sharpening. He's never looked at me like that before. "Just *say it*, Erin. Say the *fucking* words."

"Silas, I love you. But I—"

"*But*. But *what*, Erin? Get it off your chest." The derision in his voice makes me feels like he's calling me out—like he knows the intervention isn't for him; it's for us, our guilt pushing us to play out this pitiful charade.

"I—I can't let you do this anymore—"

"*You can't see it yet*," he cuts me off. "See *them*. But you will."

His eyes—I can see how dilated his pupils are. A pair of black holes. "You're high right now, aren't you? *Aren't you?*"

"Not high. *Haunted*."

Something within me comes undone. Like tugging on a loose thread that unravels an entire sweater, the words tumble out all at once. "I asked you here and you—what? Shoot up? What are you on?"

He's smiling. Smiling that same fucking smug grin he's worn his whole life.

"I am *done*, Silas." I can't stop myself. "I am so *sick* and *tired* of your cryptic *bullshit!*" The rage rises up into my chest so quickly, I can't hold back. "I want you out of my life!"

What am I doing? This was supposed to be for Silas—"Get out!" I shove him. Hard. His body offers little resistance. He feels oddly soft, almost pliant, like Play-Doh. I expected his chest to puff up, to repel me somehow, but I get the sense his body will fold if I push any harder. But I can't control myself—can't stop. I only push him harder. *Harder.*

"*Erin*," Amara calls out from behind me. "Don't—"

"Get the fuck out of my apartment! NOW!"

Something has taken over. I keep pushing him. Silas is out of the living room now.

"OUT! GET OUT!"

He's in the hall, stumbling back with each shove. His plastic bag crackles when it scrapes against the wall. My eyes sear into his. I'm staring him down as I keep pushing—exorcising this sick spirit from my apartment—expelling his presence.

"I'm fucking *through* with you! DON'T EVER—*EVER*—COME BACK!"

He looks wounded. Confused. How can I do this to him?

"You are *dead* to me!"

His back slaps against the front door. Without a word he opens it, walks through, and slams it shut. Suddenly he's gone. Truly gone.

That doesn't keep me from screaming at the door: "DEAD TO ME!"

The McMartin Agency took over the red brick warehouse that was once an ironworks that built steam locomotives. They started producing iron plating for Confederate warships during the Civil War. I only know this because of the brass plaque in the waiting area.

There's something obscenely chic about the whole industrial vibe going on in here. The decommissioned furnace still sits in the center of the lobby, now painted a sleek, oily black. If Robert E. Lee had spooged in an Office Depot, I imagine this would be their bastard love child.

I pass the time before my interview by reading the plaque for the fifth time: *Evacuation fires swept the district, but workers diligently remained at their posts to protect the foundry against rampaging looters. Their heroic efforts to save the ironworks succeeded in sparing the factory from capture by Union soldiers, but tragically not from the flames.*

I can only imagine what those foundry workers might think if they knew the factory they burned to death in is where the jingles for Little Debbie Swiss Rolls are born.

I bought a dress just for today. My job interview dress. Simple, black, cinched waist. Round neck and long sleeves. Zipper running down the back. As I slipped it on this morning, I found myself taking on the identity of someone ready to show initiative. Someone with drive.

I like this person. I can *be* this person.

My phone rings. The chime echoes through the waiting area. I cringe, as if the receptionist is going to dock me points.

It's Silas.

I'm about to answer, feeling myself getting pulled in. The undertow of Silas is strong. But I can't give in—not this morning, not anymore. I can't let him hold this power over me.

Cut him off, Erin.

Silas says give me your love and devotion.

Cut him out.

Silas says bend over backward for me.

Cut him.

Silas says . . .

"Ms. Hill?" the receptionist says.

I smile. I am a beam of radiant, golden light. Time to shine.

She escorts me through the open-plan office before handing me off to Mr. Gidding. He's all smiles as he closes his office door behind me. The buzz from the hive of hipster copywriters fades away. "Thanks for coming in, Erin."

"Thank *you* for meeting with me," I say with practiced enthusiasm. The front wall of his office is nothing but window. I feel like a butterfly pinned and framed behind glass.

"Have a seat." He holds out his hand, offering me the chair in front of his desk. His body is sinewy and tanned from years of cycling, as all the picture frames hanging from his wall attest. He's two notches shy of silver fox status—let's say gray fox—which, *ew*, gross thought.

"You wouldn't remember but I've known you since you were just yea tall." He holds up his hand. "I was invited to a birthday party or two."

"I hope the present was a write-off." He doesn't laugh at my joke. That was supposed to be a joke, wasn't it? Where the hell did my sense of humor run off to?

He fills the conversational void with the agency's history. "We started off small, but our client base has grown. Got ourselves some real heavy hitters. Toyota, Marlboro. National play."

An abrupt trill erupts from my bag, startling me.

"Sorry." I pull my phone out and switch it to vibrate, giving me a chance to glance at the caller ID. It's Silas again. *Fuck.*

"We're quite competitive with the folks up in New York." Mr. Gidding keeps talking, paying my phone no mind. "We're giving those Yankees a real run for their money."

"It's interesting that you should say that." *Oof, awful segue.* "Something I'm extremely passionate about is bringing social awareness to larger corporations."

"Oh?" I can't tell if he's impressed or merely amused. How many other grads have waltzed into his office and delivered a similarly rehearsed spiel?

Too late to back down now. I launch right into the intersectionality of marketing and street art. "Ever since I read *Underworld,* I've been obsessed with the idea of *getting the consumer by the eyeballs.*" Silas would despise me for dragging DeLillo into a job interview. So what if I'm misappropriating his critique on advertising? I'm pretty positive Mr. Gidding's never read him, so I skip the novel's commentary and deliver my sales pitch. "Billboards are a thing of the past. The pre-existing surfaces of our public spaces are ripe for advertising. We can't be overt about it, obviously. It can't feel like a promo spot for Bud Light. It needs to be organic, a visual extension of the environment. Which is why I propose something more grassroots . . ."

"That so? Do tell."

"The McMartin Agency should hire an army of graffiti artists to hit the streets and create ad campaigns that don't *feel* like ad campaigns. Consumers will assume they're looking at the work of a teenager. But when that same tag appears on our client's corporate Instagram account, or in the background of a TV spot for their product, consumers will subconsciously link it to the image they've been walking by every day. It looks like graffiti, feels like graffiti—but what's really being vandalized are our eyes."

Mr. Gidding doesn't say a word. His grin hasn't slipped a fraction of an inch but his lips somehow look thinner. I forge ahead, determined to show initiative. "I think we're noticing a trend now, at least on social media, where customers want to interact with the brands—"

He holds out his hand to silence me. "Let me stop you there, Erin."

My breath hitches. "Sorry?"

"You've got the job, I promise. Don't sweat it. Your father has been such a good friend, it's the least I can do. Your dad actually asked if we could have a chat, you and me, to see if I might offer any career advice. Just to set you on the right path. I told him I'd be happy to. What're friends for?"

Well, this is certainly news to me. "Oh?"

He stands and walks around his desk, leaning against the front of it. I have to crane my neck back if I want to meet his eyes, but I can't quite decide if I want to. "So, for starters, I have to ask—have you put much thought into what your five-year plan might be?"

I don't know what I'm doing five days from now, let alone five years. Is he for real? Should I have brought my vision board along with my resume? "Well, sir, I haven't written anything down, specifically, but I have considered—"

His hand finds my shoulder. He has to lean over to reach me, edging off his desk. "That's why I'm here. I can provide some friendly suggestions on how to get you started."

I offer a stiff smile. He still hasn't let go—and for the life of me, I can't tell if this guy is trying to be paternal or pick me up. He's friends with my fucking father and he's pulling this shit on a job interview? Is my radar way off here? Am I just reading him all wrong? How can I hint at my discomfort without deep-sixing this gig?

"Thank you, sir."

"I always thought DeLillo was being pretty cruel to us advertisers," he says with a wink, as if to say *your secret's safe with me*. "But I never took *Underworld* personally. As a matter of fact, we ran an ad campaign for Adidas back in '97 that deployed graffiti artists, right after the book came out. I actually came up with the idea after reading it."

Fuck a postmodern duck. I really screwed that one up.

He's putting me in my place. He wants me to believe he's mentoring me, but it's a total power play. And he totally knows if I go crying back to Daddy, I'll never land this job.

"I see a bright future for you here, Erin. I look at you and I feel like our firm can be your home." *A home?* His grip on my shoulder tightens. "I hire people I consider fam—"

My phone vibrates again—Silas calling for the third fucking time. Mr. Gidding finally lets go.

"Sorry." *Jesus, Erin, stop apologizing!* I pull my phone out and send Silas straight to voicemail. Why is Silas calling me? Is he hurt? Is he in trouble? *Cut him off, Erin, cut, cut, cut—*

If Mr. Gidding pretended not to notice before, he certainly does now. "Do you need to get that?"

I don't listen to Silas's message until I'm out of the building. The rear wall has been bombed with a wheat paste mural. A raven the length of the building stares down at me, as if I'm a worm it's eyeing to uproot from the earth.

When I was only four I found a dead crow in our backyard. Its wings were frozen open, its clawed feet clasping at the air. I thought it was sleeping on its back. I tried to wake it, tapping at its chest. The crow's ribcage suddenly gave way, my index finger slipping past its feathers and into the squiggly bits of its body. I could've sworn I felt its toothpick ribs tighten, closing around my knuckle, as if it wanted me to stay inside. It felt so cold. Its wet organs thrummed, intestines squirming with life. Not the crow's . . . but something else. Just beneath the sheath of oily black feathers, this dead bird's body housed a

62 clay mcleod chapman

writhing mass of maggots.

When I showed my mother, she shooed me back inside. I kept my index finger extended all day—the one I'd inserted into the bird— even after Mom insisted I wash my hands under scalding hot water for well over five minutes. She recoiled when I reached out to her, her expression full of horror. I had touched a dead thing.

Good girls don't discuss such topics publicly, dear, she said whenever I brought the crow up during polite conversation. *Death is a personal matter. It's better kept private.*

We don't talk about death in our family. It never touches us.

But I touched *it*.

I lean against the mural and bring the phone up to my ear. There are a few seconds of ambient sound, then Silas's labored breathing. I can't tell if he even knows he's called me. When he finally speaks, the words drift in and out, as if he can't hold his own phone to his mouth.

"There are things I can't tell you . . . This isn't going to make sense yet . . . I want you to find me, Erin. I know you can . . . I know you—"

I delete the message before listening to the rest.

memorial

They discovered Silas's body below the overpass where Interstates 95 and 64 intersect in a cloverleaf knot in downtown Richmond.

The floodwall for the James River is directly below, creating a space that isn't used for much beyond skaters tagging the overpass's underbelly. Slashes of spray paint form crosses and lacy RIPs. Skulls resembling toadstools sprout from the asphalt.

And a new tag, left just for yours truly, which Tobias would tell me about later:

SILAS AND ERIN ARE HERE

I try to picture how the police found him. What his body looked like: the robin's-egg cast to his face, the whites of his eyes dried to a milky gray.

The service is tasteful, I have to imagine: family and close friends only, homilies and hymns, a framed photograph of Silas from healthier days perched on top of his closed casket.

I don't go.

I can't leave my apartment. I want to pay my respects, say good-bye. I've even pulled out an outfit to wear, laying my job interview dress on my bed. I stare at it for I don't know how long. I know I'm supposed to slip it on but something within me keeps stalling.

The service is starting. All I have to do is move. One foot in front of the other.

When is my body going to wake up? When will I start going through the motions of living again? I know Silas won't answer his phone, not ever again, but I call him anyway. I listen to his greeting—*Surprise, you caught me*—over and over—*You know what to do.*

I just want to hear his voice, even if it's prerecorded. Those words are enough to conjure him up. For a fleeting second, I trick myself into believing he's actually on the other end of the line. *Surprise, you caught me, you know what to do, surprise, you caught me . . .*

I don't know what to do.

The tears come without warning, burning my cheeks. My stomach seizes and I collapse across my bed, curling into myself and wailing until my throat is raw. I cut Silas off. I cut him out, didn't I? Just when I was making a clean break, just when I was about to move on with my life. This is all my fault. Everyone at the service will know I did this to him. If I had just been there for Silas, if I'd given him one more day, *just one more*, he'd still be alive.

Instead, I ignored his calls and he overdosed alone.

I imagine a ghost slipping through my dress's sleeves, the fabric filling on its own and levitating around the room. Maybe my phantom dress can go to the memorial without me. Everyone will believe it's me: my invisible self, floating between Tobias and Amara, flipping through the program while listening to every scripture reading and piano solo. My dress can endure all the memories recounted by old high school buds, hear distant cousins share their personal stories of how Silas changed their lives. *He was such a good boy . . . He lived his life to the fullest . . . He seized the day, you know?*

I wonder if my dress can step up to the podium and share one of our memories. Maybe it will tell everyone about the time Silas and I broke into the Richmond Public Library. The woefully underpaid security guard didn't notice the two of us tucked under the table in the research room. We held our breath and tried hard not to snicker as he flipped on the lights, surveyed the room, then turned them back off, leaving us in the dark. The library was all ours. We slipped through the aisles to unearth whatever book Silas was hunting for. He was always on the prowl for some dusty tome, yet another out-of-print edition to add to his collection.

Will his family appreciate my dress telling that story? How the two of us tiptoed through the rows? How we spent the night curled up together on the floor, flipping through the book's yellowed pages until the custodian rolled in? Would Silas's sister laugh like we laughed as we burst through the emergency exit, sounding the library's fire alarm, racing out into the early morning light and waking up the rest of Richmond, Silas's new book in hand?

Silas never saw me in this dress. I don't know if he'll recognize me. But who'll recognize him in his funeral suit? That isn't Silas—not the Silas I know. That's just some silly boy in his Sunday best. Silas despised the idea of going to church.

I imagine my dress draping itself over his casket. The fabric is thin enough to slip between its hinges. My dress will wrap around his suit and we'll lie there. I'll be his funeral shroud. We can be buried in the ground together.

I blink back to my room, my dress still empty on the bed. He's gone, I think. He's really gone. Silas is never coming back. Not this time. What were the last words I said to him?

Dead to me.

I can't be around others who are ready to move on. I can't let him go. I can't let go of the here and now and the breaths in between. Opening the front door would let the air—let him—escape and I just can't do that. Not yet. I keep coming up on recollections of him as I wander through the living room, like loose change buried in the couch cushions: *That's where Silas crashed last week and there's the coffee mug he would drink red wine from and there's the T-shirt that still smells like him and there's . . . there's . . .*

So I decide to have my own memorial service, right here in my apartment, populated by all the memories of Silas I can muster. It's a low-key affair—just me in my job interview dress, now a funeral dress. I'm the first to speak. *Growing up*, I imagine myself saying, *I always wondered if what I looked like on the outside didn't match up with what I was on the inside. Silas was the first person to see me for who I wanted to be. Not the person everyone saw me as, but what I felt like. Silas wasn't afraid of what he saw. He saw to the very center of me.*

During my imagined memorial, my phone chimes with a text. It's Tanner.

Thinking bout u.

I haven't thought about him since our date, to be honest. That night feels like eons ago—so much so, it takes me a moment to even remember who Tanner is. I don't text back.

I notice I have a voicemail. I can't remember hearing my phone ring.

Hi, this is Lorraine Watkins at the McMartin Agency. Just reaching out to follow up on a few things before you start on Monday. Work. Right. There's a life waiting for me out there.

When my phone rings again—I hear it this time—Silas's name manifests itself on my caller ID and I swear all the air in my lungs evaporates. He's calling me. *How is he calling me?*

"Silas?"

"Where were you?" Callie asks, her voice dulled from grief. No preamble; she just launches right in. Of course she'd have his phone. She must've inherited his personal affects—what little there was. And I've been calling and calling. "Why didn't you come today?"

Ever since Silas's rehab breakout I've become persona non fuckoff for her. I enabled him. I absconded with him—then kicked him right out into the street.

"I wanted to be there, but . . ." I don't have an answer. Everyone else was capable of mustering the strength to show up. Why couldn't I?

"You were his friend. He loved you so much. Why? Why weren't you there for him?"

She means the memorial, but in my mind, the question cuts

deeper than that—*Why weren't you there for him when he needed you? How could you abandon him like that?*

"Callie, please, let me explain—"

"He's gone and you weren't there. He's never coming back."

I open my mouth to say something, but the thought evaporates before I can give it voice. There's nothing I can say that will help her heal. Callie's breath catches on the other end of the line, wet and jagged. I have nothing to offer, nothing that will help take her pain away.

"Callie, I—"

"You'll never be happy," she says. "You've always gotten everything you ever wanted, but you're so fucking empty and my brother is dead because of you." She hangs up.

I glance around my apartment, phone still in hand, even though I can't feel it anymore.

"I'm sorry," I say. "I'm sorry. I'm sorry, I—" Who am I apologizing to? Maybe it's Callie. Maybe Silas. Is there anyone else I should atone to? Who else's karmic shit list am I on? I haven't spoken with Tobias or Amara since we found out. I know I've broken some unspoken contract between the three of us, abandoned my post by not going to the service. How can I tell them I can't leave my apartment? That this is my life now?

Mom calls and I can't keep myself from picking up. I just need to talk to someone. We go through the motions of our weekly conversation, repeating the same script we always do.

"Just checking in," she starts. "We haven't heard from you lately."

"I'm fine," I say, staring at my laptop as I pretend to pay attention.

"You certainly don't sound fine."

I can't bring myself to tell her he passed away. I can't tell anyone. Maybe, just maybe, if I keep it to myself—keep silent—it didn't happen. Maybe I can take his death back.

Silas says don't forget me.

Silas says don't let me go.

Silas says . . .

Find me. On the voicemail he said *find me.* What did he mean by that? Find him where?

"Your father's birthday is coming up next week. You know how much it means to him."

I ignore her and pull up Facebook. I've intentionally kept off social media, avoided all the posts about Silas. Another thing that would make it feel too real. *You can look at his page once,* I say to myself. *Just once,* I promise. Just to see the photos of him still lingering online.

It's such a shoddy excuse for a profile. He was always a self-professed Luddite. I had to drag his ass into the twenty-first century and finally sign him up like the rest of world. I even picked out his profile picture—a photo I'd taken myself. He barely paid attention as I plugged all the pertinent details into his newly digitized life. He probably forgot his own password.

I shouldn't be surprised that his wall is filled with bite-sized eulogies from distant acquaintances; people from college sharing their condolences with a goddamn algorithm.

Miss U . . . Gone but not forgotten . . . Where'd you go, bro? Always in our hearts.

Then I see a reply from Silas. *Missing u 2!*

". . . Erin? Erin, are you there?"

Someone's writing as Silas. Not for him, *as* him.

You're not getting rid of me that easily!

"Are you listening to me? The celebration is on Monday."

Death is not the end, trust me!

"I gotta go, Mom." I end the call before she can protest. Scrolling through, I can see that someone has hacked Silas's account and is commenting on all the condolence posts.

I'll be baaack!

Who the hell is doing this? Who has access to his account other than me? This is disgusting. They don't even sound remotely like Silas. He'd never write *See you soon!!!*

Before I can second-guess myself, I type: *WHO IS THIS?* I stare at the screen, arms crossed, as if I'll just sit here and wait for a reply. I refresh the page. Stare at the screen.

There's a knock at the door. I slap my laptop shut, as if I've been caught spying. Slowly making my way down the hall, I strain to hear voices. I don't have any deliveries. I'm not expecting anyone. Before I peer through the peephole, I hesitate. In that breath, I feel a slight flutter of hope, a hummingbird within my ribcage. *What if it's . . . ?* I look through and find . . .

Tobias. I notice the six-pack tucked under his arm: India pale ale. Silas's favorite, now Tobias's. It's not like Tobias to show up out of the blue, alone, with no advance warning. He's still in his suit from the service—starched collared shirt unbuttoned at the top, tie loosened like a noose around his neck. I wouldn't have given him a second glance if we passed each other on the street. Then again, it's tough to spot Toby even when he's standing three inches in front of you.

I open the door with the chain lock in place. He holds the six-pack up as an offering. "You gonna make me drink this alone?"

Sweet, gawky Tobias. He spent years lingering in Silas's shadow. He *was* Silas's shadow. Somehow Silas convinced him that there was a novel somewhere inside him. There's a fabled seven-hundred-page manuscript buried under Tobias's bed that he only shared with Silas; his magnum opus. Silas told me it was terrible.

Now Tobias photocopies files for minimum wage. His days are spent tracking the same green light as it passes across page after page, wincing with each sheet as if he's *Un Chien Andalou*ed his eyeballs over and over. I imagine it's pretty lonely to be Tobias these days.

I slide the chain lock, letting the links drop. "Come on in."

"You going out?"

I look down and discover I'm still wearing my job interview dress turned funeral dress. "No. Staying in."

"Long time—"

"No see."

"I figured we could drink to the Man." Chitchat's never been one of Tobias's strengths. In college, it literally took him weeks to work up the courage to talk to me when Silas wasn't around. Even so, he'd habitually slip off his glasses to clean them with his shirt. Anything to avoid eye contact.

"Sure. Let's pour one out for him."

We bring the six-pack to the fire escape and watch the RCU kids drunkenly stumbling around below. I spot a cluster of dusty gutter punks squatting on the sidewalk, their ratty camp set up in front of the café across the street. There's a couple huddled into one another on a sleeping bag, unzipped and spread out over the pavement. She leans on him and flicks a lighter while he strums an acoustic guitar for change. A cardboard sign in front of them reads: SILAS HATES ME. Sorry. Scratch that. It actually says: SONGS FOR FREE.

"Cheers." Tobias clinks his bottle against mine, eyes elsewhere.

"Eye contact," I say. "Bad luck otherwise."

"Sorry." He brings his beer back for a second time, his eyes on me.

We don't say much for a while. Typical Tobias. Clearly there's something on his mind. He came here for a reason, but whatever his agenda is, he can't come right out and say it.

"You haven't hacked Silas's Facebook account, have you?" I have to fill the silence with something. "Somebody's responding to people's posts like it's him. Fucking creep show."

"Maybe it's Silas," Tobias mumbles.

"Yeah. Like his ghost would go on Facebook. That'd be hell for him." I leave it at that, listening to the disembodied voices of a couple bickering on the sidewalk below.

Richmond Commonwealth University has been a slow-moving cancer on the downtown scene, its campus spreading another few blocks every year. Before long it'll take over all of Richmond. A lot of the buildings that once belonged to the wealthy gentility have been renovated into offices for professors or student affairs spaces, most of them haunted.

Grace Street is where the student body bleeds into the bars. In

high school, everyone wants to live on Grace. Teens from the Southside break curfew to sneak into the all-ages shows at the Metro, then
grab a meal from the vegan buffet at Panda Express. Definitely not
my parents' first choice of domestic bliss, but they were happy that
campus security has their office across the street. It's hard not to look
down the sidewalk and remember Silas and me shuffling back to my
apartment to crack open another beer right here.

"So . . . what gives?" Tobias asks, snapping me out of it. "You lying
low? Hiding out?"

"No," I lie as I light a cigarette with Silas's lighter—REHAB IS FOR
QUITTERS—which I've somehow inherited.

"It's pretty messed up that you weren't there today."

"*Don't*. I've already been chewed out about it."

"Where were you?"

"Here."

"Why?"

There's no answer to give. No explanation matters. They're just
excuses: because I'm scared, because I'm not ready to let go, because
if I saw his body, open casket or not, there'd be no denying the truth.
He's dead. Because I can pretend—*believe*—that he's still alive.

Silas is here. With me. I *feel* him.

"It sucked, if you're curious." Tobias sips, swallows. "Gloomy as
shit. If I die—"

"*If?*"

"*When* I die, promise me I get a better sendoff."

"Deal."

"His sister was just . . . just *bawling* all over the place. Some cousin
had to hold her up."

I imagine mascara running down her cheeks. The black holes
of her eyes. The low moan escaping her mouth while her brother
molders in his casket. A month ago, Callie was asking me for advice
on which classes to enroll in and which gropey professors to avoid
at RCU. Silas always said she looked up to me. She'd spit in my face

now, if she could.

"Who spoke?"

"Amara read a poem she wrote for him," he says, then adds, "It sucked."

I can't help but laugh. Amara's poetry *does* suck. "You?"

"*Speak?* Yeah, right . . ."

The argument between the bickering couple below us escalates, their voices echoing down the block. They have no idea that I am listening in on them, totally unaware of my ringside seat to their drunken squabble. I can't see them, but I sure can hear them.

Death hasn't touched you yet.

You're making grief sound like it's some kind of medal of honor. A Red Badge of Bereavement. Something about this argument echoes in my mind, faint but familiar.

You don't even know what it's like to lose someone.

I do, too! My grandparents died . . .

Grandparents don't count.

I know this argument. I've heard it before. I lean over and glance down at the street. The couple below—that's me and Silas. Jesus, I'm looping an old squabble we had years ago.

"I keep seeing him," I say. "He's come back to haunt me for skipping his funeral."

Tobias doesn't say anything at first. He take another sip, then, "What if he was?"

"What? Haunting me?" I let out a hollow laugh.

"Don't put it past him."

"I'm thinking of commissioning some street artist to throw up a mural for him."

"For Silas?"

"Yeah. Under the overpass. Where they. . ."

Found him.

"Nothing huge. Just a memorial. There are some old classmates who'd do it for cheap. His name, his face. Maybe you can help me pick out a photo of him to use?" Truth is, I'll never visit his grave. I'll go to the spot where Silas died when I'm ready. If I'm ever ready. That patch of asphalt beneath the overpass is where his spirit lies; his true tomb. What will it look like a year from now? Ten years? A hundred? Will it crack and crumble apart? Will the weeds weave through the fractures in the concrete? Will it return to dirt when we're all dead and gone? Will his last words fade away? *Silas and Erin are here.* Spray-painted on the concrete. For me.

"I dunno," Tobias says.

"What? I'll pay for it. It's something I want to do. For him."

Tobias finishes his liquid courage. For what, though? "There's something I want to show you. Promise not to tell Amara, okay? Not yet."

"Why not?"

Tobias swallows. His eyes seem to retreat behind his glasses. "I was with Silas."

"When?" My chest suddenly seizes. "Wait. You were *with him? Are you serious?* What were you two doing? Did you watch him—"

I can't finish the thought. I don't have to—the answer is already on Tobias's face. He looks back at me with a blank expression.

"Why didn't you call an ambulance? Jesus, why didn't you try to *help* him?"

"I did." Tobias reaches into the same leather satchel he's had since college and pulls out one of Silas's marble composition books. I recognize it right away, still bound by a rubber band.

"How did you get that?"

"Just hear me out, okay?" His voice remains maddeningly calm, every word level with the next, like he's trying to talk me out of jumping off the fire escape. "I know how this is going to sound, but you're just going to have to find a way to believe me."

"Believe *what?*" I'm losing my patience for Tobias's meandering, his inability to *just fucking come out and say what he wants to say already.* "What am I supposed to believe?"

"Have you ever heard of Ghost?"

PART TWO

finding

a home

vessel

A haunted drug? The words didn't make sense.

"You're the one who's haunted," Tobias said. "Ghost just lets you see who's haunting you."

Our friend just died of an overdose and now Tobias wants to get high?

Not high. *Haunted.*

Silas discovered something. A miracle, Tobias said. But when I asked him to explain, he clammed up and wouldn't say any more. Not on my fire escape, where people could be listening. We needed seclusion, where no one would bother us, a safe space to be alone with our ghosts.

A clean slate, he called it. A house without a history.

"This is what Silas wanted us to do for him," Tobias said. "It's not me asking, it's Silas."

His dying wish.

I want you to find me, Erin, he said on his last voicemail.

Tobias tells me to take I-95 toward Hopewell. The town had been nicknamed the "Wonder City" back in the early 1900s, thanks to its mushrooming growth in manufacturing. The DuPont company even set up their own gunpowder plant during World War I, only for the factory to catch fire in the dead of night. Most of Hopewell burned down with it. A civilian-spawned militia took it upon themselves to lynch any looters they apprehended, stringing them up in the streets as their city burned. DuPont pulled up stakes shortly thereafter, before the embers cooled, leaving what was left of its homeless citizens and cindered buildings behind.

No hope in Hopewell now, folks always joked.

"What's the big mystery?" Amara has the backseat to herself, lounging like a bored Cleopatra. She rolls down her window and hangs her arm out, fingers gliding through the air.

"It's easier if you just see for yourself," Tobias says. He and I agreed to keep mum on the finer points of our weekend getaway. Better not to freak Amara out before we even get started. Not that Toby's been totally up-front with his itinerary with me, either. "Take this exit."

Why he couldn't drive is beyond me, but Toby wants me to chauffer. He's keeping his focus out the window, sinking low into his seat, as if he's worried someone's following.

"Are we being tailed?" I ask, hoping a joke might drag him out from his shell.

"Just keep your eyes on the road."

The zombie subdivision is less than thirty minutes from Richmond. Hundreds of acres of woodland were developed during the last housing boom—the woods cut down, the land platted and zoned—only for the whole suburb to go bust. Construction on these homes halted the second its developers went belly-up. The abandoned development is now nothing more than vacant lots and half-finished homes. A faded sign reads SHADY ACRES: LOTS AVAILABLE. Below that—PRIVATE PROPERTY. NO TRESPASSING. VIOLATORS WILL BE PROSECUTED.

Amara leans out her window and marvels at the skeletal homes. "We're house hunting?"

"Keep going straight," Tobias says.

"Which Suburban Barbie Dream House do you pick?" Amara asks.

"I'll take that one." I point to the bones of a home whose window frames bloom with blue tarps. Pine stakes connected with guide strings and fluorescent-pink streamers map out the rest of the lot, tinder ribs reaching out from the soil.

"Spacious. What about you, Tobes? Which house do you have your heart set on?" Amara flosses her fingers through the headrest to tickle his neck. When I'm feeling spiteful, I'll remind her about that one time in college they hooked up. Amara was drunk and bored. Tobias was too timid to say no, a deer in the headlights of Amara's sixteen-wheel libido, the two colliding head-on in his dorm. *Worst mistake of my life*, she moaned the morning after and ever since.

"Take this left," he says to me as he bats Amara's hand away, shoulders scrunching.

I turn onto Wakefield Road, plunging deeper into the empty neighborhood. Already I feel lost in this labyrinth. Every block looks the same to me. I don't think I could find my way out.

Amara slumps back in her seat and sings that Peggy Lee song, "Is that all there is . . ."

"Turn right." Tobias doesn't say it soon enough, so I have to stand on the brakes to make the turn onto Shoreham Drive. The road ends in a cul-de-sac. A cluster of half-built homes sit empty.

Perfect for Tobias's plans, apparently. No nosy neighbors. No prying eyes.

A house without a history.

"Here we are."

Our home away from home is a two-story modular townhouse nestled in the center of the cul-de-sac.

"*This* one?" Amara scoffs. "We passed, like, a dozen better-looking houses."

"This is the one."

We all climb out of the car and take the house in. I'm reminded of a transparent model of the human body, one of those see-through plastic kits that details each layer of our insides, our organs, the red and blue pathways of veins and arteries. I picture myself pulling out the circulatory system, then the nervous system, exposing the bones and guts of this place: the concrete foundation, the plywood sheathing on the exterior walls and roof, covered with plastic house wrap to prevent wood rot. Rolls of fiberglass insulation that may as well be muscle tissue pad the walls. But somewhere along the way of this house becoming a home, on some cellular level, everything halted. The life of this house just . . . *stopped.* It has no soul, no family: a Pinocchio house yearning to become real. That's all houses truly want, right? To one day become a home?

"Sure hope you got a good deal on it." Amara punts an empty Mountain Dew bottle down the street. Patches of crabgrass dot the yard. Boot prints are scattered about the mud like a how-to diagram for some sort of frantic ballroom dance. Whoever had been working on this home just walked away—*or ran,* I can't help but think—leaving their supplies behind.

A clear plastic tarp is wrapped around a pallet of bricks in the front yard. One end has loosened itself, flapping haplessly in the wind like the canvas sail on a schooner lashing against its mast. The pallet's bindings have snapped, bricks spilling out from their tight stack, like tiny red headstones tumbling into the mud. The whole lawn is a cemetery, its forgotten monuments toppled over and sinking into the soil.

"Is there an Indian burial ground under our feet?" I can't help myself. It's more for Amara's sake than mine, which by the smirk on her face I can see she appreciates. "Did the developers only move the headstones?"

"These houses are clean," Tobias says, not getting the joke. "Nothing haunts them yet."

"Glad we got the Indian burial ground convo out of the way," Amara says.

I don't want to rain on Tobias's parade, but there probably isn't a square foot left in Virginia that isn't haunted by now. Not this blood-soaked soil. *Watch your step*, I want to say. *I bet we're waltzing over a long-forgotten Civil War battlefield right now.* Why stop there? Hopewell hosted its fair share of KKK rallies. Maybe the Grand Dragon himself led a lynching on this very stretch of soil before it was zoned for housing. Not to mention Jamestown is just up the river. Maybe a Powhatan army was massacred right under our feet and we just don't know.

"Park your car in the back," Tobias says.

"Why?"

"There's a security service that comes through here every few days, making sure no squatters burn any of the houses down or whatever."

I'm about to ask, *How do you know?*, but Tobias is already pulling back the tarp over the front window and slipping inside. Amara looks at me and shrugs. "See you inside," she says.

The plan, as much as Tobias has shared with me, is to send Silas off into the afterlife in style. He spoke of our little weekend wake as if it were a camping trip. Instead of tents, we'd be roughing it inside this empty house. There was no running water, he warned. No electricity. We packed our sleeping bags, with enough food and beer for a couple nights.

Tobias is offering catharsis. A chance to say goodbye.

Say I'm sorry. Forgive me. Please. Even now, I can't get this niggling voice out of my head: *If you hadn't kicked him out of your apartment, if you'd just been there for him, if you . . .*

I'm the last to slip inside the house after moving my car. The windows have yet to be installed, sealed with a transparent membrane of clear plastic. Someone has sliced through the tarp that opens into the dining room. Or what will be the dining room one day. Will it still?

There's no carpeting in the house. Just plywood subfloor. The house doesn't absorb sound the same way normal houses do, so every step echoes off the walls. Whatever natural light slips through the window frames is filtered through greasy plastic tarps. A dull, washed-out dollhouse.

There's a viscosity to the air. Every breath coats my windpipe with sawdust. I don't mind the smell. I have a fuzzy memory of my dad sweating over a piece of furniture in his woodshop when I was little. Sawdust suspended itself in the air, drifting about—like snow, almost—getting in my hair and all over my clothes. The smell of raw wood steeped itself into my sweater. For days afterward, I'd bring my sleeve up to my nose and breathe in deeply, inhaling the memory of fresh pine. I loved that smell. Then Mom went ahead and dry-cleaned it away.

"Toby!" Amara calls. "You gonna give us the grand tour or what?"

He's in the living room. Calling it that—*living*—feels wrong. There's no life in this place.

From the candy bar wrappers and potato chip bags scattered across the floor, to the water bottles lined along the wall, it's as if he's been camping already. "Have you been crashing here?"

"Just a couple nights."

"Since when?"

Tobias doesn't respond.

Amara heads to the kitchen to unpack. A couple Igloo coolers will have to suffice for a fridge, since there isn't one. We'll be dining on beef jerky, M&Ms, and gallon jugs of bottled water. The beer was Amara's idea and Tobias didn't argue. "Anyone thirsty?" she asks.

"Not me," he calls from the living room.

"Erin? It's five o'clock somewhere."

"No, thanks."

"Well, I'm starting. I'm day-drinking this whole weekend away and none of you are going to stop me. Are we all clear on that?"

"Crystal." I find my way to the first-floor bathroom, the guts of its plumbing exposed. The toilet has been installed but the cistern is empty. I test the handle, jiggling it to see if it might flush. Nothing happens. "Guess we'll be peeing out the window?"

"I spotted a porta-potty in the backyard," Amara calls out from the kitchen. Her voice draws me in and I find her glancing out the rear window frame. "Whatever turds are floating in that pool of blue chemicals have probably pickled themselves by now."

"Guess I'll just hold it in."

"I brought a pot," Tobias calls from down the hall.

"*Welp*, at least we can say we've got a pot to piss in." Amara cracks a can of Brooklyn Lager, the snap of aluminum bouncing off the walls. I can't help but wince.

Amara holds the can out. "Still cold. Sure you don't wanna toast to our dream home?"

"Yeah, no, I'm good."

"Here's to domestic bliss." She raises her can, toasting no one. I make eye contact even without a drink. Force of habit. Amara sips, then hesitates. "What's behind door number one?"

There's another door in the kitchen. When I open it, I'm greeted by shadows. Cool air spreads across my face. A new smell drifts up from the darkness, like dried milk. I flick the exposed light switch once, twice. Nothing. "Nope. Not going down there."

"You hungry?" Amara pulls out a bag of beef jerky, ripping open the package with her teeth while juggling her beer. "I wonder if they deliver out here."

"No outside contact," Tobias calls from down the hall.

Amara rolls her eyes. She picks an unfinished cabinet and tosses the bag of jerky in, then a bag of trail mix, humming to herself, "Is that all there is?"

I decide to wander up to the second floor.

"If that's all there is, my friend . . ."

"Be careful upstairs," Tobias nags.

I keep playing house and try to imagine the family that will move in one day. The life they'll make for themselves here. Could it be my family? What kind of life could I have here?

I navigate through my daydream family, moving in for us all and mapping out our lives inside. *This room's for the kids, this room is mom and dad's, and this room is for guests.*

The second floor is far more skeletal than downstairs. In the bedrooms, pieces of Sheetrock have been nailed in place, while other walls are nothing but wooden framing. The drywall has yet to be sanded and primed. Tape seals off the seams between the sheets.

I can see faint scribblings in grease pencil along the corners of the plaster to show where they cut through the Sheetrock. I spot numbers—dimensions—penciled along the edges with annotations: *Master B. Guest B. Bathroom.* They read like secret messages left behind for someone to find.

When I'm sure nobody's looking—who would be?—I pull out my Sharpie and find a corner in what would've been a closet to leave my own note:

ERIN IS HERE

Open wide, Silas whispers in my ear.

I spin around and find nothing but thick sheets of pink-and-yellow insulation stuffing the inner cavities like cotton candy. I know you're not supposed to touch insulation—your skin will itch for hours—but I'm tempted to pinch a bit, pop it in my mouth, and swallow. Suddenly I'm at the county fair with Silas again. We split a tab of acid before coming, marveling at the spiral of lights chemtrailing off the rides. Now we're sharing a cotton candy. Silas tugs a pink tuft and holds it out to me: "Say *aaah*." I do as he says and he places it on my tongue. The fibrous threads dissolve in my mouth. The melted sugar runs down my throat as I swallow, and my entire mind expands. My eyes never leave Silas as an explosion of sugar radiates through the rest of me. My turn. I pluck a tuft and wait for him to stick out his tongue, but instead of placing the cotton candy in his mouth, I smash it against his nose. "Rude!" he says. I laugh out loud, remembering the moment, startling myself when I hear the sound of my own voice echoing throughout the hollow house.

"Erin!" Tobias's voice reaches up the stairs. "We're ready!"

"Coming!"

As I make to leave, something shifts behind me.

I turn and find a clear plastic tarp stapled over the exposed window frame, flexing in the breeze. The loose sheet of polyethylene expands and contracts with the wind, breathing almost, a gray translucent lung. When I walk back into the hall, faster than I need to, I hear the tarp contracting from over my shoulder, billowing from the draft and pulling taut.

In and out. In and out. In—

—*out.*

séance

The gloaming sun retreats through the tarpaulin enclosing the window frames, its colors dulling to a bruised purple. Tobias lights a Coleman camping lantern before we join him on the floor, crossing our legs. He positions the lamp in the center of our triangle. The exposed beams cast their shadows. Our limbs spindle across the ceiling like daddy longlegs.

There's such a slumber party vibe to all this, as if we're kids spending the night in our sleeping bags and telling each other ghost stories. Next up: Light as a feather, stiff as a board.

"What if I told you there's a way we can contact Silas?" Tobias brandishes Silas's marble composition book once more, keeping its secrets from us—from me. Since when did he become the executor of Silas's literary estate?

"How did you get his notebook?" Amara asks.

"Silas asked if I'd do this for him. He wanted us here. Together. It's all laid out here."

Maybe I'm just jealous Silas trusted Tobias with his words over me. Maybe I'm still holding out hope that, hidden within his notebook, there's something written about me.

I reach for the composition book. "Can I see?"

Tobias pulls back. "Silas was very clear. He wanted me to walk us through this part."

"To do what?" Amara asks.

"Okay. Hear me out." Now or never, Tobias . . . "Religious movements have been built entirely around the belief that the living and dead can communicate with one another."

Amara snorts. "Silas had his own brand of hipster spiritualism? *Hipsteritualism*? Nice."

"We've gotten haunted houses all wrong. It's *people* who are really haunted."

"But isn't that just the memory of Silas, though?" Amara is ready to wade into this phantasmagorical debate. "That's not a ghost. Memories and spirits aren't the same thing."

Tobias points at me like I'm Exhibit A. "Do you feel like Silas is with you right now?"

The tarp sealing the windows respires, flexing just over my shoulder. "Yes."

"Do you still feel connected to him?"

We're in my apartment. In my bed. I can't remember which epoch of our relationship this is—it could be the first era, it could easily be the tenth. Silas has nestled behind me, wrapping his arms around my chest, so that his chin slips over my shoulder. We're playing a game we always play, debating our future together. *If I die first*, I say, *I'd want you to meet someone else. I'd be okay with you moving on. Falling in love again.* Silas huffs. *If I die first*, he says, *you better believe I'm haunting your ass.*

"Yes," I say. There's the gauziest logic to what Tobias suggests. Real ghosts transcend a particular place; trauma transfers to the living. I'm the one who's haunted, not some house.

"That's where we start," he says. "We need that personal connection to draw him in."

"Draw him in." I repeat the words. "Draw him in *how?*"

Tobias holds up a white gelcap. "This will unlock our spirits."

"What the hell's that?" Amara asks.

"Ghost."

"Never heard of it."

"You wouldn't have. This is something new and old at the same time."

"*Très chic.*" She turns to me, suddenly suspect. "Wait. Did you know about this?"

"Not really," I half lie.

"I needed to get you both here first so I could explain. Shamans believe they can open a portal to elevated levels of consciousness by taking ayahuasca, which is sort of—"

"So you want to trip?" Amara interrupts.

"It's not tripping. It's a *haunting*. Ghost brings us even closer to the dead. It allows us to communicate with them."

"So . . . I'm sorry." Amara just won't let up. "Is this a séance thing? You dragged our asses out here just to perform a séance? Seriously?"

"Don't get caught up in words like *séance*. This isn't some Victorian parlor game. We make contact as a group. We can look after each other while we're haunted, make sure we don't—"

Amara gasps. She seizes my arm, squeezing tight, and I can't help but feel infected by her panic. She spins her head around the room. "Do you hear that? *Silas?* Is that you?"

There's a moment—just a breath—where I believe her.

Amara busts out laughing. "Sorry . . . I just had to, sorry."

Tobias isn't impressed. "You done?"

"Yeah. Sorry. I'm done."

"Let me see," I say, holding out my hand. Tobias drops the pill in my palm. Two translucent shells, the cap and body, sealed together. The upper shell has a slightly larger diameter than the lower. The gelatin casing captures the lantern light in a crystalline sheen.

"Where'd you get them?" I ask as I roll the gelcap around my palm, watching the off-white powder tumble inside. It looks like ashes in a pill-sized urn.

"Does it matter?"

"Um, *yeah*," Amara chimes in. "Pretty safe to say I've taken a fuckton more drugs than both of you combined, and I never *ever* take anything before I know what it is."

"The dead are always inside us. Think of your mind as a doorway to the other side, but it's locked and our ghosts can't get through. We need a key."

I take in the emptiness of the room, the wooden cavities of the house. There's nothing here, I think, this place is completely hollow. "Is Silas here? Right now?"

"He's trying to find his way back. If our connection is strong, we can make contact. That's why it's best to use a house that's not already haunted. There's less interference, less static." Just as a pitcher is filled with water, he explains, all a ghost wants is to be contained. The feeling of enclosure. Of walls. A home. "And we've got the perfect vessel. It's clean. We don't have to worry about any external interference. We'll be the first to haunt this house."

With Silas—like planting a seed.

"*Fuuuck.*" Amara golf claps. "That's some intense necromantic mansplaining. Where'd you learn all this?"

"Look, I didn't believe him at first, either. Silas told me he made contact with his mother. *His mother.* I thought he'd lost it, but then I saw for myself . . ."

What if it's all complete hocus-pocus bullshit and we're just making fools of ourselves out in here in the middle of Hopewell? It's not like anyone else is around to notice.

And if it works? Actually *works*? What if I can talk to Silas—say I'm sorry?

The gelcap is still in my hand. I can feel my palm starting to sweat. The gelatin clings to my skin. I'm suddenly worried the capsule will dissolve and burst and I'll ruin the dose. If we're going to do this, we need to do it before I start to second-guess myself and lose my nerve.

"I'm in."

"I don't know," Amara starts.

I bring my hand up to my mouth. Amara notices, her eyes widening. "Erin, wait—"

I pop the cap. The plastic shell rolls over my tongue, tumbling down, down, and I—

"*Don't!*"

—swallow.

"What the fuck're you thinking? You don't even know what this shit is!"

How many times had Silas handed me something and I just took it on blind faith? From his hands to mine, I'd pop whatever he offered. How is this any different?

Silas says take this.

Silas says try this.

Silas says I want you to find me.

And Tobias just handed me a key. "You in?" he asks Amara, holding out a pill for her.

"*Fine.*" Amara sighs and grabs it. "Fuck it. Let's get haunted."

She pops the pill into her mouth. She sips her water before jerking her head back and swallowing it all down. "If anything happens to me? If I die or go crazy, my parents will sue your scrawny ass into poverty."

Tobias seems genuinely happy to be sharing this experience with us. He swallows his cap, drum-rolling his palms on his knees. "Here we go . . ."

"So what happens now?" I ask.

"We open the door; invite Silas in. I'll guide you through. Just follow my voice, okay?"

A sharp exhale from Amara. "Tobias the spirit guide. Splendid."

Tobias doesn't pay any attention to her, focusing on me. He takes my hand into both of his, squeezing my fingers. "This is up to you," he says. "You're the linchpin here."

"Why me?"

"Because you two were kindred spirits. Silas always said that."

"He did?" We might as well be in middle school and Tobias just told me my sixth-grade crush thinks I'm cute. *Kindred spirits*. Did Silas actually say that?

"If he senses you, he'll come through. Can you try? For Silas?"

I nod. Yes—I can. Silas picked me. I'm the one who can bring him back. Time to summon my supernatural plus-one.

Tobias asks us to take one another's hands. He closes his eyes, bowing his head. "Silas," he calls out to the room. "We have come together to establish contact."

This gives Amara and me an opportunity to take each other in without Tobias watching over us. Her eyes widen. Is that panic or laughter? *Abandon ship*, her eyes silently say to me.

Too late. Tobias starts again. "Can you hear us, Silas?"

"Is the séance talk really necessary?" Amara whispers.

"It helps channel our energy."

"Energy. Right. How long before this shit kicks in, Mr. Leary?"

"Just give it time."

Silence.

"Anybody else getting hungry?" Amara whispers. "I've got the Ouija munchies . . ."

"*Please.*" Tobias struggles to maintain his composure. Amara's really getting under his skin. What's even holding our circle—a triangle now—together? What's the point of *us*?

"I think I need to peeee."

"*Amara*," I lazily snap. "You're ruining the trip for the rest of us."

"It's not a trip," Tobias corrects me. "We're not tripping."

"Fine. *Haunting*. Whatever."

Something like a low-grade nausea begins to boil over in my stomach. I step outside of myself for a sober assessment of what's actually happening here: three pals just broke into a half-finished house in an abandoned development, taking some off-brand ayahuasca in order to perform a séance to chat with their dead fuck-up phantom of a friend. If anyone told me a week ago I'd subject myself to something as ridiculous as this, I would've laughed. But look how quickly

I tagged along for Tobias's psychedelic walkabout, like some desperate Heaven's Gater trying to toss back the vodka and phenobarbital before Hale–Bopp passes over.

"If you can hear us, Silas, give us a sign."

Amara bites her bottom lip in silent laughter. Tobias has no idea what a laughingstock he is right now, eyes still closed, consigning himself to becoming the butt of every joke and jab from Amara for all eternity. "Silas—we're here. We are standing by the door."

I am so embarrassed at myself for believing this could bring Silas back.

"Erin is here. Can you feel her, Silas? Can you sense her presence? She wishes to speak with you, Silas. Show yourself. Make your presence known, Silas. Give us a sign, Silas."

Each time Tobias invokes his name it feels like a nail in my chest. This is the type of bullshit reserved for old biddies wishing to hit up their dead husbands, the kind of pushovers gullible enough to do anything to say one last goodbye. They'll dial up 1-900 numbers to chat with TV psychics, fork over cash to speak to storefront palm readers. Such easy marks, overcome by grief, blinded by loss, sitting ducks just waiting to be taken advantage of.

"Show us that you can hear us. That you're with us, Silas."

If there were hidden cameras installed around the room, a production crew hiding in the basement, filming everything—*Surprise, you're on* Phantasm Camera!—I'd almost be relieved.

"Show us a sign, Silas."

What the hell is a ghost supposed to be, anyway? The past still clinging to the present? A sinkhole that swallows us up? That's what I bet it feels like to be haunted. Truly haunted. I've been consumed by a shadow in the shape of Silas—not his ghost. There are no real spirits. It's just *me*. My selfish need to drag his dead ass back and absolve myself.

"We're here, Silas. Erin is here. Amara is here. We're all waiting for a sign."

I can't take much more of Tobias's posturing. He might believe the crap spouting from his own mouth, but I've heard enough.

"Silas—please—show us . . ."

I have to get out of this house, this abandoned neighborhood. I need to leave. *Now.*

I start to pick myself up from the floor, but the wood ripples beneath me. Or maybe it's just my legs. Nothing feels as solid as it's supposed to anymore.

The emptiness of the living room suddenly feels endless. The surrounding shadows of the afternoon stretch beyond the dimensions of the space itself. How far does this darkness go? Is the room expanding?

My eye is drawn to the far corner by the window. A breeze presses against the clear plastic tarp, pushing the polyethylene forward.

There's a light on the other side of the plastic. A soft glow seeps through the translucent seal. My mind immediately leaps to the obvious explanation: *It's a streetlamp.*

But there are no streetlamps along the block. I remember noticing there weren't any light posts outside—they hadn't been installed yet. When the sun goes down and night sweeps over the street, there will be nothing but darkness surrounding us.

None of the houses have electricity.

Tobias's lantern. It has to be reflecting off the plastic. Clearly that's the answer. I turn to face Tobias's lamp in front of me, just to make sure. Then I turn back to the window frame.

I'm sitting in front of it. My body is situated between the light and the tarp. There's no way the lantern's glow can reach the reflective surface of the plastic sheet—I'm in the way, and the beam isn't powerful enough to weave around me and fill up the rest of the room.

So where's this light coming from?

How is it growing brighter?

I realize the light isn't on the other side of the tarp. *It's inside the house.* Whatever the source is, the light is in the living room. It hovers a few feet from the floor. No wires, no plugs, no bulb. The glow is simply, inexplicably—*there.* Just a small orb the size of my fist. Pulsing.

My mouth opens to say something, but I stop myself.

The light is coming from me. My chest. The glow bounces off the clear plastic tarp.

My heartbeat picks up, mimicking the light's pulse, thump for thump. I can feel the throb in my temples now. The temperature in the room has lifted somehow, even though there's no heating. My face feels hot. My ribs glow white-hot like the filaments on a light bulb.

I glance at Tobias, blind to all of this. "Silas? Are you here?"

Amara's chin dips to her chest. Not out of focus, but sheer bemusement. Her eyes are closed, stifling her smile. Her lips pinch. She wouldn't believe me. I'm not sure if I even believe it. What's happening here? *What the hell is this?*

A radiating globe of light peels away from my body and grows even brighter. Expands. Tendrils extend from its pulsing sphere, strong enough to cast shadows.

Looking at the far wall on the opposite side of the room, I see the silhouettes of ourselves—my shadow next to Amara's thin frame, along with Tobias's slumped one. We look like tenebrous monoliths against the living room wall.

There is a fourth shadow. A silhouette of someone who doesn't belong with the rest of us.

Someone is sitting right next to me.

contact

"*Damnit!*" Tobias pitches Silas's composition book across the room. The pages fan through the air, a marbled osprey struggling to take flight. It hits the wall behind my shoulder, nicking the plaster, then falls facedown on the floor, just a few inches away from my left knee.

"I did everything I was supposed to." He drags the lantern closer, his shadow expanding as Amara's and mine diminish. His silhouette looms over us, a sullen hunchback. "Just like Silas said . . ."

I glance at our shadows along the wall. Only three forms flicker across the plaster.

Amara knows better than to laugh. Tobias has always been fragile. In our freshman creative writing workshop, he would always shut down when a classmate criticized his short stories. Not that Silas ever heeded it—he fanned the flames. *Fuck 'em if they can't see it.*

See what? Tobias wanted—needed—to know.

They don't get you. 'I don't understand your narrator's motivation.' 'Maybe you should try writing in third person.' Conventional bullshit. Silas planted the seed in Tobias's mind that he was a misunderstood genius. If Silas saw it, then it must be true. Now Amara and I are left to deal with the rotten fruit of Tobias's bruised ego. Thanks, Silas.

"Hey . . ." Amara treads carefully. "Toby, it's okay. Don't beat yourself up about it."

Amara rests her hand on his shoulder, hoping to console him.

Tobias jerks back. "Don't."

Tell them what you saw, I think. *Tell them about the light, tell them about—*

"Why didn't it work?" I ask.

"I—I don't know. It takes time for the drug to take root, I think? Maybe it needs to . . . to acclimate to your brain chemistry or something. Silas and I were still beta testing."

"*Testing.*" Amara says. Not a question. Even if Tobias doesn't pick up on it, I sure can: Once was enough. Amara tried, Amara's out. Stick a fork in her 'cause this girl is done.

Tobias doesn't pick up on it. "Until we establish contact, we'll have to keep trying."

"I'm not too keen on being your spiritualist guinea pig, Toby." Amara does her best not to roll her eyes. Whenever she's frustrated or pissed or incredulous or all the above, you know it. She turns over onto her hands and knees before picking herself up from the floor so Tobias won't see her face. "I need a cigarette break. Wanna join me?"

Tobias springs up. "You can't go outside."

"Toby. *Chill.* I'll go in the backyard." Never get between Amara and her American Spirits.

"Somebody will see you."

". . . You're not going to let me go outside? To smoke?" Amara's temper is spiking. This really isn't going to end well. I want to become invisible, to be as translucent as a plastic tarp.

"We'll go upstairs," I suggest. "Nobody will see us, okay?"

"Don't bother." Amara exits the living room without another word. I hear her footsteps on the stairs. The house strains beneath her silent anger. We listen to her clomping on the other side of the ceiling. Suddenly I'm reminded of how my parents would fight in complete silence. Entire wars were waged between my mom and dad without a single word exchanged between them. They'd lob passive-aggressive glances and stiff-lipped looks for days on end, and there I was, caught in the crossfire, aware of how loud a house could be in the absence of sound.

Tobias and I remain where we are, marinating in the quiet. He reminds me of a ten-year-old mad scientist moping over his botched experiment. "We're so close."

"Is this what you two were doing before Silas died? Is this what killed him?"

"Ghost doesn't work like that."

I want to ask: *Then how does it work?*

"If we're able to establish contact, just think about the implications. We can reconnect people with anyone they've ever lost. Death doesn't have to be the end. Not anymore."

I want to tell him about the shadow—about Silas. It was Silas, wasn't it? Tobias will believe me. He'll probably feel vindicated, even. *Told you so*, he'll say to Amara.

What if I'm wrong? What if I didn't see him? It could've been just a trick of the light. That's all it was—light, shadows shifting. Nothing more. "Maybe we should try again," I say.

Tobias doesn't understand. "You mean, like, *right now*?"

"Yeah."

"Tomorrow," he says. "We should get some rest. I need to . . . need to figure this out."

Nobody's asked Tobias how he's taking Silas's absence, how hard it's hit him. Who is Tobias without Silas around to prop him up? He might need Silas even more than I do.

"Hey." I place my hand on top of his, drawing his attention. "I believe in you."

His mouth hangs open, empty of any words for a moment. Of breath. "You . . . you do?"

"You'll figure this out. I know you'll—"

I don't notice Tobias lean in until his lips press against mine. The gesture is so tentative, as if a moth has brushed its wings against my mouth.

I pull back. "*No*."

The word seems to wake him up. Even in the dim light of the lantern, I see his cheeks flood with blood. *What the hell just happened?* Tobias has never tried to kiss me before. I try filtering through all my memories of us alone, just to see if there was ever a moment of me feeding into his belief that he could do something like *that*.

"I'm sorry. I'm—"

"It's okay," I try to recover. "I—I just don't—"

Tobias retreats into himself, the snail back in his shell, shooting up from the floor. His pants are covered in sawdust that drifts off his body like snow. "It's late. I . . ."

"Toby—"

"I'm going to pick a room upstairs. Good night." He doesn't wait for me to respond, heading out without looking back. I can't tell if he's ashamed or frustrated or both.

I listen to his footsteps march up the stairs, wood buckling under the weight of his body.

Now I have the living room all to myself.

And its shadows.

You know what a real haunted house is? I remember my mother drunkenly mumbling to me—or over me—after I asked if there was a ghost hiding under my bed. *It's where we suffer in silence. When you're older, you'll see. Trust me. You'll see for yourself.* She pressed her finger to her lips and smiled a smile that wasn't a smile. *Shhh.* When I was a girl I always felt there were so many stories my mother wasn't telling me: secrets that existed in the house alongside us, things just out of reach of my understanding, simply waiting for me when I finally grew up and became a woman. I always felt so fed up with her because I thought she was living in the past, living some antiquated housewife life, but now I'm not so sure. Maybe she's always been the one trapped in our house, left to wander its halls like a lonely ghost.

I'm sitting in the silence of this empty house and I can't help myself. I have to ask it—

"Silas? Are you there?"

———————

Hssss.

Sleep didn't come easy for me last night—not on these hardwood floors. I feel like a Hot Pocket tucked in the sleeve of my sleeping bag, fresh out of the microwave and drenched in sweat.

Hsssss. At first, I figure a snake has been let loose in the living room. Then I hear the metallic *clack-clack-clack* of the ball bearing rattling within a can of spray paint. *Hssss.*

The axe blade of a migraine splits my skull wide open. I've had plenty of hangover headaches before, but this one feels operatic—downright Wagnerian. All that's left of me is this desiccated husk of a human being.

Hssss. Tobias is tagging the living room. The plywood floor is covered in a pattern of graffiti that stretches toward the walls and reaches for the ceiling. The fumes burn my lungs.

"What do you think?" he asks, rather pleased with himself. Pink letters bloom like weeds across the floor, still wet. On one wall, Tobias has painted YES in bold letters, while NO dries across the opposite wall, and GOODBYE on the third. Tobias has turned the entire room into a massive Ouija board.

"Impressive. Did you fashion a planchette the size of a surfboard, too?"

"We don't need one," he says, as if that's supposed to make sense. "We've got you."

"So I'm the planchette? Got it." I nod a little too quickly, my neck bones popping like bubble wrap. "Got any coffee? Or a shotgun?"

"We're pretty dried out." He hands me a water bottle. "We need to rehydrate."

I feel like ass is such an understatement. No matter how much water I drink, I can't wash this loamy flavor away. A cat died in my mouth; no other explanation works. "I don't want to know what I look like. If it's half as bad as how I feel, put me out of my misery."

"Did you know humans are the only creatures alive that know about death?"

"*Toby*," I groan. "I don't think I'm awake enough for a philosophical treatise on death at the moment." Not that I have much of a choice. Tobias is already well on his way.

"Other animals sense danger and the need for self-preservation, but we're the only ones who know death is coming. We know it's there, always there, just waiting for us."

"Lucky us."

"What if it's a gift? Knowing?"

"I'd keep the receipt."

"What the hell." Amara walks into the living room. "You're redecorating?"

"Just refocusing our energy. Helping set the mood."

"How romantic."

"I figured out what went wrong last night," he says with total confidence. The resilience of the male ego is a stunning thing. "Let's try again."

"I'm gonna need a minute before I do anything," Amara mutters.

But Tobias doesn't waste any time. "I want you to sit here." Taking our hands, he guides us to sit in a freshly painted circle in the center of the living room. "Amara, you sit next to her."

"Is this where we'll *refocus our energy*?"

"The person with the strongest connection has to be the one who reaches out. That's why you're leading us today."

He's looking at me. "*Me?* Why me?"

"Because you love him." He says as if the answer is obvious. "You don't have to hide it."

"I'm not *hiding* anything."

Tobias turns to Amara for a little backup. "Am I wrong?"

Amara doesn't say a word.

"Your denial is what's blocking us from contacting him. If you accept—"

"Don't blame *me*."

"It has to be you." Tobias scoots even closer, until I can smell his breath. He really needs to brush his teeth. We all do. "If he hears you—senses you—you can draw him in."

If Amara finds any of this even remotely amusing, she's keeping it to herself. She's too tired to resist Tobias anymore. That makes two of us. "So what am I supposed to say?"

"Don't worry, I'll walk you through."

Amara has clearly checked out this morning. I can tell she's counting down the hours—maybe the minutes—until this weekend is over. The most painless way to make this all go away is to do whatever Tobias says—then ghost.

He doles out another dose for each of us. "One for you . . . one for you . . . one for me."

"Eye contact," I say, trying to bring some levity to our drug-induced séance.

"Cheers," Amara mumbles, not meeting my eyes. We all pop the pills in our mouths and swallow without another word, chasing them down with as much water as we can stomach.

The living room feels different in the daylight. Smaller. The night before, the room itself seemed to expand, the wooden beams stretching over our heads. It felt like we'd been devoured by some prehistoric plywood beast. Everything looks harsh and dusty in the sunlight.

"Close your eyes," Tobias starts. I glance at Amara before I do, but she won't look at me.

"We wish to speak with someone we've lost," Tobias announces. His voice sounds far away, as if it's coming from the corner of the living room, even though I can still feel his knee pressed against mine. "Silas—if you can hear us, we want you to know we are here."

I strain my ears as much as I can. I want to hear something—hear him, his voice.

"Erin." Tobias squeezes my hand. "It's your turn. Reach out to Silas."

I don't know what do to. What am I supposed to say? If my eyes were open, I'd feel like a complete idiot, but behind my eyelids, any feelings of self-consciousness begin to ebb. The presence of both Amara and Tobias slowly recedes from my mind's eye. There's no one else now. It's just me and—

"Silas? Can you hear me?"

The longer my eyes are closed, the more I notice certain patterns. Diamond-shaped helixes emerge from the darkness and spiral across my eyelids.

"It's me . . . Erin."

The helixes twirl faster at the sound of Silas's name. They fluctuate in color, red to purple to green, as they gain speed.

"Are you there?"

The temperature rises up my back before radiating through the rest of my body. The room is muggier now. The plastic tarps trap the warmth of the sun in the room. It feels like a sauna overheating.

"Silas," Tobias says. "We're here. Can you hear us?"

"Silas," I jump in. I don't want Tobias to reach him first. "I know you're there."

The presence of my body, the very sensation of my skin, fades. I'm dissolving. I can't tell where my skin is anymore, where I stop and the house starts.

"Silas, if you can hear me, I want you—I want you to know that I never left you."

I am the house. Every room is a chamber of my heart, every hallway an artery, every beam a bone. All I need now is a ghost. I'm ready to be haunted. For Silas's spirit to possess this vessel.

"I never let you go, Silas. I never meant to hurt you."

The fluctuating colors behind my eyelids compress themselves, taking shape.

A silhouette.

"I wish I could take back everything I said that night. I wish I could go back and—"

The floor creaks behind me—a footstep. It's such an abrupt sound I can't help but open my eyes. I'm immediately met by harsh sunlight. The sun has shifted, seemingly in a matter of minutes—or have we been sitting here for hours? Long enough for the sun to move along its path, the light sliding across the living room.

"I love you, Silas. I miss you . . . I . . ."

A pocket of shadow remains in the far corner. The sun can't reach that far into the room. There's something palpable within the darkness, something growing, gaining potency. Then the shadow starts to move. Something—*someone*—is standing in the corner.

"Do you see that?" I hear myself ask, but it doesn't sound like the words are coming from me.

Tobias glances around the room. "See what?"

"In the corner. Right *there*."

Amara won't look behind her. She refuses to see. Her focus remains on the floor. The walls. The ceiling. Anything but that far corner of the living room, anywhere but there.

The silhouette steps forward. Out from the shadows. The darkness follows, as if it somehow drags the shadows with it, tugging on that black, a web spindling out from the wall.

I see him. I see *him*. "Silas?"

"Where? Where is he?" Tobias asks, unable to hide his anxiety. His head whips around the room, desperate to see—and when he finally does see him the stillness that takes over his face is so sudden it's as if someone pressed pause on his body. Only his eyes move, frenzied. He whispers, "*It's him.*"

"Silas, I . . ." My throat is too dry. I need water, but I can't look away from him. I can't bring myself to break contact—he might disappear again. "Silas, it's me. It's Erin!"

Saying his name out loud seems to give him life—*I'm giving him life*—as if it's enough to endow him with existence once more. "Can you hear me, Silas? Can you see me?"

A name is a vessel. It holds certain syllables, certain cadences. If you say them in a certain order, in a certain rhythm, you're able to invoke the very breath of God. And I want to say Silas's name with life again. I want to say his name out loud and have it sound the way I used to say it when he was alive. I want to say his name with all my heart. To endow every letter with love, everlasting love.

"Silas—"

I cough. There's something caught in my throat, but I can't look away from him.

"Silas, it's me. I'm here, Silas. I—"

Something thick moves up my esophagus. I can hear myself retch. It's wet, labored.

"Erin?" Amara's hand tightens its grip around mine, squeezing my fingers.

Whatever is rising up my throat now blocks the airway. I can't breathe. Amara yanks on my arm. I pray that the pleading look in my eyes broadcasts my absolute inability to inhale.

I can't breathe.

My chest heaves once, twice.

Can't breathe.

The bulge in my throat works its way up.

Can't . . .

Silas is gone, if he'd even been here. He was, though, wasn't he? Hadn't I seen him?

"What's wrong?" Tobias asks, kneeling before me. "What is—"

I retch once more. My entire body starts to seize.

"Erin!"

A tendril of white, wet substance pushes past my lips. It coils and oscillates in front of my tear-stained face, branching out and upwards, a root reaching for sunlight.

"*Holy shit.*" Tobias pushes away from me, his eyes fixated on the tendril. My jaw locks, unable to close as I continue to expel this substance from deep within me. It just keeps coming and coming, whatever it is—*unspooling*—blooming in the air above our heads.

I can't breathe. Can't breathe. Can't—

Amara reaches out to touch it.

"*Don't,*" Tobias starts.

The tip of her index finger barely grazes the surface of the writhing mass, wet and alive.

Tobias tries to pull Amara's hand away. "Don't touch it—"

The mass ruptures.

Whatever suspended itself in the air immediately loses its hold the moment Amara touches its slippery surface. It falls to the floor and bursts into a yellowish liquid that appears to contain the contents of my last meal. Trail mix and bile splash across the floorboards.

I feel as if I just broke through the surface of a body of water, finally able to breathe again. I gasp for air, drawing in deep, ragged breaths as I expel the last of the drug from my stomach.

"Erin. *Erin.*"

I finally look at Amara. The terror in her expression is unmistakable.

"What—" I say, hacking uncontrollably. I hold out my arms to her. I need to hold someone. Need to feel safe. "What—"

"It's okay, it's okay, I got you." Amara opens her arms and I collapse into her, letting her take my trembling body and keep me from shaking. I can't stop. She combs the wet hair out of my face with her fingers, using her sleeve to wipe the vomit from my cheeks.

"What *was* that?" I shriek.

Tobias is practically hyperventilating. The elation on his face sends a chill through me—I know exactly what that expression means.

It works.

stash

The mushroom cap is a creamy off-white, a gauzy veil draped over its stalk. When I hold it up to the sunlight, it's nearly translucent.

It even resembles a ghost, I think.

"Shrooms?" Amara is incapable of hiding her disbelief. "Are you kidding me? We've been taking fucking *shrooms*?"

"*Hebeloma sarcophyllum*." Tobias's jaw clenches as he enunciates its name. "They're very rare. They don't grow on just anything."

I try repeating the name. "Sarco . . ."

"Phyllum. You can't even find them in the US. Silas had to order a batch from—"

"I don't give a shit where they came from," Amara interrupts. "You lied to us!"

"How? I've told you everything. You're just not *listening* to me."

"You didn't tell us we'd be shrooming. We're not in college, tripping our balls off."

"Taking Ghost isn't *shrooming*."

"Stop." I can't keep from trembling. My sleeping bag is draped over my shoulders, but the cold reaches my bones and now my whole body is vibrating like a tuning fork. "Just . . . *stop*."

A stale, meaty aroma has seeped into my skin. Amara leans in to take a whiff of the mushroom cap, then pulls back, her expression souring. "No wonder you puked."

"That wasn't vomit," Tobias says. "That was ectoplasm."

"I'm sorry?" Amara's expression sours.

"*Ectoplasm*," Tobias repeats. "A substance that exudes from the body during a trance—"

"Oh, *come on.*"

"It must be some kind of side effect of the—"

"I'm surprised Erin didn't purge pink elephants!"

"We all saw him, right?"

"I didn't see shit." Amara says it way too quickly, as in *end of discussion.*

"That was Silas! Do you know how amazing this is? The séance worked. Ghost *works*—"

"Erin puking is not a religious experience and you're sure as shit not some shaman."

"This is why I didn't want to tell you. I knew, *I just knew*, you'd latch onto this infantile idea that it's all a bad trip."

"That's *exactly* what happened—"

"If I wanted us all to shroom, I would've bought us some shrooms!" Tobias isn't getting anywhere with Amara, so he turns to me. "Erin—you experienced it. What did it feel like?"

"I don't know." I focus on the mushroom. Pinching its stalk, I roll it between my fingers so the cap spirals. All I think about is the shadow in the corner of the room. How it moved toward me—reached for me. I nearly *touched* him. "Can we do it again?"

"*Excuse* me?" Amara nearly shouts. "Are you out of your *mind*?"

"I want to try again."

"Whoa, whoa," Tobias cuts in. "Slow down. I'm not sure what the side effects are . . ."

"I've got a pretty good idea," Amara says.

"We need to stay hydrated and get some rest before we dose."

"When?" I fail to suppress the eagerness that even I don't totally recognize. The *need.*

"Tomorrow."

"*Tomorrow?*" I can see it click in Amara's mind that this isn't over yet. Not as far as Tobias is concerned—or me. It's only Saturday. We have a whole weekend ahead of us. "I'm out," she says.

"You *saw* him," I insist. Silas materialized for me. *Silas picked me.* It was my voice that drew him in—not Tobias's. It was my words that lured him toward our house. *Mine.*

"No, I didn't." Amara's digging in. She's not going to cede any ground. She's scared.

"We're *this* close," Tobias says, nearly pleading with her.

"*I—am—not—doing—it—again.*"

This isn't the response Tobias was expecting. He reaches for her. "Amara. Please. We—"

Amara yanks her hands back. "Don't you touch me."

"We can't leave until we—"

"You can't keep me here!"

It seems to collectively dawn on us all that I'm the one with the car. Both Amara and Tobias turn to me, identical pleading looks in their eyes.

"Amara . . ."

Amara steps back, the walls closing in on her. "I'll call a cab."

"You know what we saw." Tobias says it in the calmest voice possible.

Amara looks back at me.

"Please, Amara," I say.

I understand how she must feel like I let her down; that I'm on Tobias's side now and she's all alone in this house with no skin. She heads to the kitchen by herself. I hear her stifle a sob, but the house lets her anguish echo through its hollow halls.

Tobias turns to me. "If she leaves, we'll break—"

"I'll talk to her. *Jesus*, just calm down."

I find Amara leaning against what would've been the sink. "Amara . . . ? You okay?"

She stares through the window frame instead of at me. The late afternoon sun seeps through the tarp, casting a gray pallor over her face. She looks exhausted. Spent.

"This isn't what friends do to each other. This isn't healthy. You know that, right?"

She's right. Of course. What none of us have said—not out loud, at least—is that our friendship has felt extremely lopsided ever since Silas died. Our quartet is now a trio and we haven't found our footing yet. But hearing Amara say it, hearing the words out loud, cuts deep.

"So what're you saying?" I try to make a joke out of it. "You breaking up with us now?"

She is, I realize. Oh god, Amara is letting go. She's cutting *me* out.

"I'm only doing this for you. Not for Tobias, and definitely not Silas. Silas is dead." Amara says it so matter-of-factly, it angers me. "He's gone and this isn't going to bring him back."

"I saw him, Amara. You did, too, didn't you?"

"No."

Liar.

———

I can just barely spot the lights from Richmond burning on the horizon through the clear plastic tarps. Crickets chirp in a steady, mechanical thrum outside the house, dampened by the plastic.

We all agreed to stick together, just in case one of us—meaning me—gets sick. Amara wants to keep an eye on me, I can tell, even if the conversation between us is pretty brittle for the rest of the night. We've held each other's hair back plenty of times, helping each other through our most pukeable moments. Even now, there's a silent solidarity between us. I hope so, at least.

We're in our sleeping bags, facing the ceiling. The lamp lights up the Ouija board walls.

I'm the planchette. I wonder if I can slide from letter to letter and spell out Silas's name.

Amara finally ventures, "Anybody got any good ghost stories?"

"Does Silas count?" I ask.

"Not yet," Tobias mutters.

Amara turns until she's facing away. "Well, this slumber party's a bust."

"Ever heard of the Good Death?" Tobias asks. I immediately sense we should all gear up for a lecture. "Look back to the Civil War—"

"I wanted to be scared to death, Toby," Amara says, burying her face in her sleeping bag, "not bored to death."

But he's off and running, talking at the ceiling whether we want to listen or not. "Up to that point, when someone passed away, it happened at home. Your family gathered all around your bed while you just gently slipped off this mortal coil. Everyone got to say their goodbyes. Then came the Civil War. Soldiers were dying miles away from home, from their families. Nobody got the Good Death anymore. All those souls were . . . lost."

Tobias holds his hands up, conducting a symphony. "Then came Maggie and Kate Fox. Only fourteen and eleven years old, but they could communicate with the spirit world."

"Bull," Amara moans into her sleeping bag, "shit."

The Fox sisters were one of Silas's favorite stories. Tobias sounds just like him, to be honest. I can nearly hear Silas's voice. The Fox sisters let the parents of departed soldiers know they died a valiant death, spirited away by the graceful hands of God. If it was good enough for Mary Todd Lincoln, it was good enough for the rest of America.

A silence insinuates itself into the living room. Tobias has put both himself and Amara to sleep with his history lesson. I should turn the lantern off, conserve the propane for tomorrow, but I keep it on, listening to the hiss of its cylinder. I feel the plywood floor through my sleeping bag.

I slip out of my sleeping bag and grab the can of spray paint. Finding an empty space for myself, I tag the corner.

ERIN IS HERE

I step back to admire my handiwork, the pink letters bleeding all the way down to the floor. I am here. In this house. In the—

The light from the lantern suddenly pulses and moves across the wall, drawing my attention along with it. It lands on Tobias's satchel. The leather bag rests next to him, unbuckled, its flaps pulled back just enough to expose the books within.

There's Silas's composition book. I recognize the black-and-white cover right away.

"Tobias?" I wait to see if he'll wake but he's fast asleep.

As I tug on Silas's notebook, a Ziploc bag falls out of the satchel. There are six gelcaps inside. I pry one open and an earthy aroma rushes out, like the trapped gases from a corpse's bloated stomach. The smell clings to my skin, seeping in.

The mushroom he showed us earlier is in the bag too. I bring it to my nose, breathing in its earthiness.

I pop the mushroom in my mouth.

I taste dirt. Loam. My tongue runs over the cap's gills. I gag as soon as I start to chew but I manage to force myself to swallow. I empty a whole bottle of water to keep myself from bringing it back up.

I'm going to puke, oh god, I'm going to—

I fight the nausea back. I can feel the water sloshing around my stomach. I know it'll take some time for the Ghost to kick in, so I open Silas's notebook.

It's empty.

Every last page—completely blank. No poems or notes or hidden thoughts from Silas. Not even a single pencil mark. Tobias has been waving around a blank book this entire time.

Why would Tobias lie to us? To me? Because he couldn't con-vince us to come along if I didn't believe Silas had planned this all out? Because I needed to believe that it was—

The propane lamp sputters and everything goes dark. The shadows in the far reaches of the living room rush toward me, swallowing me whole. I fumble for my cell—it's on the floor somewhere. I left it just next to my sleeping bag, which is bound to be only a few inches from where I'm sitting. I pat blindly at the wood floor.

My fingers graze against something soft, spongey, like a—

mushroom

—and I yank my hand back. Just nylon. My sleeping bag, of course. A few more pats in the dark and I finally find my phone. The blue light of the lock screen pushes the shadows back a bit. The notebook is still open on the floor where I dropped it.

A single word is now written across the page:

ERIN

I swear it hadn't been there before. I flipped through the whole composition book and found nothing. There's no way, absolutely no way I would have missed it. I flip to the next page.

ARE YOU HERE

The tarp over the window seems to respire behind me. I turn on my phone's flashlight and aim it at the window. The translucent sheet slowly expands and contracts, as if someone is standing on the other side of it, inhaling so hard the plastic sucks into their mouth, then exhaling out again.

I don't know how long I stare at it. *In, out.* Air hisses through the plastic.

Turning back to the composition book, I flip to the next page.

FIND ME

A floorboard creaks over my head. I let out a gasp, startled by the abrupt sound.

It came from upstairs. I double-check that Amara and Tobias are still there in the living room with me. Neither of them has moved. Neither is awake. I try to rationalize the sound away—the house is just settling, that's all. No one's here. No one else was—

I hear it again, louder this time. More pronounced. The sound of wood giving under pressure, followed by another.

Footsteps. Someone is walking along the second floor.

I hold my breath, eager—*yearning* to hear it again. Daring it to happen. *Come on.*

There it is. Another step. *Someone is upstairs!*

I rush up the steps on my tiptoes, trying in vain not to make a sound. But the wood won't stay quiet. I hold my phone out before me, letting its flashlight illuminate my way down the hall. I shine the beam in each room, sweeping the light across the closet and—

The light catches something that wasn't—shouldn't—be there.

I'm not sure if I actually see anything at first. I'm probably making it up, imagining things, but just to be sure, I glide the light back over the walls and—

There. In the far corner. In the closet. Scrawled across the walls. Words.

I don't care how loud my footsteps sound, don't care if I wake anyone else up now. Each step I take reverberates through the house as I rush for the closet and hold my phone up.

I AM HERE

It's Silas. Even scrawled on the wall, pencil on plaster, I'm positive it's his handwriting.

WHERE ARE YOU

I'd been in this room earlier and I swear I hadn't seen anything. Did I just miss it? Had—

Silas

—written it when we were downstairs? As if the answer isn't obvious—as if it isn't clear.

"Silas?" I call out to the room, shining the light all around me. "I'm here. I'm right here!"

The shadows shift with the light from my phone, slipping behind the exposed planks that hold up the room. They look like limbs. No, they are becoming arms and legs—taking shape.

Walking toward me. Standing before me.

Silas says get on your feet . . .

Silas says come to me . . .

He cups my jaw in both of his hands. He leans over and kisses my forehead.

Silas says:

"Hey there, Li'l Deb."

comedown

Silas is in the waiting room. I've spent the last hour in the recovery room by myself, thinking of what I'll say to him, knowing that he's still out there, the same magazine in his hands, flipping through its pages without reading a single word, waiting for me so we can escape together.

A nurse checks on me twice. She smiles sympathetically whenever she ducks her head in. "Feel okay, hon?" Does she want me to say yes? "It's okay to go now, if you feel up to it."

They give me pamphlets. A prescription. Reassurances that I'll be fine.

I spot Silas before he sees me. It's rare to see him worried. Anxiety is never something he exudes, but for that split second before he notices me, I watch his gaze travel from one place to the next, never settling.

Then he finds me and—oh god—his face brightens. There's joy in his eyes. Not relief, *joy*. He's radiating it. Absolutely ecstatic. Leaping to his feet, he runs over, holding out his hands as if I'm about to fall, even if I'm not. Silas stands ready to catch me. I almost let him.

"Hey," he says. "You okay?"

"I'm fine. Can we go?"

Silas nods and holds open the door for me. We step out into the sun. My eyes sting from the sudden flood of light and I bring my hand up to shade them. When my vision recalibrates, I notice a group of people standing on the opposite end of the parking lot. It's just a trick of the light, but for a brief moment, they all look like maggots to me. Each one holds a homemade cardboard sign over their head. I try not to look at them but certain phrases leap out at me.

HAUNT YOU

IN HELL

SOULS

Silas guides me to my car, away from the crowd. Instead of hopping behind the wheel, I sit shotgun while he drives. We ride in silence until we're finally on the highway.

"Can we go somewhere?" I ask. The doctor told me that it would be best if I rest for the remainder of the day. She told me to expect some bleeding, but that was about it. Perhaps some cramping. I can go back to classes as early as tomorrow, as long as I feel up for it.

"Where do you wanna go?" Silas asks.

"Anywhere. I don't care. Just . . . not back to my apartment yet."

We cross the Lee Bridge on our way to Belle Isle. Yet another memorial to a dead Confederate general, a ragged stitch connecting the Southside to the rest of the city. The James River flows beneath us and curves around fifty acres of public park.

I shouldn't be walking but there isn't a single part of me that wants to rest right now. I want to be outside, out of my head, in the open where I can breathe. I don't want to be alone.

We take each step slowly across a footbridge that runs under the interstate. You can hear the hum of traffic passing along the highway overhead—but once you've set foot on Belle Isle, the sounds melt away. It's like the city doesn't exist anymore.

"You know this used to be a prison camp?" Silas says. "Thousands of soldiers froze their asses off right here."

"Since when did you become such a Civil War buff?"

"I'm from Richmond," he says. "Of course I'm a Civil War buff." He has a point. You can't live in this city without its history seeping into the fabric of your everyday existence. It's a fact of life here. You simply accept all those Confederate skeletons in our collective closet.

"Can we slow down?" I ask. "Just a little?"

"Of course."

You have to get to Belle Isle super early on the weekends if you want to beat the sunbathers and claim one of the broad rocks along the riverbank. Luckily for us, it's a Tuesday in October. I pick a flattened slab right at the river's edge. I can barely make out a couple's spray-painted names across the rock's broadside, faded to a dull, brown algae—ESTELLE + CALEB 1986.

Silas notices me wince as I lower myself. He holds out his hand for me. "Here. Easy."

Neither of us say much of anything for a while. Which is fine. We end up watching the river in silence, the currents roiling all around, until Silas finally asks, "Want to talk about it?"

"Not much to say, is there?" What's done is done.

I'd been terrified to tell him at first, unsure how he'd react. There was a part of me that could've easily just not said anything and dealt with it all by myself. But I knew I couldn't keep it a secret from Silas forever. He would've found out eventually. He deserved to know. He listened intently when I told him the news at my place, quietly nodding along. Never interrupting, just listening to me. I waited for him to react. Was he going to panic? Run away?

We ended up spending the rest of the night together, holding each other.

The next morning I scheduled the appointment.

It must've happened the night of our graveyard raid in Hollywood Cemetery. This had to be our, what, eighth breakup? Tenth? What was the point of keeping count anymore? Our sporadic postmortem sexual encounters were de rigueur. The past still clinging to the present. The ghosts of our love that wouldn't let us go.

I never told anyone. Not my parents. Not my friends.

Only Silas knew.

"I don't want Amara to know," I finally say. "Or Toby. Okay? Promise you won't tell."

"Of course," he says. "Cross my heart."

"Hope to die," I say back.

When there isn't much to say, Silas fills the silence with more history. "They'd bring a surgeon out to check the prisoners, figuring out which frostbitten limbs to saw off."

"Everybody in this city's a goddamn Civil War aficionado," I mutter.

"You're the daughter of the Confederacy here, not me."

"Do you love me for who I am, or is it just because of my birthright?" I mean it as a joke, but plenty of dudes have wanted to date me solely on the basis of my Southern heritage. Not to mention I just tossed out the L-word at Silas, a big no-no on my part.

"Just you." Silas slides across the rock and positions himself directly behind me. His legs now stretch out alongside mine. He wraps his arms around my chest and I lean back against his. The two of us nestle into one another as we watch the currents slip by.

We fall quiet again until Silas says, "I never left you, you know?"

"I know."

"What if I told you we could be together forever?" His breath is warm against my neck. "All you have to do is stay. Stay with me."

This isn't how I remember that morning on Belle Isle. There's an undertow to his breath that's pulling me in. His arms continue to slither around my chest, tightening.

"This can be our house. *Our home.*"

"I'd like that." Would I? I never said any of this. What's going on here?

I glance up at Silas.

His eyes have gone completely milky. His skin is a pale robin's-egg blue.

"I knew you'd bring me back." His purple lips don't move. His mouth simply hangs open. His tongue blooms out of his mouth, like a mushroom cap.

I push him away but a sharp pain stabs me below. I press my hand against my pelvis, hoping to halt the sting, but I lose my balance. I'm falling. Falling—

My shoulder hits the rock as I slip into the river.

Cold water swallows me. My insides seize. I try to find the surface but I keep tumbling, spiraling end over end through water the color of ashes.

When I finally find the surface, I'm no longer in Richmond. I'm surrounded by black, churning waves. A sea of shadows that reaches as far as the horizon, where gray clouds gather against a soot-colored sky. My arms thrash in the water—

"Erin!"

But I'm getting nowhere—

"Erin—wake up!"

I'm spiraling, tumbling back under—

"Erin!"

My eyes fly open to find Tobias leaning over me. His glasses reflect the light of the lantern and nearly blind me. I feel the plywood floor against my shoulders.

I'm in the living room back at the house.

I could've sworn it was the James River . . . Or something else. *Somewhere* else. A different place. A cold place.

My muscles ache but I swear I can still feel Silas's arms tightening around my chest.

"Erin." Tobias can barely hide his excitement. "Erin, he's here!"

I can't speak just yet. My throat's too dry.

"We *saw* him, Erin! Silas is home!"

There's still a part of me that hasn't come back yet, trapped in the remnants of—what was that? A dream? A hallucination? I felt everything from that day, stronger than any sense of déjà vu. Silas holding me, the wind on my skin, the rock beneath us, the cutting of the currents.

I must've gone further. *Deeper.* Into the cold.

Amara is in the living room but she's not present. She's no longer participating, merely yielding to Tobias. I know this is the end of our friendship, and I am okay with letting her go.

Silas is back, that's all that matters. *Silas is here.* Silas is in
our home

—away from home away from home away from home.

PART THREE

withdrawal

clear plastic tarp

"*Let's go.*" Amara's voice rebounds throughout the house like she's shouting from every room at once. Usually she's the one dragging her heels when it comes to heading out, but she's packed before the rest of us, ready to get the hell out of Hopewell.

Tobias won't budge. "I wouldn't go out there if I were you."

"Why?"

"There's no telling what you're going to see."

"I'm so fucking done. Have a blast, Toby. Erin, come on. Let's go home."

But I am home, I want to say. I just brought Silas back and now we're leaving him? Here? All alone in Hopewell? I still feel his spirit buzzing through my body, like a sparkler in my heart. Can't I take him with me? If all it takes is a dose of Ghost, can't I contact him wherever I want?

I'll be Silas's haunted house.

Tobias doesn't seem all that sad to stay behind. We're abandoning him.

"I can come back for you," I offer.

"Don't worry about me. Just get back to your life."

Your life. What a funny way of putting it.

I want to say Amara and I have some heart-to-heart during the ride back to Richmond, but things remain pretty quiet in the car.

She rolls down her window and lights an American Spirit with Silas's REHAB IS FOR QUITTERS lighter, then tosses it onto the dash.

The shrill hiss of wind cuts through the cabin as we drive down the interstate.

"Mind if I bum one?"

Amara takes a long drag before passing it to me without a word.

"I know you don't believe—"

"*Don't*," Amara cuts me off. She silently occupies herself with the stereo for the rest of the ride, shifting from station to station, never settling on one song long enough to listen. Static crackles through the speakers every time she changes the station and I can't help but drift a bit behind the wheel, my thoughts lost in a gray ocean.

When we pull up to her apartment, I try one last time. "You saw him, didn't you?"

"I didn't see anything." Amara flicks her cigarette through the window before climbing out. She doesn't look back.

I wait for her to safely enter her building before driving off. What I failed to mention, what I hoped to tell Amara on the ride back but couldn't was that . . .

I stole Tobias's stash.

I honestly hadn't planned on taking it. I saw his satchel on the living room floor, flap still open, the Ziploc baggie tucked within. Only a handful of Ghost left: three gelcaps.

Tobias will be pissed when he finds out, but he'll forgive me. I don't want him dosing out there alone. I expect he'll call and chew me out and I'll have to explain why—*I'm trying to protect you, Toby*—and eventually he'll come around and get over it. Tobias always gets over it.

I didn't plan on dosing on Ghost.

At least I don't think I did. It isn't until after I drop Amara off that I even begin to consider the week ahead. My new job beckons like a beam of light. *Go toward the light, Erin! Go toward the light!* I can see the New Me reaching out, calling, *Take my hand, Old Erin!*

So why do I feel so listless?

I have nowhere to go. Nowhere to be. Whenever this happened before, this itch taking root within me, Silas would always show up and whisk me away on one of his adventures.

But that's not happening anymore, is it, Erin?

What if it can? Who says it has to be over?

The notion firmly takes hold by the time I reach my apartment. I can have Silas all to myself now, can't I? Really make an evening out of it, too. No interference, no nagging from Amara, no mansplaining from Tobias. Just Silas and me, alone at last.

I start thinking about the possibilities between us—all the things we can talk about with a little privacy. I think back to those nights where Silas guided me through the city, showing me every bygone spot Richmond itself had forgotten. We were making our own history in those moments, exploring the ruins of Richmond, reading its graffiti together, and I can't help but wonder if we can have that experience anytime I want now. I can take Silas with me wherever I go. What's stopping me from conjuring up his ghost whenever I dose? He'll have a home in me.

I lock the door, switch my cell to vibrate, and fetch a half-finished bottle of merlot. Light some candles. Fire up some Belle and Sebastian before slipping into bed.

Everything is perfect. All I need is Silas. So I drop some Ghost and wait for him to arrive.

And wait.

And . . .

I'm bored with Belle and Sebastian. I decide to shift to the Smiths, which feels more appropriate for the mood I'm trying to evoke here. Then I turn the music off altogether.

At one point, I think I hear something down the hall. I bolt up in bed. "Silas?"

No response.

"Silas—it's me." I second-guess myself, so I add, "Erin."

Still nothing. Some other tenant must've wandered through the main hall. I lie back in bed, feeling extremely present—*Erin is here*—trying to pinpoint every stray sound in and out of the building. There's too much noise outside my window. I can't push out the sounds of cars and frat bros emerging from Twisters on Grace Street. I can't concentrate on my own connection.

I find myself yearning to be back—

home

—in Hopewell, where everything is quieter. Where I can focus on my own ghosts.

"Silas, can you hear me?"

Thirty minutes later, still nothing. What am I doing wrong? Why can't I connect?

"Silas. I'm *here*. Where are you?"

Nothing.

"Why aren't you listening to me?"

Nothing.

It's possible he just can't hear me. That we have a weak connection. What if my body is developing a tolerance against my phantoms? Do I need to take more? Double my dose?

I pinch a second pill from the baggie and roll it between my fingers, watching the gray powder tumble like grains of sand in an hourglass.

A half dose, I say to myself. Just a little bump to get over the hump. I try prying the gelcap apart. The shell casing is just another vessel, I think.

I tug too hard. The gelcap tears open abruptly, sending ash scattering all over my nightstand. *Shit.* I can't waste it. I only have one cap left. *Fuck fuck fuck what should I do*—

Guess I'm hoovering it. I lower my head to the nightstand, press one finger against my left nostril and snort through the right. The burn reaches deep down into my nasal cavity. I feel the drip at the back of my throat, a septic echo that resonates through my skull.

He'll hear me this time, I know it. I just have to focus my energy. "Silas?"

I have to call upon him. Summon him.

"Silas, please . . . I need you."

Our connection is strong. Tobias told me so. *I found him.* I brought him back.

So where the hell is he?

"It's Erin. Please, Silas, come to me." Am I supposed to repeat whatever incantation Tobias said? I thought my voice was strong enough. "*Silas.* Please. Where are you?"

Nothing. I can't feel him. He's not here.

"Screw you, Silas." He's a total no-show. "Asshole," I mutter just before falling asleep.

———————

When I peel open my eyes, I'm met by the morning's gray haze. Everything seems suspended in a fog, but that's just my head. I can't think straight. My entire body has dried out. My mouth feels like a tundra. I yawn and the skin around my lips cracks like a brittle shell. My alarm clock says it's already ten. *Jesus.* I've blacked out before, but this feels like a total solar eclipse in my skull. All I want is to lie in bed, bury my head under my pillow, and pronounce myself dead for the foreseeable future.

I'm revived by the vibration of a new text. I reach for it, only for my hand to touch—

soft plastic

—and recoil. I sit up far too fast, feeling my mind lag behind the rest of my body. I need to take a moment for the bedroom to stop spinning. Let the walls settle down once more.

It's only the Ziploc baggie on my nightstand.

One gelcap left.

The text is from Tanner: *Still up for drinks this week, killer?* I don't have the stamina to text a pithy comeback. Tanner will just have to wait. I have three new voicemails from Mom. I was so dead to the world I must not have heard her calling last night. Or this morning. As I listen to the messages, I can hear her tone tighten with each voicemail:

Hon, is everything alright? This isn't like you . . . Give your mother a ring, will you?

I don't know why you can't simply pick up your phone . . . Should I be taking offense? Just promise me you'll be there tomorrow. You know how important this is for your father . . .

Tonight. As in Monday. Seven p.m. Sharp. Don't forget. For your father's sake, not mine.

I can't understand why this party is so important to her. Dad doesn't care. Even at twelve, I sensed my parents were destined for divorce—or should be. They could've put our family out of its collective misery just by separating, but instead, they've gone through the motions of marriage with ghoulish devotion.

No texts from Amara. Guess the last ten hours haven't lifted her mood. I call her but her phone goes straight to voicemail. She's probably still asleep. Lord knows I want to be.

My skull is pounding but I desperately need to get up and get some water. When I lift my head, I notice the tag I'd scribbled on my wall in Sharpie weeks ago:

ERIN WAS HERE

What the fuck? What kind of sick joke is this? Who rewrote *is* as *was*?

I lick my thumb and rub at the *was* to see if the marker will come off. It smears across the wall, the Sharpie coating my thumb.

My phone vibrates again, a call this time, startling me. It's not a number programmed into my contacts but I pick it up anyway.

"Uh . . . Hi?" The woman's voice sounds hesitant on the other end. "This is Lorraine? At the McMartin Agency? Just calling to check in, see when we should expect you this morning."

Oh shit. My first day of work. I'm so screwed. I could lie—tell her I'm feeling sick. Loraine would understand, right? She'd let me come in tomorrow. I need one day, *just a day*, so I can get my head on straight and get my life together. "I—think I came down with something?"

"Ah. Oh, okay. Well . . ."

It's slipping. My future. My fucking five-year plan. My opportunity to move on with my life. It's all slipping through my fingers right now and I'll lose everything if I don't grab it back.

"You know what," I hear myself say, "false alarm."

". . . You sure?"

"No. Yeah. Food poisoning. Nothing big. I'm feeling better." I sit up and open the blinds. Too much sun comes flooding into the apartment all at once. It stings to look out the window.

As I blink against the harsh light, I notice a figure standing in the middle of the street directly below my apartment window. A woman enshrouded in plastic. A clear plastic tarp.

"Great," I hear Lorraine say. "So . . . I guess we'll see you in the office soon?"

"You got it," my voice trails off as I slowly step away from the window. I keep my eyes on the woman in plastic for as long as I can—*who is that who is that who*—until I'm in the hallway and she finally disappears from sight. I can almost convince myself that she's no longer there. Out of sight, out of (my) fucking mind. I compel myself to let the notion of her go. It's too early and I'm way too hungover to give the thought of who she might be any mental real estate.

I head to the kitchenette. *I'm seeing things, that's all. I just need to eat something. Clear my head.* But the fridge is empty, save for a plate of cheese speckled in blue fuzz.

I fill a glass of water and try sipping some but it tastes far too metallic.

I wander over to the living room window, which gives the same view of the street below as my bedroom. Just to see.

The woman wrapped in plastic is still there. Still staring up at me. *What. The. Fuck.*

Compartmentalize, Mom would say in this situation. I watched her do the exact same thing for years. It's easy to place whatever we wish to dismiss in tiny boxes and stow them away in our minds where we can't dwell on them. All it takes is finding a space within yourself to house these particularly unpleasant feelings and simply . . . lock them up. Throw away the key.

That's all I need to do right now: *Don't be afraid, Erin. Simply . . . compartmentalize.*

I repeat the word, my new mantra—*compartmentalize, compartmentalize*—as I finally extract myself from my apartment to head off to my first day at my new job—my new *life*.

She hasn't moved. The woman in plastic is still standing in the street. Waiting for me.

You're not compartmentalizing, Erin, Mom tsk-tsks.

The elderly woman's head tilts toward me. Now I can see she's completely naked underneath her tarp. She's well into her eighties. Pale blue veins branch across her skin. Her hair is wet with sweat as it clings to the tarp's underside.

She's still breathing. I say *still* because, despite her physicality— despite the way her breath clouds her face beneath the tarp as she exhales—I know she isn't alive. Who is she?

". . . Ma'am? Are you hurt?" I don't know what else to say. What am I supposed to say?

What am I supposed to fucking *do*? I don't understand what's going on here. I just want to—

Compartmentalize, Erin, Mom chimes in. *Pack these thoughts away and move on . . .*

The tarp crinkles along her body as she steps forward, dragging the plastic with her.

Instinctively, I step back. My unconscious mind knows it's best to put as much space between us as humanly possible. But she keeps coming for me. Slowly closing in. She keeps staring at me through the tarp. Even through the gray haze of plastic, I can see her eyes are filled with a yearning look. I don't know her, I've never seen this woman before, so why is she looking at me like that? Does she think we're related? Her lips move slowly beneath the sheet. She's muttering but I can't make out the words.

"I can't hear you. Do you want me to . . ." Want me to *what*? What am I even doing?

Her lips are moving faster now. Before I think twice—*what're you doing Erin what*—I reach out for the tarp.

Free her, I think as I pull the sheet from her face.

The shroud slowly slides off her head. The last inch of plastic slips away. Her gray eyes widen. She's finally out. This must be what she wanted . . . Right? I've freed her from her sheet. I imagine she'll take in a lungful of fresh air—*bless you, child*—but the woman begins to claw at herself. She smells like the shallows along the James River. Still water festering in the heat, breeding mosquitoes.

Panic rises in my chest as I step back. "Are . . . are you okay?"

The woman drags her fingers over her pruned breasts, her distended belly. She won't stop. She keeps scratching at herself, overcome by some hideous itch, her bloated body and the latticework of veins in full view. Her mouth opens as if she's moaning, but I can't hear a sound.

"What's wrong? What can I—"

Gray water spills from her lips. It dribbles down her chin in thin rivulets.

Does she want the plastic back? Is that it? I look down at the tarp in my hand and it crinkles between my fingers. I can still feel the warmth of her trapped in the plastic, the heat from her breath. But the tarp quickly cools until it's just a sheet of plastic.

I look up and—she's gone. The smell of her lingers, stagnant water still in the air.

Where did she go? Where the fuck did she go? How did she—

I drop the tarp. It collapses across the pavement, empty.

I don't know what's happened but a sick feeling in my stomach tells me I've done something wrong. I hurry away, abandoning the plastic on the sidewalk. I don't turn back.

A stray wind blows by. I hear the breeze fill the tarp and drag it down the sidewalk behind me. I can *feel* the scraping sound of the sheet on asphalt in my teeth, *sskrrrch*.

Without turning, I sense the plastic phantom drifting on its own as if it's following me.

Don't look back, I say to myself. *Whatever you do, please, Erin, don't look, just . . .*

Compartmentalize.

nine-to-five

"Here's your own slice of heaven." Lorraine does her best Vanna White impression as she gestures at our workstation table. Her tattoos and vintage horn-rimmed glasses break the illusion but also make me think we could be friends. I could really use a friend right now.

"These are your tablemates, Tomás and Becca." Tomás barely looks up from his laptop. He's assessed me with a glance and is already moving on with his workday.

I at least get a half smile from Becca. I can tell she's a recent RCU grad. The McMartin Agency employs a workforce of primarily young twentysomethings. I wonder if anyone else's dad got them their job or if I'm the only one who doesn't belong? Jesus, my imposter syndrome is thick this morning, separating my body from my sense of self.

"Here's your key card to get into the building." Lorraine hands me a laminated ID card with my picture on it. I glance at my photo and can barely recognize myself staring back. *Who the hell is that? Is that me?* "Your training sesh will be in the boardroom. We had an emergency meeting this morning, some unhappy client stuff, so now I've got to set everything up again. Why don't you just get settled in here and I'll swing by in a few minutes to pick you up, 'kay?"

"Thanks." I manage to smile, even though I know I shouldn't be here. I should be in my apartment. Hiding. Not outside. Not where—

"There's coffee in the break room." Lorraine leans in. "Trust me, it sucks. The café around the corner is much, much better. Let me know if you wanna—"

get haunted

"—and I'll pick you up something. We take turns on coffee runs."

"Great, thanks."

I watch Lorraine hustle down the remodeled work floor of the factory. Everyone pecks away at the keys of their laptops, tap-tapping like crows jabbing at carrion, beaks hitting bone.

Move on with your life. I keep repeating my mother's mantra, *Compartmentalize . . .* This job is the first step into my future, my newly forged path as a real adult. *Don't screw this up, Erin.* I can do this. I just have to keep calm and carry on, keep cool, keep breathing, and . . .

Compartmentalize.

There. Easy peasy.

Tomás and Becca ignore me. Totally fine. I get it. I kill the time by figuring out how to sign on to my computer. Once I'm in, I search every absurd combo of words that comes to mind:

haunted drug

spirit hallucinogenic

drug séance

I better remember to clear my search history before the day ends. My phone buzzes. *Drinks tonight? 11 PM. Poe's.*

I feel a rush of relief. Amara's still talking to me. Friends 'til the end. I exhale all the pent-up breath I didn't even realize I was holding on to, suddenly weightless. I text back: *I'm in.* Dad's birthday dinner party is at seven so I'll stop by after. Three dots ripple across my screen—Amara writing back—then vanish. Whatever message she was about to send never materializes.

None of my search results turn up a thing. There's bound to be something written about Ghost, isn't there? An article or blog post? *Anything?* I try to remember what Tobias said about where Silas found it, but there's no fighting through the fog in my head. I suddenly catch a whiff of somebody's lunch takeout, pulled pork or pit BBQ or some other kind of burnt meat, which doesn't settle so well with my stomach at this particular moment. Is it lunch break already?

mushroom ghost drug

I see dead people

spirit pill

Nothing. Not a single goddamn hit.

Even now I find myself silently calling out to Silas. Where is he? Why won't he answer me? I'm trying to perform my own silent séance without my tablemates catching on. Why does it suddenly smell like a brisket joint? Should I say something? Complain to my tablemates?

Becca could be a friend. I find myself staring at her without realizing it, watching as she clacks away at her keyboard. She possesses a self-serious air and an intense collection of canvas tote bags. Looks like a *Weekend Edition* listener. Probably sews her own reusable tea bags. Maybe we could get after-work drinks—with Lorraine? I lose myself in the fantasy of Workplace Me when Becca catches me staring. I smile—*oops, hey*—then look away, pretending as if I'm not—

The smile fades from my lips.

There's a figure partially eclipsed by the water cooler. What's left of his clothes seem baked into his blackened body. I can make out his mottled flesh from where I'm sitting.

I gasp. Tomás glances up, then follows my eyes.

"Something wrong?" Becca asks, doing the same. They don't see him. *Can't* see him. But he's right there, staring back at me. A coworker leans over to refill his water bottle, inches away from the man's crisped skin, charred bones piercing through his chest. He just can't see. No one can. I'm the only one. *Because you're the only one tripping their ass off right now, Erin . . .*

"Sorry." I try playing it off with a light cough. "Just thought I saw someone I knew."

Tomás raises an eyebrow. I don't even have time to be embarrassed before I catch sight of another figure sitting at the far end of our worktable. The skin on the right side of his body has been stripped away—a scabrous landscape that looks more like badly molded clay than flesh.

I turn away. Focus on the floor. I count to ten before I lift my head back to see if—

He's staring now. He found me. I have a feeling I'm only giving him power by looking back. *So don't look*, I hear my mother say, as if these figures are simply vagrants asking for pocket change. She would tilt her chin and pretend not to smell the acrid aroma of burnt meat.

These ghosts won't bother me if I don't bother them, right? That's just a general rule of the wild. I can think of them as bears—the trick is to not pay them any attention.

I'm trying hard to hold it together. Compartmentalize the absolute insanity around me.

Why am I seeing ghosts when I can't even seem to summon Silas? Where the hell is he? If he was here he'd tell them all to go away *get the hell away leave her the fuck alone shoo!*

Tobias tried to warn us about this, didn't he? What did he say?

There's no telling what you're going to see.

He knew. Tobias fucking *knew*. That's why he didn't want us to leave the house. He knew what was out here. What we might see. *But they're not real. They're just hallucinations.*

I count six dead officemates scattered through the room. They know I can see them—sense it, somehow. It's like my presence provokes them, like there's a smell rising off of me.

It's Ghost, I realize. I take out my phone, even though that's a company no-no. No personal calls during the workday. I struggle to keep my wrists steady as I fumble through a text to Tobias under the table: *can ghosts smell drug on me?* I can't believe I'm even asking such an idiotic question, but what other choice do I have? I don't know what the hell is going on with me. I keep staring at the screen, yearning for Tobias to answer. *Please.*

The rack of ribs by the water cooler starts walking toward me, but I will myself not to look. I just have to keep calm and *compartmentalize*—and whatever I do, do not fucking look.

Is he still walking this way?

Don't look don't look.

Is he getting closer?

Don't look don'tlookdon't . . .

Where is he now?

Dontlookdontlookdooooon't . . .

Becca reaches her hand across the table, drawing my attention, and asks very quietly, "How's it going?"

I purse my lips and nod. I know if I say something, my voice will break. I have to keep my panic inside, keep it contained. *Lock that shit down, Erin. Play it cool. Compartmentalize.*

Becca studies me as the man with the burned, clay-like body stands behind her. "You seem—I don't know—a little distressed?"

"First day jitters," I manage to say. *She can't see she just can't see what I see.*

"I had 'em, too," she whispers, as if she doesn't want Tomás to hear. But of course he does. Not that he says anything, no, he just continues to *peck peck peck* away at his laptop.

The man with the clay body is trying to say something but his mouth is a melted mass. He moves around the table until he's standing next to me. I refuse to acknowledge his presence. I try to breathe evenly through my nose, *inhale, exhale, steady your breath and don't scream. They aren't real. They're just hallucinations. Photocopies on two feet. It's only in your head . . .*

What did the plaque in the lobby say? *Fire.* The Burning of Richmond. How many ironworkers died here? Where are they now?

Everywhere.

I'm tripping. That's all this is—just another bad trip. Of course it's all in my mind. Nobody else sees what I'm seeing, clearly, so I just need to keep cool and not panic. *Why did I double my dose of Ghost?*

Stupid, stupid Erin what the hell were you thinking—

"They bring the juniors in to walk them through the new accounts and see if we can—"

get haunted

"—so don't forget to bring your laptop."

"Thanks," I say to Becca as if I've been paying attention this whole time.

A sudden gust of singed steak fills my nose. Someone is standing next to me, but I'm not going to look. I refuse to look. Not even from the corner of my eye. They lean forward, whoever they are. *What are they doing*, I ask, and suddenly can't stop asking, the litany repeating in my head, *God, what are they doing. What're they doing whatretheydoingwhatretheydoingwhat* . . .

The man with the Play-Doh face approaches from the other side. He leans in and sniffs, *he's smelling me oh god he's smelling me*, as if I'm exuding some phantasmal pheromone.

My stomach lunges. Oh—not this again. Please, God, not now. The Ghost wants to come back up, I can feel it. The first lurch tightens my belly and I force myself to swallow.

There's a third burnt spirit now. They're all leaning in—smelling me. They want a taste.

They're not there not there not there—

I'm going to be sick. I feel it coming—rising. My throat tightens as I keep swallowing it down. *Please don't do this, not now. Not here.*

These spirits smell the Ghost on me. *In me.*

"How's it going over here?" Lorraine says. I slap my laptop shut so she can't see my search for *dead drugs mushroom ghost séance.* "Everything all right?"

"Yeah. Becca's just giving me the lay of the land." I smile at Becca, but she's clearly distancing herself, returning to her work with barely a nod.

Bile rises in my throat. It has the taste of loam and it takes all the strength I can muster to gulp it back down. I smile even as the scalded spirits close in, sealing off the suffocating space around us, pressing their noses against my face, running their shriveled tongues across my cheeks, reaching into my earlobes, over my forehead, all the nooks and crannies of my body, just trying to find that yumminess within me, whatever it is, surging up my throat.

"Don't stress over figuring everything out right away," Lorraine says. "It took me a—"

I can't do it. I can't hold back anymore. I'm going to vomit. I need to—

Need to—

"Is there a ladies room?"

Lorraine blinks. "Yeah. Right over here. I'll take you."

I don't want her to *take me*. I need to be *alone*. I abandon my seat, pushing past my entourage of phantoms as I try to breathe steadily through my nose.

Standing settles my stomach. That's better. At least I won't get sick on the work floor.

"You smoke?" Lorraine asks as she guides me to the restroom.

"No. I mean, yeah, sometimes." *Smoke means fire means cindered skin.*

"That makes two of us. Strength in numbers. The higher-ups really get in a pinch over the number of smokers and I'm all like, well, *helloooo*, one of our own accounts is Marlboro."

There's an octopus in my stomach. I can feel it. I remember the mural painted across the side of Fan Thrift as its pale tentacles slip around my intestines, searching for a way out.

Almost there, I say to myself. *Don't make a fool out of yourself and puke in front of all these people, all your so-called coworkers, don't you do it, Erin, don't you fucking dare—*

I glance over my shoulder to see how far Lorraine is behind me, and I realize we're being followed. There's a spirit trailing after us. Ol' rack of ribs doesn't want to part company just yet.

I pick up the pace and push through the door before Lorraine can. The restroom walls are a slate gray illuminated by fluorescent lights overhead. Three stalls and three sinks.

Lorraine takes the first stall while I head for the third. She's still talking, for Christ's sake. Her voice bounces off the slate. "—here for a couple years. Who'd you interview with?"

I press my palm against my chest as I manage to say, "Mr. Gidding?"

"*Wow.*" She whistles. "Outta the frying pan—"

"—into the fire."

I push open the stall door and immediately freeze when I realize someone is already standing inside. "Sorry," I say purely on reflex.

But the door was unlatched. And it's not a woman—it's a man. He's not sitting on the toilet, just standing there, staring. The right side of his face has cratered. His cheeks have sloughed away. His exposed jaw reveals a row of blackened teeth. It almost looks like he's smiling at me. I press the back of my hand firmly against my mouth to keep from retching on the floor. *How long has he been waiting there? Jesus, how many of them are there in this building?*

"You okay?" Lorraine cautiously asks from her stall. She's probably asking herself what she did in a previous life to deserve getting stuck training a screwup like me.

"Yeah. Fine." I'm still standing outside the third stall, struggling to maintain the chipperness in my voice while my insides roil. "First day jitters is all."

Didn't I already say that? How many times can I repeat the same excuse?

"We all get them." Everyone here is just politely going through the motions, but they just don't know—*they don't see*—what's surrounding them, always surrounding them.

Here it comes oh it's coming oh god I'm going to puke I'm going to—

Lorraine's still chatting as I run into the middle stall and slam the door, latch rattling. "Just between you and me, I'd steer clear of him. His hands have a way of, well, *finding you.*"

I feel the Ghost surge through my esophagus. It's coming up and nothing I can do will stop it. Everything within me twists. My body turns inside out. *What's happening to me . . .*

"Make sure you're never in his office alone. As soon as that door closes . . ."

The thick stalk drags itself up my throat like an uprooted flower, tugging up clods of my intestines with it. I don't believe I've ever felt anything as painful as this. *Please make it stop . . .*

"He's done it to just about every one of us. It's a rite of passage. HR has a whole fucking dossier on the bastard, but they won't touch him because it's his company. Makes me sick."

I lean against the door and press both hands against the walls in hopes of pinning myself in place as my body rocks through its convulsions, expelling this tendril of viscous matter into the air. I pray Lorraine can't hear me gagging. I just want this thing out of me *get it out get it out.*

"Guess you can get away with murder when you're the cofounder, am I right?"

I grip the stem of ectoplasm and try pulling it free, hand over hand, like a magician pulling handkerchiefs out of his sleeve at a children's birthday party. But there's just too much of it. There's no end. This root reaches down deep, all the way to my core. The tendril ripples against my lips, pulsing as it moves sinuously through the air above my head in a hovering coil.

It turns toward me. It's *looking* at me. I see eyes—hints of them, at least. The thinnest slit of a mouth. *It has a face.* It glides over me before winding around my waist and coiling through my legs. *I'm coming for your cooooooch, coochie-coochie-cooooooooooo,* it whispers.

I bite through it as hard as I can. I have no choice. It's the only way. My teeth sink into the stalk like the intestinal sheathing of a sausage, and I don't let up until the slippery skin breaks, sending the ectopede splattering across the far wall of the stall, just behind the toilet.

The wet splat echoes throughout the bathroom and I know there's nothing I can do to keep Lorraine from hearing me puke all over the place. All over the floor. The stall walls. Me.

"*Erin*? Oh god, are you okay?"

"I'm fine," I manage to gasp before releasing the rest into the toilet bowl. "I'm okay."

"Here, let me help—"

"Don't come in!" I lift my feet onto the toilet. I wrap my arms around my shins, slowly rocking back and forth. I can't stop myself from trembling. I just want to hide. Hide inside myself. I shake my head before burying my face between my knees.

"It's just us." Loraine doesn't have a clue. "Don't worry, okay? You can let me in."

"No. Please. I'm fine, I promise. Still a little sick is all. Food poisoning. I just—"

I lift my head.

Look down.

The man with the melted face is on the floor. On his back. He slid under the gap between the stalls. He's staring up at me with his one remaining eye. His jaw swings open and his tongue tumbles to the floor with a flaccid slap and I scream, oh god, I scream so loud, I can just imagine the sound of it echoing out into the rest of the office where everyone can hear but I can't stop.

He's lapping at the puddle. He can't contain himself, frantically licking every drop of what I've just expelled. He looks so happy. *It tastes soooo goooood*, his blissful expression says.

I leap off the toilet, screaming louder and louder. I can't stop myself. My shoulder hits the door and I bounce back, falling to the floor. I hit my head against the side of the toilet.

Lorraine is pounding her palm on the stall door. "*Erin?* What's wrong?"

My head. I can't see straight. Can't stop spinning. I have to pick myself up. I have to—

The man licks my face. Sandpaper at my cheek. His tongue reaches into my ear.

I scream as I lurch onto my hands and knees. So does the melted man. Our movements mirror each other. My vomit dribbles down his chin. I watch as his gray tongue rubs over his exposed jaw and licks it away. His one good eye rolls up into his skull, as if he's in absolute ecstasy, as if he's high—*oh my god, he's getting high off me*—and my scream lifts an octave.

There is nothing left within me, no air left to use, but I find a way to shriek even louder.

"Erin! Open the door! Please!"

Rather than reach up for the latch and unlock the door, I crawl through the gap under the stall. I find Lorraine standing just on the other side and I use my hands to climb up the front of her body, scaling her frame until we're face-to-face. She looks absolutely terrified, but she doesn't see—*good god, she doesn't see them*—all the burnt bodies now crammed inside the bathroom, all the ghosts pressing against one another, shoulder to shoulder, leering at me.

They all want a taste.

There's no space in here. No air to breathe. There's just too many of them. They're everywhere. I haven't stopped screaming. I can't stop screaming. I'll never stop screaming.

coatroom

"Fashionably late as always," Mom says as she presses a drink into my hand. She really has this routine down pat. I glance at the guests—the same ones that have been coming to my parents' soirees my entire life—and marvel at how they've gone through the social motions for decades. On any other night I wouldn't be caught dead at one of their dinner parties, but I can't be alone right now—not after what happened at work. Lorraine tried to take me to the emergency room. Somehow I convinced her I was okay—*food poisoning, ha-ha*—that I'd be better off going home and resting instead of sitting in a waiting room for hours. She reluctantly agreed but insisted on calling me an Uber and walking me to the car, which might've just been her way of making sure I quietly exited the building without making any more of a scene than I already had.

How am I going to show my face there tomorrow? Do I even have a job anymore? I'm crash-and-burning through my future before it even begins . . . all because of some fucking drug.

Because of Silas.

"I was wondering if I could crash upstairs," I ask Mom. "I'm not feeling—"

"Nonsense. We have guests." She leads me in a lap around the room, an elegant hostess in a three-quarter sleeve beaded tulle illusion gown with a bateau neckline and a V-cut back. She leans in and whispers, "Could you at least attempt to dress for the occasion? You look like you're going to a funeral."

I look down and realize I'm wearing my job interview dress turned funeral dress turned dinner party dress. I didn't realize I'd slipped it on. I want to tell her she's lucky I'm still holding on to whatever scrap of sanity I have left after the horror show that unfolded during my first day at my job—*keep telling yourself you've still got a job, Erin*—but there isn't any time before she presents me to the rest of the party. "Our daughter finally graces us with her presence!"

I make polite conversation. That's the deal with my parents—they help with rent as long as I play the show pony. They trot me out for their country club comrades whenever they host one of their suburban soirees.

Erin, our pride and joy.

Erin, our darling angel.

Erin, our—

"Li'l Deb," Silas whispers in my ear. The chill of his breath spreads down my neck. I turn to see who's standing behind me, but no one's there.

"God, I could pack my whole wardrobe in those bags under your eyes," Mom mutters.

"I think I should lie down . . ."

"Don't dillydally. There's someone I'm dying for you to meet." Mom guides me from one golf pal to the next as I shake their hands with a trembling wrist. I go through the motions, repeating everyone's name before quickly forgetting them. Their faces blur. Gleaming teeth.

I can feel a migraine gaining traction in my head. "Do you have any Advil?"

"We can ask Loretta to fetch some." But Mom never does, guiding me to the next guest.

Salisbury is a neighborhood built around its own country club. It's a bit chicken and egg: *What came first? The suburb or the green?* I grew up among these palatial, mass-produced McMansions, remarkable only for their architectural blandness. There's no history here. One good breeze could blow them all down.

In high school, I'd sneak out in the middle of the night to meet up with the other neighborhood kids on the golf course. We formed our own suburban cabal, just a bunch of bored boys and girls with nothing better to do but get drunk and mess around. We'd bring whatever bottles were gathering dust in our parents' liquor cabinets. Usually the fruity stuff—peach schnapps or coconut rum. It tasted absolutely disgusting, but it was our only shot at breaking up the monotony. Most Salisbury guys were merely looking for a chance to get to second base. The schnapps was just a warm-up. We'd all start off in a circle, passing around a bottle of you-name-it before falling onto our backs and staring up at the stars. I'd glance at my so-called friends making out and see the next generation of privileged date rapists. They'd move into houses exactly like the ones I was desperate to escape, raising their own 2.5 kids with the same values their parents imposed upon them, voting for the same presidents and attending the same private schools, repeating the cycle all over again.

Some guy would suddenly slither up next to me. Then on top of me. I could always smell the candied alcohol on his breath, then taste its sweet burn when he'd press his lips to mine.

I remember puking into the ninth hole with Benjamin Pendleton's hand tangled in my bra strap. I probably puked on him, too. Served him right. He never asked if I was okay, if I needed any help. He simply yanked his hand out from under my shirt and said, "Whoooa."

I never told Mom I'd been with Benjamin Pendleton all those years ago, but the memory instantly resurfaces the second she reintroduces me to his parents. I have to hear the rundown of how good ol' Benji is doing, married with one daughter and another bundle of joy on the way.

"He's making a killing in finance." His mother beams. "We should all get together for dinner. Benji was always so fond of you, Erin," she says. "Frankly, I'm surprised you two never dated—but that's ancient history now, I suppose. Tell us: Is there anyone special in *your* life?"

Yes, I want to say. *As a matter of fact, there is. He should materialize any minute now.*

"Erin just started working at the McMartin Agency today," Mom interjects, slyly steering the conversation away from my lack of a *certain special someone*. I refuse to receive her telepathic broadcast commanding me to lock down a marriage proposal *this instant*. Which descendent of whatever dead Confederate general will I be pawned off to this evening, I wonder?

"Care for anything to drink, ma'am?" a boy-bartender asks. I assume he's a caddy at the country club. In another life, we might've made out on the golf course during a midnight rendezvous. I get lost in his face, flushed with acne. The constellation of pimples is mesmerizing.

"Water, please?" My throat is always so dry now. No amount of hydration seems to help.

He nods. "Do you want—"

to get haunted

"—ma'am?"

"What the fuck did you just say?"

Bartender Boy stares back with his deer-in-the-headlight eyes. ". . . Ice?"

"Oh! Erin, darling," Mom beckons. "Come say hello to Mr. and Mrs. Blankenship!"

And just like that, I'm spirited away to the other side of the room. I try to be polite but these people are all empty to me, sheets hanging on a clothesline, nothing but suburban phantoms cycling through the same dull conversations they have every week. Nothing changes.

I count ten guests. *An intimate gathering*, Mom called it. Everyone congregates in the parlor. I pick up stray strands of conversation, unsure who's even talking to me anymore.

"It's absolutely *atrocious* what they've done to the monuments," one woman says with a sigh.

"Just gone to waste," another Daughter of the Confederacy replies. "Every last statue . . . And for what? Just so a bunch of protestors can have their way?"

"*All* lives matter. You don't see anyone spray-painting Arthur Ashe, do you?"

A string quartet plays an innocuous concerto in the background, but all I hear are horsehair bows shrieking over catgut strings, sending their high-frequency tremors through the air. I have to force the sounds out of my head just to keep my balance.

"Easy does it, dear." Mom holds me by the arm, like I'm too drunk to stand on my own. It's a subtle gesture but it's not lost on me. She guides me exactly where she wants to go, gripping my forearm tightly so I can't escape, her nails digging into my flesh.

I notice the window next to Dad's bookshelf. The glass has gone gray, an eye cloudy with cataracts. The other windows seem fine, but this one's fogged completely over.

"Are you doing some work on the house?" I hear myself ask.

"Pardon?" Mom has no idea what I'm talking about.

"The window. Did it break, or . . . ?"

"What's come over you?" Mom asks in a hushed tone. "You're not acting like yourself."

"I told you, I'm not . . . not feeling well."

She examines my face. "Your eyes—your pupils are dilated. Erin!"

"What?"

"Are you *on* something? Look at me."

"Mom—"

"*Look at me.*" Her voice, even at a low decibel, carries enough tonnage to let me know she's displeased as she studies one eye, then the next. "You came to your father's party *high*?"

Not high, Mom.

Haunted.

"What on earth were you *thinking*? Haven't we given you everything you ever wanted? Do you have a care in the world that we haven't taken care of? What more could you need?"

"Mom, I'm not—"

"Just don't let your father know. You could at least show a little respect for your *family*."

I could mention plenty of prescription pills that passed through her hands over the years, how she self-medicated her way through my entire childhood. She drifted throughout this house, day after day, zonked out of her skull. I'd hear the rattle of gelcaps in the morning, then later in the afternoon, and then again at night. I want to ask her in front of all her guests if she's haunted—truly haunted. I want to ask if she believes in ghosts, but before I can say a word—

I wake at the dinner table.

The laughter filling the room picks up; hyenas cackling over their carrion. I have no recollection of leaving the living room. I'm sitting next to a man I don't know—or don't remember. "If you'd like, I could see if there are any openings at our downtown office."

He doesn't seem to notice I've drifted. I close my eyes in hopes of focusing on the words but I can't catch any of them.

"I would be happy to put in a good word." The side of his leg presses against mine underneath the table. "Your father is such a *dear friend*."

I nod. Smile. Someone leans over my shoulder and I let out a shout. My place setting rattles, drawing everyone's attention my way. A hand deposits a bowl of soup on the table before me. I hadn't noticed the worker bees drifting around the dining room. Mom's really gone all out, hiring an entire waitstaff so she can sit back and bask. She laughs breathlessly from across the table, saying to everyone, "And here I thought it was just *my* cooking that made Erin scream."

This gets the appropriate chortle from the rest of her guests and away we all go, drifting back to our droll conversations. "It's our legacy I worry over," I hear Mom say to her neighbor, who thoughtfully nods along. "How else will our grandchildren know about their heritage? We can't erase our history simply because it makes *some folks* feel uncomfortable."

The color of my soup sends my stomach roiling. It's an off-green cream with dollops of white floating along the surface chilled phlegm. Something undigested wants to rise up my throat and claw its way out of my mouth. I force myself to swallow it back down.

Clink clink.

I bring my fingers to my temples to knead out the sound of cutlery on crystal.

Clink clink.

"Can I get everyone's attention?" Mom continues to tap a spoon against her wineglass. "If I may, I'd like to say a few words about the man of the hour . . ."

The waitstaff take their cue to halt and line up along the back wall, almost as if they aim to disappear into the woodwork. Their expressions are blank, offering no emotion.

"As most of you know, Bill has been grousing over this occasion for months now."

Polite laughter rises from the guests. *So true,* they all seem to say. It's all a performance. Everybody knows their part and how they're supposed to act, having done this ritual time and time again over the decades.

"I wasn't about to let the big six-oh slip by without marking the occasion," Mom titters, her eyes locking onto Dad, practically beaming at him. Dad gives a polite smile back. He endures these soirees for her sake. All of this—the whole godawful party—it's just for her.

I look at the waitstaff, curious over what they might think of all this. But their resting expressions show they know better than to let on about what's really going on in their minds. If Amara was working this catering gig, I'd motion to her to sneak out back so we could get—

haunted

—high behind our house. The thought makes me laugh as I reach for my glass. Empty. I need more water. I glance at the waitstaff just to see which server's attention I can get without disrupting my mother's toast. I can't make eye contact with any of them. They're all staring off at the same vacant spot in the ether, their bodies present but not here.

Except him. There's one more waiter standing directly behind my mother. He's tucked into a shadowy recess, his back pressed against the wall. I hadn't even noticed him before. Jesus, just how many servers are there? It's not like Mom needed to hire an army to feed ten people.

At least he's making eye contact with me. I gingerly lift my empty glass, beckoning him for a refill. He seems to get the message loud and clear because he takes a step forward and—

I see the long gash across his throat.

"Oh god." It just comes spilling out of me. I can't stop myself.

Mom glares at me before continuing. She thinks I'm trying to sabotage her toast. She can't see who's behind her, even when he comes closer. "Bill has been terrified of what Tom might say about his blood pressure, so we just *had* to invite him and Cathy. Tom—you brought your monitor, yes? The—what is it? With the Velcro cuff? The hand pump?" She squeezes her fist to mimic the pumping of an invisible sphygmomanometer. The guests all laugh on cue.

The man reminds me of my high school mascot, a bastardized version of a Monacan warrior. Centuries before this suburb was built, well before Midlothian was settled by Europeans in the seventeenth century, this land belonged to the Monacan tribe. I should know because I got an A-plus on my fifth-grade history project, making a shoebox diorama of their tribe battling the French Huguenot settlers who were themselves escaping religious persecution. I used my mother's nail polish for blood, dripping the cherry acrylic over their bodies. My inspiration for the project had been my father's prized cigar-store Indian. He keeps it in his home office. Still there. The older I got, the more I'd give him shit for it, complaining that there's no difference between this representation of Native Americans and, say, a lawn jockey, to which my father always shrugged and muttered under his breath, *Used to have one of those in our front yard, too . . .*

The man stands mere inches behind Mom as she raises her glass, beckoning us to toast. His focus remains on me as his head begins to lean back, exposing the crevasse of flesh along his neck—an extra set of lips more than ready to scream while the rest of him remains mute. Whatever slit his throat wasn't sharp enough.

I try so hard not to react. I try very, *very* hard to *compartmentalize*. I look down at my place setting. I see my soup has started to boil over and I need to look away before I retch. I'm wrestling against my own insides now, so I invoke a silent prayer. *Please don't puke please . . .*

"To Bill," Mom says. "May you have many, many more happy years ahead of you."

"I hope to God not," Dad jests, eliciting chuckles from all the men in the dining room. *Kill us now*, they silently plead. *Put us out of our misery.*

The Monacan moves around my mother and nears the table. His eyes are on me now, inflamed with desire. Someone *sees* him. He looks so stunned, so eager to have eyes on him.

"Happy birthday, dear." Mom's cheeks are fully flushed with merlot. Everyone taps their wineglasses over the table. The clinking of Waterford crystal is like an icepick in my ear drum.

I toast with an empty glass, which I know is bad luck. *Eye contact*, I remind myself, even though the only person gazing my way is dead. His mucous-colored eyes are fixed on me. His gray lips crack open, hungrily. Both pairs. The gash along his throat widens and widens and . . .

Don't look Erin please don't look don't look—

The Monacan climbs onto the table, but no one else notices. The rest of the guests simply go about eating and drinking, laughing amongst themselves as he crawls toward me. *Please, stay away, please* . . . It takes every ounce of strength I have left not to leap up from the table and run.

He won't touch me, I think. *Won't hurt me.* The spirits at the office didn't harm me, did they? All they wanted was the Ghost. To taste it, that's all. There's probably so little left in my system by now, this spirit will simply drift on as soon as he realizes I have nothing to offer.

But he can't *do anything* to me, right? He can't *hurt* me? I'm breathing deeper through my nose, clamping my jaw so I won't scream. I bite my tongue. *He can't hurt me* . . . He's inches from my face, but I'm too terrified to move. All I do is sit and pretend like he's not here. I look everywhere else. Just not at him. *He can't hurt me* . . . I dig my nails into the meat of my thigh, focusing on the pain and funneling all my thoughts away from the man as he tilts his head *back, back, back*, the lips of his sawn-open throat parting and, oh, I feel his breath spread across my cheeks, drifting out from his neck, not his mouth, his neck and *oh god I can't*.

I'm about to push my chair away from the table. Just as I plant my legs to push my chair back, the man takes my head in both of his hands. It happens so fast, there's no time to react. To pull back. There's a chill to his skin. It seeps into my skull. Everything within me freezes as I feel his fingertips against my temples and for a second it's as if they're burrowing through, plunging into my cranium. I can't move. Can't scream. All I can do is look at him as he stares back.

His eyes. I can't look away from his eyes. I'm about to lose myself within them. Fall in.

His throat sputters. The gash peels back as far as the wound will allow—and in that moment, I believe he's about to kiss me—but not with his mouth. His tongue, an ashen maggot, slips past his larynx and dangles through the wound.

My stomach recoils. I'm going to be sick—but I can't breathe. I can't escape.

Why can't I scream? Why can't I—

The man breathes in deep. Something in the way he inhales tugs at the very center of me, like he's breathing me in.

I feel my own tongue swell. It's expanding. *Growing.* The root presses against my jaw and pushes past my lips. There it is. Oh god, I see it now. I can't help but frantically stare at my tongue as it winds into the air, the tip flattening then expanding into a pink mushroom cap.

My eyes sting and water. *Make it stop please make this stop make it all stop pleeeease . . .* All I can see is the underside of my tongue, gills rippling beneath the cap.

A stem of ectoplasm branches from my left nostril. It's quickly followed by another creeping out of my right. The two stems thread throughout the air, thin and quivering, until they form a latticework over my head. This man is drawing it out from me, tugging on what's left.

I can't see the roots coming out of my ears but I certainly *feel* them, looping around the lobes and extending outward. My bones have locked in place but I feel myself budding. *Blossoming.* Pressure builds behind my eyes. Something inside my skull is forcing its way out and the only way to escape is through my eye sockets. I can feel my eyeballs swelling and popping out of my skull, floating into the air like balloons tethered to my body by optic nerves.

All these stems drift through the dining room, twisting and converging above the table—above my body—like a fungal colony extending for miles below the earth's surface. These phantasmal toadstools explode from every orifice and reach for the air, sucking the life out of—

"Erin!" My mother shrieks from across the dinner table, snapping me back.

I'm surrounded by petrified guests. The dining room has gone so quiet, so deathly still, that the only sound I hear is the faint drip of my vomit trickling off my empty glass and onto the fine china. It runs down my job interview dress turned funeral dress turned dinner party dress.

They still don't see the Monacan as he greedily laps up what I've just regurgitated over the dinner table. His tongue writhes like a waterlogged worm caught in a puddle.

He's not using his mouth. It's all happening within his neck and I feel like I'm going to be sick all over again—I can feel it coming. My chair tips over as I spring to my feet, knocking my neighbor's glass over. Wine spills onto the table. The guests focus on dabbing the merlot bleeding through the tablecloth with their napkins, the linen turning deep red.

Mom hasn't moved from the head of the table. No one has. "Erin, my god . . ."

I have to say something. *He's right there.* Why haven't they said anything? *Why can't they see?* He's smashing his throat desperately against the table, starved into insanity.

"I—"

The sound of my voice startles the man. His head snaps up at me, furious that I've interrupted his meal.

"I'm sorry, I—" I rush out of the dining room. "Excuse me."

"Erin!"

"Let her go," I hear Dad mutter. "Will someone please clean this mess up?"

My parents haven't touched my bedroom since I left for college. It's still technically mine, as if they're waiting for me to move back in.

The room feels like a memorial. Posters of bands I can't bring myself to listen to anymore, indie movies I thought made me look more intelligent than I actually was.

I flip the light switch and find my bed completely covered in coats. Lots of black. Some fawny, tawny brown. Cigarette-ash gray. I fall directly on top of the pile and sob. I can't stop crying. I bring my hands to my face and try to hide inside the hovel of my palms. I'm losing my mind. I can't keep doing this. I can't keep running away if I'm going to keep hallucinating.

But he touched me. I felt his fingers reach in.

This is just a never-ending trip. That's all this is. I just need to be alone. Somewhere safe. I try to balance my breathing. I need to calm down. Rest. If I can power through this nightmare, flush all the Ghost out of my system, I'll be okay. I'll survive. I can sleep it off. Sweat it out.

No more dosing. That's a promise. *I, Erin Hill, do solemnly swear to go cold turkey.*

I'll stay the night in my old bedroom and head out in the morning. I just want to get—

haunted

—some rest. I glance at the poster for Godard's *Contempt* next to my bed and notice that the tape sealing the lower left corner is curling off. I peel it back and discover—

ERIN WAS HERE

—hiding beneath the poster. I used to be here. In the past.

So where am I now? Why can't I find myself anymore?

A woman laughs downstairs. I've heard that cackle before. The party's moved back into the parlor. Mom's voice projects throughout the house, filling the cavities of every empty room.

Please Jesus, I pray, *I promise never to take another drug for as long as I live. Just let me get through this. Let me ride this out and I swear I'll never dose on Ghost for the rest of my life.*

Sleep. That's it. That's all I need. Already I can feel my body relaxing. The tension in my muscles melts, my head growing heavier. Just . . . *sleep*. I'll feel much, much better after some—

Something squirms under my left leg. Something trying to wriggle away.

I tug a fur coat out from under me. *What're you supposed to be?* Whatever animal it had been before it became this hideous coat is a total mystery. I'm not even sure if it's real fur or not, but it feels warm as I run my fingers through it. So cozy. I bundle it up into a ball for a pillow.

I sprawl out on the pile of jackets and close my eyes. I even tug a couple coats off the top and cover myself with them, like a patchwork blankie. There's a stretch of leather against my cheek—the sleeve of someone's bomber jacket. It gradually warms against my face as I drift.

Goodnight. Sleep tight. Don't let the—

The sleeve slithers. This time I'm positive it moves on its own. The bomber ripples across my cheek, *undulates*, as if it wants to free itself from under the weight of my head.

Something loosens against my fingers. Snakeskin.

All at once, the coats are moving. *Writhing.* A nest of serpents wakes, their leather-skinned bodies slinking over each other. The entire pile inhales. Empty pockets fill with air like the chambers of a dozen lungs. I scramble across the bed to the headboard, my heart racing.

This can't be happening, none of this is happening, I'm trapped in this trip—

The patchwork of coats rises from the bed and reaches for me. Some coats fall to the floor and rise again. Sleeves form tangled tentacles that slip and slink across my thighs, inching under my shirt and snaking up my chest, wrapping around my waist, my neck, my arms . . .

Vessels. I hear Tobias say the word in my head. Something has slipped inside and made a home in this pile of coats. A pair of hands push their way out of a jacket. Now there are three hands. *Five.* Each one emerges from its own sleeve. So many of them, manhandling me, working their way across my skin, groping and tugging. How many bodies are buried under this house, under all the McMansions in the neighborhood? How many men and women were massacred, never to appear in any history book, any ledger, any cemetery? Have they ever been at rest?

I'm waking them. Stirring them up—and now they're pulling me in. Pulling me down. *Deeper.* The mattress opens and welcomes me in. Its quilted rictus loosens as it swallows.

The room goes dark. I can't see. *I can't see.*

When I try to scream, a leather sleeve shoves itself into my mouth. It works its way down my throat, down into the pit of my stomach. I'm drowning, drowning in the dark.

I hear Mom clink her glass for another toast, the tipsy lilt in her voice when she says, "To our legacy living beyond us. To our birthright and many more birthdays to come! Cheers."

"Cheers," the guests echo—

clink, clink, clink

I pull the sleeve from my throat. I have to grip it with both hands and pull hard. *Harder.* The sleeve eases out of my mouth. Saliva-slicked leather glides against my esophagus until I can finally gasp for air.

I find the strength to pry free from the pile of coats and fall to the floor. Their hands keep reaching for me, clutching for any part of my body they can grasp.

I need to get out of this room. Out of this house. Don't look back, just run. *Just go.*

I lose my grip on the banister as I slip down the steps. I burst through the front door and don't bother closing it. I hear my mother calling from behind me but I don't look back. *Just run.*

I need help. But who's left? I'm all alone now. There's no one. Not Tobias. Not even—

Amara.

going away

Poe's is packed. Apparently I'm at a going-away party? Only Amara could pull something together like this with twenty-four hours' notice. On a Monday night, no less. Amara would host her own funeral if she could, just so she could get plastered with her pals.

She's telling everyone else she's leaving for New York within a week but I know what's really happening.

She's running away. Amara saw something in the house and it scared her enough to finally leave Richmond. *But you can't outrun what haunts you*, I think. *Your ghosts will find you*.

"*Whatsup, bitches!*" she shouts every time someone she knows arrives. She tipsily shrieked it at me as I entered with a group of strangers. Or I thought she did. She hugs the others, so I make a beeline to the bathroom. Her squeals follow me. I've known Amara long enough to know when she's trying too hard. She's keeping a brave party face on, wearing a high-necked, pink floral-print cheongsam that demands attention. All eyes are on her. The belle of the ball.

I thought our circle of friends was the universe and Silas was our sun, but Amara has this entire other reality of work pals.

I wasn't going to come. Not after Dad's birthday party, but the idea of going—

home

—back to my apartment and being alone terrifies me. Now that

I'm here, I know I should leave. I don't think I can do this, but I want to be around familiar faces. Even just one.

I need to get Amara by herself. I'll ask if she's seeing *them*, too. Why else would she be surrounding herself with so many people? Why else would she be leaving so suddenly?

I need to talk to someone, *anyone*, who'll understand what's happening to me. This nightmare. Tobias isn't picking up his phone. His roommates haven't seen him since last week. *He's still out there*. In Hopewell. In the house. I don't know for sure but I'd bet my life on it.

Everyone here gives me a wide berth. I haven't looked at myself in the mirror in a hot minute, but I can imagine the strung-out vibes I'm giving off right about now. I'm repelling every living soul while all the dead ones can't seem to leave me alone.

The bathroom walls are covered in the scabs of stickers for local bands and graffiti. Even I contributed a little something to the walls. You'd never know I was there unless you knew where to look for me, which is exactly the way I like it.

There I am. It's the little things that remind you you're still alive, only now it says:

ERIN WAS HERE

Someone changed it, like all the others, editing my graffiti so that I exist in the past tense. This is . . . this is insane. Who's doing this? Why are they acting like I'm not here? Like I'm—

dead

It's beyond fucked. Nobody else even knows about these tags but me and it's not like I'd do this to myself.

It's the drug. It has to be the drug. I'm hallucinating these edits. Maybe I'm hallucinating the ghosts, too. Wouldn't that be an absolute gas? After all the shit that I've gone through today? Wrecking everything in my life? But they're attacking me. I have the bruises to prove it now.

No more Ghost, I can tell you that right fucking now. No more letting these spirits in.

This house is officially closed from future hauntings, fuck you very much.

After a survey of each stall, I pull out the Ziploc bag and hold it up to the bare bulb.

One gelcap left.

Even now, after everything, I still—*still*—feel the desire to pop it. The tug on my insides. Just holding Ghost gives me this tingle down my spine.

Is Silas on the other side of this pill? If I just try harder to contact him—

Call out louder—

Shout for—

Quit it, Erin. I can't stop making excuses to justify taking another hit, as if all of this is perfectly normal. *None of this is normal.* I'm losing my mind and it's all because of this drug.

I have to flush it. *Now.* Don't think twice.

But what about Silas—

Just dump it.

Silas is waiting—

NOW.

I toss the last cap into the toilet. *Plink.* It bobs along the surface of the water until I use the toe of my sandal to hit the flusher and watch it spiral down the drain with a hiss.

There. I step out of the stall, triumphant. No turning back now. What's done is done. No more Ghost. Time to detox. Or a goddamn exorcism. I'll do whatever it takes to clean myself—

Wait. Was that the sound of a baby? The toilet gurgles over my shoulder. I turn back to the stall, staring into the bowl as it refills with foggy water.

Nothing's there. Of course.

I walk back into the bar with the slightest sense of triumph. *I won, motherfucker.* I flushed that shit straight out of my life. Even if I wanted to take it, too late, there's none left.

I'll take the small victory wherever I can get it. Now I just need to tackle Amara.

Poe's is one of the last holdouts in the entire state where you can still smoke indoors. It won't be long before the law cracks down and forces everyone to step outside for a cigarette, but for Amara's final night in Richmond, a thick, gray haze suspends itself over everyone.

Mondays are karaoke night. James the bartender dragged out a stool and a battered laptop, and Amara is currently belting out "Fever" by Peggy Lee. Her mouth is too close to the mic, her slurring words crackling through the crappy sound system. It's a less sultry version of the song, for sure—a punked-up rendition that has everyone shrieking, "You give me FEVER."

The floral pattern on her form-fitting dress seems to be shifting across her lithe body, the flowers unfolding and closing over and over. There's a hypnotic quality to it. If I stare too long, I'll lose myself in my very own version of "The Yellow Wallpaper."

"Long time," James shouts at me over Amara's caterwauling.

"No see," I shout back.

"What're you having? The usual?"

"Can I just get a water, please?"

"For real?"

"Yeah, sorry . . . No fun for me tonight. Need to flush some toxins." To put it mildly.

"*FEVER!*" Amara screams with a double slice of her hands through the air. The whole room belts out the lyrics right along with her. "*When you kiss them! Fever if you live you learn!*"

James slides a glass of water across the bar. "Let me know when you want to—"

get haunted

"—move onto something stronger. I got you covered."

"*WHAT A LOVELY WAY TO BURN!*"

Amara ends her song with a swell of drunken applause. She curtseys, almost losing her balance as she catches her breath, soaking up the sweaty moment. "Thanks, everybody. Y'all are the best." She must be really drunk if her Southern accent is coming out. "I'm gonna miss y'all so much, but—I'm sorry, I gotta get my ass out of the Southside before I lose my miiiiind."

The crowd laughs. There are so many people here. I can't make out their faces in the dark. There's no air to breathe—only smoke. Tendrils of gray curl up from their cigarettes and for a second it looks like thin wisps of ectoplasm are emanating from everyone's lips. *Stop, Erin.*

"There's always a place for you to crash in the Big Apple, so come and pay me a visit. I'll have a couch waiting for y'all." Is Amara starting to tear up? She uses the tip of her pinkie to wipe something from the corner of her eye. "Okay. None of that. Not gonna cry . . ."

A man's arm reaches out from the shadows and hands Amara a drink.

"Thanks," she says and sips. "Love you. All y'all. Promise I'll be back for the holidays."

This is it—my chance to corner her. I need to know if she can see them too. I need to know if I'm going crazy. And maybe, if I'm strong enough, I need to say, *Please, don't leave me.*

I can't do this alone, Amara.

I need help.

I need you . . .

"Soooooo . . ." Amara bites her bottom lip, a coquettish grin spreading across her face. "One more song from me and then I promise—*I promise*—I'll pass the mic."

Of course Amara won't abandon the spotlight.

The initial strains of "Unchained Melody" by the Righteous Brothers start. Amara's favorite song. If karaoke is ever in the cards, she dusts off this little ditty. Every. God. Damn. Time. She closes her eyes and embraces the microphone with both hands, wobbling a bit before solemnly bowing her head.

"Whoooa, my love, my darling . . ." She's way out of tune. Intensely serious. "I've hungered for . . . your touch."

"A looong," the crowd joins in a drunken chorus. "Loooonely time . . ."

"Erin?" It's Silas. I swear I hear his voice behind me.

I spin around, looking for him . . .

. . . and find James holding up one shot for me, another for himself. "Don't leave me hanging. Let's drink one for the man. To Silas."

This time I don't hesitate. I down the brown booze. I need to go scorched earth on myself. Raze it all. It tastes awful, whatever it is. Napalm cough syrup.

"Thatta girl. Want another?"

"Yeah. Sure. Why not."

"Now we're talking." He pours another shot, not paying attention to any of the other people at the bar. Several girls lean into his workspace and wave their hands in the air, but to James, they don't exist. How does he *compartmentalize* like that? "You still living on Grace?"

"Yeah. Still living." *Still alive*, I remind myself.

"Invite me over." Is he *flirting* with me? I smile weakly and motion for one more shot.

James tops me up from a bottle with no label. "What is this?"

"You're bleeding the bootlegger, baby!"

"Lonely rivers flow to the sea, to the sea . . ." Amara is seriously butchering this song but the crowd eats it up, swaying in unison. "Wait for me, wait for me, I'll be coming home . . ."

"No wonder Amara's leaving," James says. "Must be really hard on her."

"What do you mean?"

"I mean, you know . . . him passing away must've been hard on her . . . I guess I can understand why she'd want to go."

Of course it's hard on Amara. It's hard on *all of us*. Silas was *our friend*. But there's an insinuation in his words that doesn't quite settle for me. "She's moving away because of Silas?"

James is really starting to sweat. "Well, yeah. I mean, they were . . ." His voice fades.

"They were *what?*"

He clamps up. He knows he's really put his foot in it.

"*They were what?*"

I want to press him further but the woman standing next to me starts to edge into my personal space a little more than I'd like. I can't let James off the conversational hook, so I push back with my shoulder, hoping whoever this woman is, she'll get the message to back up.

"Hey, so, uh, I don't know if this is your thing or not," James keeps talking, trying to change the subject. "I scored some really strong stuff if you're looking to get—"

haunted

"—a little elevated. Wanna come to the backroom for a little pick-me-up?"

This same fucking woman pushes against me again. Harder this time. More insistent. It's almost like she's more interested in rubbing up against me than getting James's attention.

I'm about to shout something to her over the music when, from the corner of my eye, I notice her bare shoulders. Whatever she's wearing, it's ripped. Torn right down the back.

At first, I think her arms are covered in caterpillars—but no, now I realize they're scars.

I turn to look at her.

A Black woman stares back at me, never blinking. She *sees* me. I recognize the desperation in her expression, the need in her eyes. She's yearning for a connection.

She was never trying to get James's attention.

She wanted mine.

"I . . . have to go." I step back. I'm so tired. I can't keep doing this. Can't keep running. Everywhere I go, there are just more of them. They're in every house. Every building.

Where can I go now? Is there anywhere left?

The woman's expression brightens, glad that someone, *anyone*, has acknowledged her presence. She only moves when I do, as if we're syncopated. She steps forward whenever I take a step back. I shouldn't be seeing her—and *she* shouldn't be seeing *me*.

I'm not looking where I'm going, pushing through the people behind me. I bump into some guy on the dance floor, his drink spilling over my shoulder.

"Watch it!" he shouts, holding his wet hands in the air.

The woman stands in the center of the dance floor, staring back with such a longing gaze, while everyone else faces the makeshift stage, lost in their singalong—"I neeeeed your love."

How long has she been in the renovated basement of this antebellum mansion? How long has she drifted through the bar, no one ever noticing her presence?

They'll always be here, won't they? They'll always be here because they've always, *always* been here. No matter where I go, there will always be more of them. This will never end.

How can I stop myself from being haunted?

"What do you want from me?!" I shriek as loudly as I can over the sound system. Everyone surrounding us jolts, as if I just fired a shot into the crowd. "Get away from me!"

Amara stops singing. The karaoke track keeps on playing, the hollow strains of "Unchained Melody" reaching their synthesized crescendo.

"Leave me alone!"

Nobody else sees the yearning in her ashen eyes. They can't see her raise her hand. Can't see her fingers graze my cheek. She's shorter than me. I peer over her shoulder and see that her scars run down the length of her entire back—no, not scars. They're still bleeding. She'll always be bleeding. These wounds will never heal. The wounds open and flex as she touches my face.

"Leave me—"

No one sees this woman's fingers reach in, sinking through my skin. The cold immediately clenches my chest. Vertigo takes hold. I can't feel my legs. I'm falling backward.

I'm falling into—

—a gray body of water. A sea of ash. Waves of black. They reach as far as the horizon, met by gray clouds. The dull glow of what could be the sun barely penetrates the ozone.

There is no land in sight. Nothing but ink. The water boils over, creating massive summits of waves that crest and crash into one another, then fall back into themselves.

The clip lights overhead fluctuate until there's nothing left but the gray haze of smoke, and I'm plunging even further under the surface. Into an endless ocean of shadows.

The water around me is too murky to see through. Billows of wet soot. *So cold*—

I can't breathe—

Amara's friends grab my shoulders, catching me in mid-fall.

The woman's fingers slip away. Separating us.

I gasp for air. For a moment I swear I felt my heart stop. It felt like I was—

dead

"Erin?" Amara asks, her voice faint. She holds her hand up to shield her eyes from the spotlight as the karaoke track ends. Pin-drop silence descends. Everyone's staring at me.

The woman focuses on her own fingers, transfixed by the hand that sank into me—*through me*—as if she's just as bewildered by what happened as I am. She brings her fingers up to her mouth and licks. Her eyelids flutter in ecstasy, as if she's just tasted the sweetest nectar.

She crams the knot of her fist deeper into her mouth. Her jaw dislocates, lips stretching taut and sealing over her wrist as she sucks down whatever's left of the Ghost. One taste isn't enough. She wants more. She takes a woozy step forward, as though she's drunk. Reaching for me.

I spin around and force my way through the crowd of unfamiliar faces *all these faces who do these faces belong to—*

The fresh air smacks me as soon as I stumble out the door. I close my eyes and lean forward, placing both hands on my knees until I can finally slow my breathing.

I just need to get my equilibrium back. I need the world to stop spinning. I need to—

"Erin?"

Amara.

"Are you okay?"

"Did you see her?"

Amara remains silent.

"Did you?"

"I don't know what you're talking about." She's *lying.* I can see it in her face. Even now, she won't admit it. What other secrets is she keeping from me? What else is she hiding?

"Did you sleep with Silas?" The question spills out before I'm even ready to ask it.

"Erin," Amara says very calmly, "let me explain."

I moan. "*Don't.*"

"It wasn't serious, I swear—"

"How *could* you?"

"What do you want me to say?" She takes a tentative step forward. "Silas made everyone feel like they were the most important person in the world. The *only* person."

"Oh god . . ."

"We all fell under his spell, Erin. It was impossible not to."

"When?"

Amara hesitates. "Off and on."

"For how long?"

"Not long."

"College?"

"No."

"So after we graduated."

"Yeah."

"How could you do this to me?"

"To *you*?" Amara's getting pissed now. "Erin, you've been in a holding pattern for *years*. Blame me or Silas or whoever, fine, be my guest, but nobody did a fucking thing to *you*."

Our group. Our friends. Four Musketeers—one body. We always joked that Silas was the head, Amara was the balls, Tobias was the ass, and I was . . . what was I again?

The heart? This blackened, shriveled prune of a muscle? How had it been my responsibility to pump the lifeblood of our friendship through the rest of our veins?

We've been decapitated. Who are we without Silas?

Who am I?

Amara is still explaining herself. Atoning. "It wasn't serious. It just . . . happened."

"Why didn't you tell me?"

"Because . . ." Amara pauses for a second. "I knew it would hurt you and I didn't want to."

"But you did it anyway."

"Yeah. I guess I did."

"Thanks. Thanks a lot."

"Look, Erin. I know you don't want to hear this, but . . . What did you want from him? Did you think you were going to move to the suburbs and have kids with him?"

My stomach turns as I think of that day we went to the clinic.

"I saw him," I cut her off. "In the house."

"Erin . . ." Her look of pity sickens me.

"He was there," I nearly spit the words out. "With me. He came back to *me*."

"Don't, Erin."

"I found him. I brought him back. His spirit found its way to *me*. Not you. *Me*."

"*Stop*." Amara's voice echoes off the surrounding buildings. "I told you not to buy into Tobias's bullshit. Which, if we're being honest, is just more of Silas's bullshit. Now you're acting just like him, too."

"Who?"

"*Silas.*"

Amara never cared. She never thinks about anyone other than herself. She's always been *selfish, selfish, selfish* for as long as I've known her. Now she's trying to run away.

"You saw something in the house, didn't you?"

"Stop."

"That's why you're leaving, isn't it? You've been seeing them too. Just tell me you have."

"No." She slowly shakes her head, the word barely audible.

"*Tell me.*"

Amara steps back, away from me.

"Who did you see? *Who?* Was it Silas?"

Amara doesn't say another word, turning around and returning to her party.

"DID YOU SEE SILAS? IS HE WITH YOU?"

The door slams shut behind her while I stand in the middle of the street. Fuck her. I don't need her help. I start walking, fishing through my bag for my phone.

I don't see the man until I nearly collide with him.

"Jesus!"

He doesn't move, even when I shout. He simply stands in the middle of the street. I turn away the moment I realize he's naked, a toadstool plug for a penis poking out from his crotch.

I keep moving, powerwalking directly down the center of the street. Now I'm running. Faster now. His pace is so slow, I lose sight of him in a couple blocks. I can't tell if he's following me anymore, so I pull out my phone and call for a Lyft. There's one five minutes away, which means I have to stand at the corner and wait for "Roger" to pick me up.

Five minutes is nothing, I think to myself. *I can wait that long.*

I position myself underneath a streetlamp, leaning against the pole in my own pool of light. I have a good view of the block, able to see anyone coming or going from either direction. I keep a close eye on the direction I just came from. Nothing can creep up on me here. I'm safe now.

Four more minutes. I can see Roger's car moving along the map on my phone.

A text pops up. It's from Tanner: *Is it something I said?* I start writing back—*I'm just going through a lot of stuff right now*—but delete it. I could call him. He could pick me up, couldn't he? Take me—

home

I glance down both sides of the street. Things feel surprisingly quiet for this time of night, even for a Monday. Church Hill has never attracted a large nightlife crowd, but it's downright deserted now.

Still four minutes.

I look up at the streetlamp and see moths swarming around the bulb. Their bodies arc so fast that the sheen of their wings creates trails in the sky. *Don't go into the light*, I want to warn them, *whatever you do, don't go into the light.*

The crinkling is faint at first—plastic scratching against asphalt. I look both ways, but the street remains empty.

I notice a white grocery bag. There's no breeze, yet the bag keeps drifting through the air, occasionally dipping and dragging over the pavement. *Sskrrrch.* The sound sets my teeth on edge.

Every deli has a bag just like this one—a Day-Glo yellow smiley face, THANK YOU FOR SHOPPING WITH US—but something about this one conjures up a latent memory.

Silas was carrying a bag just like it.

There's no way this could be the same one—and yet, somehow, I know it is. In my bones, I just know. His plastic bag found me. I almost expect Silas's happy little phantom pal to wave back with one of its handles.

I never saw what was inside. It had to be personal belongings—

keys and wallet, his lighter. What else? The bag's handles span out like sails on a schooner, setting its scraping course over the road and aiming for my feet. It's coming for me. It's less than three feet away . . .

One foot away . . .

The bag finally skids to a halt. Now it's stock-still. Only seconds ago, I would've sworn the bag was empty, but now I'm not so sure—it seems like there's something weighing it down. The handles collapse inward, sealing the contents off.

I glance at my phone. Three minutes for Roger. His car icon is only a few blocks away from the pulsing blue dot that is me, and yet the distance between us feels insurmountable.

Two minutes and counting. *Come on, Roger, move your ass!*

The bag hasn't moved. At all. It's waiting for me to open it—*I know it, I just know it*—but I refuse to give in to temptation.

Still two minutes. Back to three minutes. *Fuck.*

I'll just take a peek. What's one peek going to hurt?

To hell with it. I'm looking.

I lean close enough to the bag to see the faint glint of someone's eyes staring back.

A woman blinks up at me from inside. Her mouth opens like a fish out of water, silently gasping for air. She wants to say something but has no voice to speak.

My mind goes to a framed photo on Silas's dorm room desk. To her car accident.

It's her. It has to be. She's staring right at me.

Silas's mother.

I lurch backward, slamming against the lamppost.

The decapitated head of Silas's mother stares up at me from the bag. This is worse than the other ghosts. I can't live with this. I can't stay here. Can't wait for Roger another minute.

I need to run. I need to go—

home

I'm racing so fast, it takes me a moment to notice the bodies dangling from the trees. At first I think they're branches. Willow oaks line the streets of Church Hill, one of the oldest neighborhoods in this city, where Patrick Henry requested liberty or death. Most have stood as long as the houses themselves, going all the way back to 1775, so it shouldn't come as such a shock to see so many suspended spirits hanging by their necks. They twist in a wind that has blown for centuries now and I just can't look. I don't want to see their eyes staring blankly back at me. Even they can smell it—the Ghost in my blood. They reach for me as their bodies sway.

I'm losing my mind. I'm losing my mind . . . There's no scrap of sanity left to cling to. I'm seeing them everywhere now. Some hide in dumpsters. Another is stuffed in a newspaper kiosk, face pressed against the glass. All the parked cars I pass are crammed full of spirits, like clown cars. Their gray eyes follow me as I run by. They lick at the windows—hungry for me.

Too many. There's just too many of them.

I pass a McDonald's and notice the drive-through windows are bursting with limbs every time the retractable flaps slide open. Whenever a patron opens the door, another lost soul slips in behind them, desperate for the safety of a vessel. Any vessel. They'd rather cram in together than spend another minute outside. But why? What's so awful about being left out in the open?

Why do they need a home this badly?

These spirits are around us all the time and no one even knows. No one sees. But dosing on Ghost changes all that, doesn't it? Ghost changes everything . . .

The city is *alive* and it's hemorrhaging centuries of ghosts everywhere I go. I see members of the Powhatan tribe. This was their home—Shocquohocan to them—before Christopher Newport set sail to explore the James River.

What about the Battle of Bloody Run in 1656, when so many Pamunkey soldiers died that the creek ran red?

I'm running through their blood right now.

I can't stomach the idea of passing the spot on Cary Street where the Main Street Hospital for the Medical, Surgical and Obstetrical Treatment of Slaves once stood.

Or where the Church Hill tunnel collapsed in 1925.

As I pass Chimborazo Hospital, which tended to Confederate soldiers, I trip over gangrenous limbs sawn off to stop the spreading infection, the streets littered with amputated arms and legs, all of them reaching up for me. My ankle twists and I lose my balance. I hop on one foot as I pull off my sandal, then the other. I carry them in my hands for a while but there's no point. I fling them away and run barefoot, trying not to see the hundreds of ghosts around me. I've never seen so many outstretched hands, all of them reaching out for me. Grabbing hold.

I want to take it back. Take it all back . . . I didn't know. I just didn't know.

Death is everywhere. *They* are everywhere.

There's only one place left.

Time to go home again.

Home again, home again—

PART FOUR

chasing

the

phantom

housewarming

Someone has painted a symbol in red across the front door. A circle with three rippling slashes cut across, like sperm burrowing into an ovum. I run my fingers over it and rust-colored crust flakes off. Spray paint doesn't crumble off like that.

It feels wrong to knock. Why do I need Tobias's permission to enter? It's not his house any more than it is mine. It doesn't belong to anyone. What's stopping me from walking in?

Honey, I'm hooooome!

Just as I reach for the knob the door opens a crack.

A loamy aroma rushes over me, and I catch a hint of mildew and sweat in the air. It smells like a locker room that's doing double duty as a mausoleum. Did it smell this bad before?

A young woman peers out from the crack. She has a porcelain complexion, like a dead Betty Boop. I wonder if she's a ghost and reflexively step back. Am I at the wrong house?

"You wanna get haunted?"

The question throws me. Who is she? "Is, uh . . . Is Tobias here?"

Dead Betty Boop shouts over her shoulder, "Tobias! Some girl's here to see you!"

Some girl? Doesn't she know I used to live *here?*

Feet shuffle down the hall. "If she wants a session, tell her to—"

Tobias cuts himself off as soon as he spots me in the doorway.

He looks thinner now, if that's even possible. Pale, but his cheeks are flushed a faint pink. He's not wearing his glasses, which is strange. I don't think I've ever seen him without them on before.

"Oh. You made it." He smiles at me, a genuine grin. "Took you long enough."

"What's with the graffiti?" I nod at the door.

"Protection," he mutters before turning back to the shadows. "Welcome home."

Dead Betty Boop gives me another once-over before shrugging and trailing after Tobias. The door stays open for me.

It's Tuesday. I left this house a little over forty-eight hours ago and yet this place feels totally transformed. It hits me the second I enter. A vague, sickly sweet scent drifts throughout the hall, like a bowl of apples left out to rot.

"Tobias," I call after him, wincing at the neediness in my voice. "I need to make it stop. I'm—I'm seeing them everywhere. Outside my apartment. In the streets."

"Told you to stay, didn't I? But you and Amara wanted to go, so . . . Maybe it's for the best. I think you needed to see the revenants for yourself."

"See *what*?"

"That's what Silas called them," he says over his shoulder, barely turning to acknowledge me as he shuffles along. "They're lost souls. Spirits with no house to haunt."

"Well, they should fucking rent like the rest of us."

"What do you think happens if you die outside? Your ghost wanders. Imagine all those homeless ghosts out there, roving the streets, just looking for something, *anything*, to call home."

That's all spirits want, apparently. To be invited in; a place to lay down their roots. Not much different than the living, I guess. Isn't that what we're all after? A home to call our own?

"Are you saying they won't go away?"

Tobias turns to face me. "They've always been there, Erin—you just couldn't see them. But now that you can, you want it to stop? What did you think would happen? You could just quit and—*poof*— they'd all fade away?"

I'm going to be haunted for the rest of my life.

"I tried to warn you." Tobias turns back with a dismissive wave, continuing his lazy shuffle to the living room. "We opened a door. It's not going to shut because you suddenly changed your mind. Sorry. Ghost just doesn't work that way."

"Then *how* does it work?"

"A vessel isn't just for bringing ghosts in. It's for keeping unwanted spirits out. No ghost is getting through that front door without an invitation."

"So you're just going to stay inside forever? Lock the doors and hope nobody slips in?"

He doesn't answer.

"*Please*, Toby. I need my life back."

"Your *life*." Tobias must still be pissed at me for stealing his stash. That's what this is about—he's punishing me. This strung-out, passive-aggressive, laissez-faire attitude is his way of getting back at me. I should come clean and confess my sins so there'll be no hard feelings. Tobias will forgive me and *then* he'll make the ghosts go away. "I'm sorry I stole your Ghost."

"Did you bring it back?"

"It's gone."

"You dropped *all of it*? Jesus, no wonder you drew so much attention! Dose on too much Ghost and you become a beacon for these spirits. They can smell that shit from a mile away."

"Yeah, well, I had to find that one out the hard way."

"You're safe here, don't worry. Plus I got the balance better now— this new batch is much smoother. Folks won't puke ectoplasm every time they dose. That shit was getting pretty nasty to mop up."

"You're making *more*?"

"There's always more Ghost where that came from." He disappears into the living room.

"Toby, how are you—" I cut myself off as soon as I notice the fluctuating glow. I peer into the living room and am immediately taken aback by the sheer number of candles—tea lights, candle tins, mason jar candles. Jasmine, vanilla sea salt, lilac bloom, honey lavender. It's a Bath and Body Works blowout sale in here.

Primitive signs that I don't recognize now adorn the wall, matching the symbol on the front door. The windows are covered with plywood sheets, nailed over the frames to seal out any external light. I immediately forget what time of day it is. Time doesn't exist the same way in a place like this.

"Take a load off." Tobias sits on the floor next to Dead Betty Boop, who won't stop staring at me.

I hesitate at the doorway. "There's got to be a way . . . right? To stop seeing them?"

"Is that why you're *really* here?"

"Yes." I hope I sound like I mean it. "Turn the tap off, Tobias. I'm done."

"Oh, man . . . That's a heartbreaker. I thought you wanted to see Silas."

"Is he here?" The sheer predictability of my emotional response to simply hearing his name makes me feel like I belong in some goddamn Brontë novel. I came here to stop this, not to see Silas.

"Right where you left him."

"Wait. You're telling me he . . . he's . . ."

"He's been waiting for you."

All this time I was out there, lost in the city, calling out for him, while he's been waiting for me to come back home. This is our house after all, isn't it? "He's here now?"

"Of course. He's missed you."

"Have you talked to him?"

"All the time. Come on. Sit down." Tobias waves his hand lazily through the air. "You're making me nervous, hovering like that. You look like a ghost." He chuckles at his own joke.

"Where are your glasses?" I ask as I lower myself onto the floor, joining them.

"I don't need them to see anymore."

Dead Betty Boop is all smiles now. I can see how young she is in the candlelight. She could be in college—Christ, high school, even. "Hi. I'm Melissa."

"This is Erin," Tobias makes my introduction for me. "She's a dear old friend."

"What's she doing here?" I ask Tobias, unnerved that there's a stranger inside—

our home

—the house.

"Just making new friends."

"Make new friends," Melissa sings on cue, out of tune, "but keep the oo-ooold . . ."

I don't know where she comes from, but I know her story already. I don't want to admit it, but I sense the same exact desperation to run away from her prefab identity that I had. That's what's brings us here, isn't it? We all want to—

get haunted

—escape our lives. And here's Tobias, taking her in with open arms. *Mi casa, su casa.*

"Toby?"

It takes him a moment to open his eyes—and when he does, it takes even longer for him to find me. His eyes drift about the room before locking onto mine. Now he's all smiles. "Yeah?"

"Have you been here this whole time?"

"Where else am I gonna go?"

He never left. This home with no electricity, no running water, nothing but his—

ghosts

—stupid drugs. "What's going on here?"

"Oh, you know . . . I've been busy, just being neighborly." He holds out his hand, a dose of Ghost pinched between his fingers. "It's a wonderful day to get haunted."

"Would you be mine," Melissa sings, "could you be mine, won't you be . . ."

"What do you say?" Tobias asks. "Wanna get haunted?"

Yes, I say to myself. "No."

"You sure?"

Yes, god, yes, I want it.

But just seeing the pill turns my stomach. I don't know if I can go through with it again.

"I'll pass."

"It's okay, Erin. Just one more time? For Silas's sake?"

"*No.*"

Tobias backs off, unable to wipe the shit-eating grin from his face. "I'm just messing with you. You don't have to do anything you don't want to. Stay, go, totally up to you."

There's a knock at the door. My shoulders spring up, startled by the sudden sound.

"You mind getting that?" Tobias has already closed his eyes, shutting me out.

I don't seem to have much of a choice. A bit pissed, I leave the living room and head back to the front door. *I need to get out of here*, I think. *I need to get as far away from this septic shithole as soon as humanly possible. I should just walk out now and never look back.*

A sinewy pair of gutter punks prop themselves up on the porch. They couldn't be older than twenty, if that. Just kids. Christ, is Tobias peddling his drugs at the playground?

Wait. I recognize these two. This couple has been squatting on the sidewalk outside my apartment, haven't they? Strumming their guitar for pocket change? I recognize her topknot of dreadlocks and his homemade face tattoos.

"Is this the haunted house?" she asks. She's wearing his leather jacket, a little too large for her diminutive frame, studded with buttons from bands I've never heard of. Crudely sewn canvas patches run along its sleeves.

"Who told you? How did you—"

The words catch in my mouth.

There's a boy standing in the center of the cul-de-sac. Just a boy. He doesn't move. Only his clear plastic tarp billows in the breeze, flapping at his feet. He stares back at me.

He hadn't there before, I swear. Did he follow me?

"I'd close the door if I were you," Tobias calls out from the living room. "Don't want any uninvited houseguests sneaking in."

The boy senses something has shifted in the air. He steps forward—toward me, the house. He wants to come in.

"Get inside," I say to the couple. My eyes never leave the boy. He steps onto the lawn. If I don't close the door, close it now, the boy will slip in. And somehow I know one lost soul will lead to two will lead to ten will lead to—

"*Hurry.*" I grab the girl by her sleeve and pull, and her boyfriend comes with her. I slam the door, sealing us in, and peer through the peephole. The boy stops, set adrift. I nearly feel a twinge of regret for him, all alone with no place to haunt, no friends to play with.

The couple has already joined the circle when I enter the living room.

"Erin"—Tobias makes introductions like a good host—"this is Adriano and Stephanie."

"Hey," Stephanie says with an awkward smile. Adriano doesn't even look at me.

"So you're selling," I say. "You're a dealer now?"

"That's a pretty crass way of putting it," Tobias admonishes me. "Ghost isn't the kind of drug you find. It finds you. You hear about it from someone who's used it. They tell you about it, then you tell someone else, like a—"

"Ghost story?"

"Exactly! That's how we're going to let it spread." He holds out his hands, presenting the living room to me in all its glowing, rippling glory. "We all have a ghost story to tell. I'm merely providing the campfire."

I force my way into the ring and sit. "How'd you hear about this house?" I ask the circle.

Dead Betty—sorry, Melissa—chimes in, happy to have an answer. "Facebook."

"Jesus, Tobias, you're *posting* about this place?"

"I got friended by Silas," Melissa says defensively. "He sent me a message—"

"*When?*"

"—asking if I wanted to get haunted." Of course. Social media is a perfect platform to reach out to people who have lost someone.

"So *you're* the one who hacked Silas's account." I'm intensely aware that I'm harshing their mellow but I don't care. Tobias used his friends list as a phone book for people in mourning after Silas's death. Imagine receiving an Evite from the afterlife. People want to believe so badly, they'll RSVP to anything. "You lied to me."

"We're *helping* people," Tobias says. "People who are hurting."

"You're exploiting their grief—"

"We're reuniting them," he says. "Silas always had this . . . this *sway* over people. Everyone listens to him. I figured I could use his account to reach out and—"

"Silas is *dead*." It's the first time I've said the words out loud.

"You think death is *really* going to stop him?"

This isn't like Tobias. This isn't like Tobias at all. He's pretending to be this chill Zen master and I don't like it.

"I'm glad you came back, Erin . . . I am. I couldn't have done this, *any of this*, without you."

"I don't want anything to do with—whatever this is."

"You brought Silas *back*! If it weren't for your connection, none of this would've worked." Something in the way he says the word *connection* makes it sound like what he means is *addiction.* "You're my good luck charm. Let me pay you back . . . Say hey to Silas."

"I told you, I don't want any more of that shit."

He raises his hands. "Suit yourself."

Tobias passes a Tupperware full of gelcaps around the circle. "We all have our own ghost stories. This"—he holds up a pill, then swallows it—"is how we tell them."

Each member takes a cap, giddy as schoolkids at snack time. Melissa forces a gelcap into my hand and smiles. "Here."

I glance at the pill between my fingers. I turn it over a couple times, up and down, up and down, the ashen powder tumbling around. I feel the mounting itch.

Even now, I want it. That chill down my spine. The gooseflesh ripple. I can't stop myself.

I want to get haunted.

Maybe this time it won't be as bad? I'm in a safe place, a controlled séance. Not out there, in the city, with all that supernatural static. I'm protected here.

Tobias said he perfected the dosage, didn't he? Maybe it was just a bad batch. *Stay away from the brown acid.* One more haunting, that's all. What's one more ghost going to hurt? Feeling Silas inside. Sensing his spirit drift through. Inhabit me. I can have that feeling back . . .

You don't have to do this, I hear Amara say. *You came here to—*

I perform a magic trick: The Vanishing Capsule. *Now you see it, now you don't . . .*

"Thatta girl," Tobias says. I didn't realize he'd been watching me. "That's my Erin."

My mouth is so dry, I can't get the pill down. The muscles in my throat wrestle with the capsule. Melissa offers me a bottle of water. It's room temperature, but by the time it hits my stomach, I can feel it boiling over—*Double, double toil and trouble.*

"This house is a safe place," Tobias says. "We can fill its rooms with those we've lost. You'll invite your own ghost inside. Your connection will draw them to us. Focus on that bond. Take each other's hand and close your eyes," he instructs. I watch everyone in the circle follow along, shutting their eyes and letting Tobias's voice send them off. "You've come here because there's someone you wish to contact on the other side. Go ahead and picture them in your mind."

I close my eyes and I immediately see Silas, as if he's been waiting for me there, hiding behind my eyelids. His face is so clear in my head—his hair hooked around his ears, his hazel eyes, that devilish grin.

"Now I want you to say their name out loud. Call out to them. Cast out that first line."

"Hutch," Stephanie says.

"Sabeen," Melissa says.

"Mark," Adriano says.

I don't call out for Silas. I keep his name inside, hidden, as if to save him for myself.

"Keep them in your mind. Hold on to them. Don't let go. Some must travel a great distance. It won't be easy. But your connection, your link, will bring them home."

I hold on to Silas. His face. His smile. His laughter fills my mind.

"This house is merely a receptacle," Tobias says. "A vessel for our ghosts to inhabit. It's *you* who are truly haunted. We need to unleash them, release them, within these walls."

The picture of Silas slips just a bit. It's hard to hold on to the mental image of him while Tobias speaks. I keep getting distracted.

"We're going to take a tour of this house in our minds, walk through each room. All of them are empty, waiting to be filled. Let's start by looking at the front door. It's closed now, but I want you to imagine it opening. Go ahead and open the door in your mind. Open it."

I swear I hear the front door slowly open on its own. The thin squeak of its hinges echoes down the hall.

"Come inside. Walk through the front door. Into the hallway . . . See the space in your mind. See its rooms waiting to be filled. Follow my voice. Can you hear me? We wish to reach out to those spirits we carry with us. We have been granted access to the other side and now we are ready to see." Tobias really has perfected his spiritual sales pitch since our last séance. Or maybe his demographic has changed. Without Amara around to call him on his shit, Tobias is in full command of the room.

I feel the grips of both of my neighbors tighten, their hands sweating against mine.

"We are ready to receive your message. Please speak to us." I sense the slightest sway in the circle. Suddenly, we're all rhythmically rocking side to side in tandem with one another. The movement gradually gains momentum the louder Tobias's voice rises. "Spirits, we wish to communicate with you. Show us a sign."

I can feel the pull and tug in each of my arms, left to right.

"Hutch: Is there someone here you wish to communicate with?"
—*back and forth*—

"Sabeen: Is there someone you wish to speak to?"
—*back and forth*—

"Mark: Is there someone you—"

The swaying halts. I feel a snap in my neck as the circle stops rocking. Someone—Melissa, maybe—gasps. I open my eyes.

There's a flicker in the center of the room. A single flame the size of a silver dollar suspends itself over our heads. There's no source that I can see.

It draws near. I reel back, frightened at first, as the free-floating flame slowly approaches me. *Me.* The rest of the circle sees it, too, marveling at it. Tobias's chest sinks as he can't stave off his exhaustion any longer.

The flame hovers in front of me, mere inches from my face, letting me take in its glow. It now fluctuates with all kinds of colors. A ring of green swirls through the orange and yellow, there and gone, now replaced by a brilliant red ribbon, then blue. There's a pulse to it.

A heartbeat.

". . . Silas?"

The light grows brighter at his name. The flame flattens itself, elongating. It's now as large as my hand, growing, deepening. I can see through it, and yet it still possesses depth.

I catch sight of Silas's face.

"Silas, is . . . is it really . . ."

Every time I say his name, a new color swells through the flame. The pulse picks up. The light now looks like a flipbook of translucent pictures. His motions are slow, segmented, but I watch as the quivering image of his hand lifts to touch my face.

"It's *you*," I say, tears suddenly running down my cheeks. "It's really you."

The light passes through me—Silas's spirit enters my body—and I swear I've never felt so warm in all my life. I gasp as the heat of him reaches through my limbs. I swear this feels like the first breath I've ever taken.

He's inside. *Possessing* me. When I look out at the room, my eyes are no longer my own. They are his eyes—*our eyes*—now. We are together, fusing as one. His spirit and my body.

I let go of my neighbors' hands and ease back onto the floor against the spray-painted Ouija board. I have always been the planchette. I feel the light spread through my bloodstream, the heat of Silas's spirit circulating throughout my entire body, touching every nerve, seeping into every cell, until there isn't a part of me that's not his.

They say your life flashes before your eyes right before you die, but all I see is Silas's. In this moment, sprawled across the floor, I bear witness to the entirety of his existence. Gravity is gone as my body separates from my consciousness. My limbs are now his, my body now his, my flesh for his past, my soul for his history. His birth. His infancy. His boyhood.

I watch Silas grow and blossom in a rapid-fire procession of memories, spiriting through his lifetime so fast, I can barely breathe. The force of his presence pins me to the floor.

Then everything halts. Time slows down all at once and I feel
Silas suddenly slip. My body's grip on his spirit loosens and I need to
tighten my bones around him. Why did we stop?

We're following a young woman, trying to catch up. There's a
bruised aura about her—something vaguely familiar. I know her
from somewhere. She radiates bands of deep purple. The atmosphere
all around her bends and warps in concentric, iridescent circles.

She is a black pearl.

Oh god . . . *it's me.* I'm looking at myself *outside* myself, through
Silas's eyes. I barely recognize myself. I look absolutely radiant, my
body somehow distorting the spectrum of light. I'm eighteen, wearing an outfit I haven't worn since—

Wait. I remember this. I'm in college. This is the first time Silas
and I ever spoke to each other. Was he tripping when he approached
me? The colors coming off my skin make me look like a human oil
slick, wrapped in undulating rings of purples and greens and blacks
and blues. I can feel his heartbeat pick up and I know it's my heart
mimicking his palpitations.

Excuse me, he says. *Erin, right? We're in Brooke Stevens's writing workshop together.*

I see the expression of my own face shift. I'm trying to remember
him. *Hey.*

*You don't remember me. That's okay. Our class is pretty forgettable. Not
a lot of Updikes in the mix.*

. . . Dykes?

*As in John Updike, the author. I'm not making any broad sweeping
statements about the sexual orientation of our classmates, I swear. Just their
talent.*

Ah . . . Glad we cleared that up.

I just wanted to say I really liked your story today. Pretty grim.

Were you expecting some sugar and spice? Sorry.

*To be honest, I was actually hoping I could read more. Something else of
yours.*

. . . Of mine?

Yeah. Give me something you've never shared with anyone else—the really dark stuff—and I'll give you something of mine. Only fair, don't you think?

So . . . what? We're playing doctor now? I'll show you mine if you show me yours?

Sure. Why not? If it blows me away, you'll never be able to get rid of me. But if it's trash . . . you'll never have to worry about me bothering you again.

How can I say no to that?

You do the same. If you think my writing's crap, then you'll know I'm not worth the oxygen. But think about it: if it's good, if I'm really good, then we can rule the world together.

You're pretty full of yourself, aren't you?

Life's too short to waste it on people who're beneath you . . . and I look at you and I can't help but think that maybe, just maybe, you're above.

Life is too short. But it doesn't have to be.

I'll . . . think about it.

Don't think. Just take the leap with me. There's a darkness in you . . . isn't there? I bet no one else has ever seen it before, or wanted to. Maybe you don't even see it in yourself.

But you can, I say—and with his eyes, now mine, I see that darkness for myself. See it radiating off me in pearlescent waves of black. He always saw me like this. This is who I am.

Silas wants me to see this. Experience this. He's showing me our life together, how our existences intertwine. This is his way of telling me that he's here, still here, that he never left. He will never leave me—he loves me, forgives me—as long as I stay inside this house.

Two spirits, two souls, communing. It's beautiful. So fucking beautiful. This is better than sex. This is being touched by God.

"Silas," I call out to the candlelit living room. "I'm here . . . *I'm home.*"

ringside seats

"I'd like you to meet Marcia," Tobias says. I'm totally thrown by the frosted blonde woman before me. She's old enough to be friends with my mother, though I can tell from her choice in clothes that they'd never be in the same social circle. This woman strikes me as some kind of working mom from the north side of Richmond—a small business owner. She could own a clothing boutique in Carytown. I've probably shopped there for all I know.

"Hello." Marcia holds out her hand to me. I can't help but dwell on her manicured fingers, the gold wedding band dully glowing in the surrounding candlelight.

She shouldn't be here. Her presence throws our home out of balance. She's harshing my haunting. High schoolers are one thing—college kids, sure—but Marcia is a goddamn *adult*. She's dressed in activewear, like she's on her way to hot yoga after our drug-induced séance.

"Marcia is going to be staying with us for a while," Tobias says. "She's hoping to make contact with her son." This is how Tobias introduces new houseguests: by who we've lost.

Marcia's lips tighten, like she's trying to hide how much it hurts to hear someone else bring up her boy.

"I wonder if you might show her around? Make Marcia feel at home."

"Sure."

Tobias rests a consoling hand on Marcia's shoulder. "Did you bring a sleeping bag?"

She nods, eyes wide as Tobias gives her his full attention.

"The money? Just for food and water while you're here . . ."

"Yes."

"Great. You're doing great, Marcia. Now . . . can I have your cell phone?"

"My . . . ?"

"It's important we restrict contact with the outside world." Tobias sounds so calm. So in control. How can Marcia say no? "There's no telling how long this process will take. It could be a day, it could be five, but until we plant your seed, we need to seal ourselves off."

This is a house rule for everyone. Tobias demands we sever ties. No phone calls to Mom and Dad, no friends or family. The people calling this house home are our family now. Give yourself over to Tobias and in return, he'll offer what you want—*need*—more than anything.

Marcia unearths her cell from her purse and hands it to Tobias, who promptly powers it down and slips it into his pocket. "You're not alone anymore," he says. "Your son—"

"*Sean.*"

"Sean is out there. Trust me, Marcia, we'll find him. We'll bring him home."

"You can really do that?" Every word is weighed down with desperation.

"We carry these ghosts with us, wherever we go. By giving them a house to haunt, we know where they'll be. We can always visit. All it takes is a key. That's what I'm offering."

"He'll be here?" The tears are already pooling in Marcia's eyes.

"All it takes is opening that door and letting them in. Nobody knows you're here, right?"

Marcia shakes her head, *no no no.*

"What about your husband?"

"We're separated. He doesn't . . . doesn't believe . . ."

"Good. We can get started right away. I've got a private session scheduled for you this evening. I want you to settle in and meet some of the other people here. Make friends, okay?"

But keep the old, I think to myself.

Marcia nods, even smiles through her tears. She wipes her eyes with her sleeve. "Okay."

This feels wrong. Seeing Tobias tap into this woman's mourning is wrong. I still feel Silas lingering within me, the residue of his spirit coating my insides like honey, but there's a cognitive dissonance to seeing others go through the same experience. Ever since I came—

home

—back, people have been coming and going. Strangers knock on the door and say they want to get haunted. Tobias sells them Ghost and sends them on their merry way. I can hear the commercial jingling through my head now, as if it's an ad campaign put together by the McMartin Agency. Maybe they'd give me the account: *Now you too, kids, can dose on Ghost in the comfort of your own home! Ghost now comes in handy travel snack packs for easy séances with your lost loved ones. Turn your own home into a haunted house today!*

Others stay. Those who need Tobias's spiritual guidance can get the elite pass, which includes exclusive sittings with the man himself.

Marcia is our first walk-in. How did she even hear about this house?

"How long have you been here?" she asks. She trails up the stairs behind me as I give her the grand tour.

"Not long." I have no idea if that's true. How many days has it been? Do I even remember? My head feels so foggy. I haven't been outside in what seems like forever.

"Who're you here for?" Marcia's question makes my skin prickle. I don't know how to engage with her. Something about her status as an adult—who should know better than to get mixed up in this kind of shit in the first place—makes me want to call her *ma'am*.

"A friend." I want to tell Marcia to run while she still can. Before it's too late. But I know she won't listen. If her grief brought her this far, nothing will change her mind.

I know that look. We all have it.

Silas just wanted to see his mom again, Tobias explained to me. That's how this all started. Silas had stumbled on a Reddit thread about an obscure hallucinogenic purported to be so potent, it actually allows you to see the dead. There were a few footnotes in anthropological texts about the Indigenous peoples of Australia using the mushroom to open up corners of their minds never accessed, allowing them to pull back the veil that separates the living from the dead.

We all assumed Silas was on some run-of-the-mill drug. Heroin or cocaine. We had no idea. By the time I sprung Silas out of rehab, he'd been off his spirits for days. No wonder he was so strung out. He was seeing ghosts he didn't want to see.

If the drug allows us a glimpse into the realm of the dead, Ghost allows the dead to glimpse back into the realm of the living . . . and it turns out they're just as hungry for it as people are. Silas needed a safe house, a *clean* house, so he reached out to Tobias for help.

They ended up here. In Hopewell.

The rest is history, as they say. I can't help but wonder what books will be written about Silas and Tobias. Their little burgeoning business.

I lead Marcia to the master bedroom, where Adriano and Stephanie have shacked up. Let them share a room together, I think. "Here you go."

Adriano is busy spray-painting the walls. I'm not going to critique his tagging style, or lack thereof, but I'm not impressed.

Marcia hesitates at the door. She wants to say more. "He wasn't even a year old. One morning I woke up and found him in his crib and his body was all blue."

I know the color. I can picture his chilled complexion.

Look how far this woman has come. Look at the lengths she'll go, the depths she'll descend to. She has nowhere else to turn. I don't know if it's the right thing to do, but I hug her. Marcia's shoulders stiffen at first, but she eventually relents, her body softening against mine.

"You're going to be okay," I lie right into her ear.

————————

Tobias asks me to sit in on Marcia's session. She's nervous and could use a friendly face, so I've been tasked with holding her hand through her first séance.

I watch Marcia's eyes wander around the living room, anxiously taking in the empty space and its cave drawings as Tobias lights the candles. She hasn't said a word since we sat, forming our triangle. I can tell she's nervous, so I squeeze her hand and offer a warm smile.

"Don't worry. I'll be right here."

She smiles back, but it quickly fades from her lips. I can't help but think about what's brought her here, the kind of grief that could lure a woman this far off the beaten path of her everyday life. Could Marcia tally all the hours of therapy, the antidepressants, the counseling with her estranged husband—everything she's about to forsake, just for a chance to see her son? I try to imagine how many memories were created between Marcia and her boy during the life they shared. It was so short. *Not even a year,* she said. Barely enough to fill a calendar. Her boy's belongings could fit in a single trunk—bath toys and tennis shoes and baseball caps smaller than your fist, soft-padded picture books and neatly folded T-shirts still crisp. And yet, it's more than enough to hold on to. Of course she'll do anything—*anything*—to see her son one last time. Who could blame her for being here?

Who would fault her for wanting to get haunted?

Tobias hands us each a dose of Ghost. I nod and Marcia swallows her pill, chasing it with a gulp of bottled water. I pretend to take mine but I pocket it instead.

"Marcia," Tobias begins. "It's very brave what you've done. Your love, your connection to your son is so strong, you're willing to reach beyond the veil to find him. To bring him back."

Marcia nods, lost in his words. It's unclear to me if she believes him or not, but his voice is drawing upon her desperation, luring her in. She wants—*craves*—this connection so badly.

"You'll need that strength for this to work, okay? Can you be strong? For your son?"

"Yes."

"Good. Now . . . I want you to start by picturing the room where you last saw your boy. See that space in your mind. Can you see it now?"

"Nursery," she says. Her eyes are closed, while mine remain open. Already I feel the itch to get haunted, but I want to watch Marcia's mystical experience with as clear a head as possible, see someone else go through Tobias's parlor games for myself.

"Tell me about that room. Show me the nursery."

Marcia opens her mouth to speak, but the words aren't there yet. It takes a moment for her to gather her thoughts, but I can tell the room manifests itself in her mind's eye. "We painted it just for him. Ships on the walls, dinosaurs. He's in his crib . . . I see him . . ."

"Good," Tobias says in a soothing tone. "Focus on the crib. I want you to bring that crib here. Into this house. Can you do that for me? Imagine one of the rooms here in our house becoming your son's nursery. You have to root Sean here, within our walls."

The muscles in Marcia's jaw slacken. She's drifting, slipping into the cavern of her own mind, with all its shadows and self-doubt and grief. Her eyes race back and forth behind their lids, as if she's already lost in the depths of REM sleep. "Yes . . ."

But Tobias won't let her go. He holds on to her, his voice luring her along. "Focus on the wooden slats. The railing. I want you to run your hand over the mattress. The sheets. Everything is so smooth and soft. Can you feel it?"

Marcia's free hand extends out before her. I watch her fingers glide along the invisible surface of the mattress and oh god, I nearly see it too.

"Yes." She tightens her other hand against mine, squeezing.

It feels so bizarre, watching someone else—a stranger—go through the motions of their own séance. I want to believe my experience contacting Silas is somehow exceptional, that no one else has the same experience as me. My ability to connect to his spirit is different, *special*. But watching Marcia wander through her own trip snatches that feeling away from me.

"Marcia," Tobias says. "Listen closely. With all your heart, all the love and strength you have, I want you to fill that space, fill the crib with all the joy your son gave you."

"Yes . . ."

"That crib is a receptacle for everything you hold dear in this world. Everything you love is right there. Inside it. So much love. You have so much love to fill it up with. Can you feel it?"

"Yes . . ."

"Just when it feels like the crib is going to break from all that love, just when you think there's no room left to fill it up with any more, just when you think you've given every last drop you have to offer, you see something at the very center of the mattress. Can you see it?"

"Yes . . ."

"It's taking shape now, isn't it? Can you see it, Marcia? Can you?"

"Yes, I . . . I can see . . ."

"Someone's there, right? Someone small? So small, they fit right in your hands . . ."

"Sean . . ."

"*Ssh.* He's sleeping. Don't wake him. Let him rest. Can you see how peaceful he is?"

"*Yes*." A complex tangle of emotions plays across her face, joy and pain intertwining, rippling across her features.

"Don't let go of him. Keep him there. In his crib. In your heart. Your son is resting now. He's been resting for a long time, but he's ready to wake . . . Are you ready to wake him, Marcia?"

"Sean, baby . . ." Her grip tightens against my hand, squeezing so hard I feel the bones in my fingers press into each other. Her back extends to the hilt as a flower reaches for sunlight.

"Your son's getting ready to open his eyes. See him wake."

"Sean . . ."

"See him open his eyes."

"It's . . . It's *you*."

"See him, Marcia. See your son."

The air gets caught in her lungs. "It's—"

"See him—"

Marcia vomits a stream of yellow bile. It erupts suddenly, but instead of striking the floor, it curves up and twists above our heads. The thin sliver of ectoplasm spindles into a bundle. It's so small, a contorting newborn, slick and slippery with phantasmal afterbirth.

Marcia gasps as the last of the viscous substance slips from her lips and coils into the air, an umbilical cord of ectoplasm. Her eyes fly open to take in the pulsing knot floating above her head but they're completely glazed over. Her consciousness is elsewhere, even as her body remains rooted to the floor. The euphoria in her face is unnerving, the look of wonder so overwhelming.

"*Sean*." Marcia lets go of my hand to reach for her ectoplasmic newborn, to take it in her arms, to embrace her boy.

"Sean, baby, baby . . . Mama's here . . ." Marcia lowers herself onto her back, pulling her son down like a cloud from the sky and bringing him to her chest.

"Mama's here." She's smiling, truly smiling, the ecstasy radiating across her face as she cradles her son.

The wet knot of ectoplasm struggles in her grip, the fluctuating coil reminding me of a maggot as it wrestles against Marcia's loving embrace. But she won't let it go. "Sean . . ."

Then the tendril of ectoplasm ruptures and spills all over Marcia's face—nothing but bile now, the partially digested remnants of her last meal. The look of ecstasy on her face never diminishes, though. Marcia is still blissfully lost in her haunting, her hands still holding on to the negative space of her son. "Sean, my baby . . ."

Tobias turns to me. It's the first time he's looked at me during the session, a grin playing across his face that might as well say, *Told you so.*

"You mind cleaning up, Erin?"

secret sauce

"Did you see him?" Marcia's glassy eyes still brim with dull wonder. She's so far gone, I wonder if she even knows who she's talking to. "Did you see my son?"

"Yes." I wipe the last fleck of vomit from the corner of her lips and comb her hair out of her face, but she doesn't notice. She stares at the ceiling, not seeing it, enraptured. Adriano's pink and black graffiti loops across the walls.

Everybody has chores in this house. My responsibility right now is to tuck Marcia into bed. Her sleeping bag comes up to her chest, her fingers gripping the nylon lip. But she's not here. Her eyes drift toward some far-off point beyond the roof, in the sky, as far as outer space for all I know. "I . . . I held him . . . in my arms. He was here . . . in my hands. I felt him."

I leave her like that, lost in the cosmos with her ghosts. "Sean," I hear her say from over my shoulder as I step out of the bedroom. "I'm here . . . I'm here, baby . . . Stay with me . . ."

Stephanie is on door detail. I hear her ask *You wanna get haunted?* every time someone knocks to pick up their Ghost to-go. If business keeps growing at this pace, we're going to need a drive-through window.

Adriano is spray-painting the living room. The *click-clack* of his aerosol can echoes through the room like a pinball. This symbol looks like a spiraling sun.

Someone found a ratty couch and dragged it in. Tobias is sprawled across its tattered red velvet cushions, his legs slung over the armrest like a king lazing on his throne. He looks almost skeletal, his eyes hollow and his flesh gray. So pale—and the poor guy can't even grow a full beard.

Melissa's on the floor at his feet, head pressed against the armrest, drifting. It's impossible to get Tobias alone these days. He's scheduling séances by the hour now. We all have to clear the living room whenever there's a session, unless we're invited to participate.

"Marcia's all settled," I say. "You got a minute?"

"For you? Always."

"Is there anywhere we can be alone?"

"*Now* you want to be alone with me." It's not a question. He isn't asking. The little dig is in his voice. "Whatever you want to say, just say it. We're all friends here."

I point to his chest. "You're bleeding."

"Huh? Oh . . ." Tobias glances down at himself and notices the blood. He absentmindedly frowns but doesn't do anything, content to keep on bleeding through his shirt.

A perfect circle of blood with three wavy lines.

"I'm worried about you, Toby . . . Don't you think this is all getting a little out of hand?"

"Seems like everything's coming together."

"But . . . what's the plan?" Even I know I'm parroting all the parental conversations I've ever had with my own family, mimicking their authority.

"You mean, like, my *five-year plan*? What're my goals for the future?" There's nothing he needs from me. Not anymore. "I'm a conduit, that's all . . . I'm just opening doors for others."

"So you're just going to keep playing haunted house out here forever? Is that it?"

"Why not?"

"What if the cops show? Shut this all down?"

"There are plenty of empty houses where this came from."

"*Toby*, I'm serious." I'm trying hard to keep my frustration out of this. "How long do you think you can keep this up? Honestly?"

"As long as supplies last." He scratches his stubbly neck, fingernails raking over dry skin. "Don't worry. You've always got an open invite. Whenever you want to get haunted, just ask."

"*This can't last.*"

"Says who?" He's taking pity on me. *Poor you*, he's thinking, *you just don't see it yet.* "I've found my calling, Erin. And look who's answering! It's amazing, don't you think? Ghost is starting to spread all on its own now. Marcia is proof of that. Soon there will be more."

"Aren't you worried about what you don't know? What the long-term side effects will be? What if it gives you cancer or brain damage or destroys your liver? What if we can never walk down the street again without seeing every last phantom that doesn't have a house to haunt? I don't want to be stuck inside this house for the rest of my life."

Tobias looks at me with a withering smile. "You've read the Bible, right? Jesus and the final supper? *Eat, for this is my body?* What if— hear me out—what if the body of Christ wasn't what we've always believed it to be? What if his disciples ate something else?"

"You mean a *mushroom*?" I say it to shoot him down, to illustrate how absurd Tobias sounds right now. If only Amara were here.

"Unless you eat the flesh of the Son of Man and drink his blood," he recites, "you have no life in you. Those who eat my flesh and drink my blood abide in me, and I in them."

So Tobias is quoting scripture now. This is new.

"How can that *not* be a mushroom? I mean, what even is manna from heaven?" He sits up, excited now. The abrupt movement sends Melissa's head skidding down the armrest. She hardly reacts. She's haunted right now, her mind off and wandering the halls with her ghost, whoever it is.

This isn't how I expected our conversation to go. Tobias is pushing into uncharted territory, and I have absolutely no idea how to drag him back. This goes way beyond Silas.

"Tobias." I soften my tone, hoping to break through to him. "I want to help."

"That's great. I can use your help around the house."

"No—I mean help *you*. *You* need help. This is getting way too big too fast."

"Why?"

"Because . . ." *Because this is crazy. There's no way this can last. It could kill you, just like it killed Silas.* But I don't say any of these things. I just stand there, wordless, trying to fight my way through the fog in my brain because I haven't dosed on Ghost in . . .

In . . .

How long has it been since my last cap? I can feel the tremors in my hands, withdrawal rattling my bones like somebody shaking a prescription bottle.

"Come with me." Tobias springs up from the couch with a sudden surge of energy. Melissa doesn't move.

I follow Tobias through the hall. He's drifting on a current of electricity that I can't quite match. "We need to find a job for you," he says. "We just have to figure out what's best."

"I'm not doing chores, Tobias. I'm not your fucking house cleaner."

Tobias stops abruptly and points down the hall to the front door. "Then just go, Erin. I'm not keeping you here. You're free to go whenever you want. *So go.*"

He's stalemating me. Making me choose. *Get haunted or get gone.* I can feel the need brewing within my body, the downright ache of it all. I can't leave the house.

I want to get haunted.

My silence admits defeat. Once Tobias realizes he's won, he says, "There's something I want to show you. Something special. I'm trusting you with this, okay?"

"What is it?" I can't stop myself from feeling the sudden surge of curiosity, no matter how much I try to resist it. Resist him.

Tobias heads for the kitchen. He's talking to me but he might as well be talking to himself. "We tried baking the mushroom in chocolate, but that just diluted the dose. Tea wasn't strong enough, either. The gelcaps were my idea." I can hear the pride in his voice. I don't like it.

The kitchen is far more cluttered than I remember. Tobias has set up a slipshod bake-sale operation. There's a padlock on the upper cabinets. The basement door, too. Rows of cookie sheets line the entire counter. Spread out evenly across each metal tray are dozens of mushrooms, stems shriveled and curled into little question marks.

"You got yourself a real Martha Stewart vibe going on." It's meant to be a joke, but it's true. This feels like a cooking demo. All Tobias is missing is a camera crew.

"Powdering is prime time. I use a coffee bean grinder. Battery powered, of course. Super simple." He's talking a mile a minute, excited to share. Even now, he's still a little kid at heart, eager to earn the approval of his peers, of me. I'm not sure I want to give it to him.

A half dozen grinders clutter the counter. I feel like I'm scanning different brands at the department store, trying to pick which one is best for my hallucinogenic needs.

"Two grams of whole mushrooms yield ten microdoses." He pops a few shriveled mushrooms into an empty grinder before sliding the clear plastic lid on top. He presses his palm down on the lid, sending the blades whirring.

"Funny story," Tobias shouts over the grinding. "Starting off, I used the same grinder I'd use for my coffee. I would end up accidentally blending a little Ghost in my morning brew."

Would you like cream with your haunted coffee?

Tobias lifts his hand off the grinder. The whir of the blades fades, but it leaves this ringing sensation in my ears. I can still hear them chewing through the soft, shriveled flesh. "Let the powder settle. If you open it right away, the whole kitchen fills with magical fairy dust."

I notice several of the other grinders have their chambers already full. Tobias picks one and slides it across the counter.

Several disposable dust masks dangle by their straps from a hook next to the sink. Tobias pulls two free. His mask has an archaic bio-hazard symbol across the front of it in Sharpie, just like the one on the front door. He tugs the grinder's lid, careful not to disturb the dust. "It's easier to adjust the dose by hand, but now that we're expanding, I need to meet the demand."

The pill dispenser is a small plastic box with rows of tiny holes lined up like a hundred hungry mouths. Tobias gingerly tips the dust out from the grinder, pouring its powdery contents across the dispenser until each hole is evenly filled. He covers it with a lid, opens it again—a child performing a magic trick—and *presto chango*. The grid is now lined with capsules, each filled with their own perfectly proportioned allotment of Ghost.

A hundred gelcapped phantoms waiting to haunt whoever ingests them.

"*Boom*. We're in business. Pretty nifty, huh?" Tobias is clearly pleased with himself. I can tell he wants me to be impressed, too.

I can taste the earthiness in the air, even with my mask on. That loamy flavor clings to my throat, like I'm tasting the dirt over my own grave. "Where are the mushrooms coming from?"

"Don't worry about that," he says. "This is all that matters."

Tobias is teaching me, showing me the ropes, so he can put me to work.

"So Silas taught you all this?" I try to sound as unimpressed as humanly possible. If I can't stop him, at least I can make him feel like shit. "Seems like his style."

Tobias pauses. I can tell he wants to tell me more, even when he knows he shouldn't. "Can you keep a secret?"

"Cross my heart," I say. *Hope to die.*

"You can't tell anyone, okay?"

"Who am I gonna tell?" It's a joke at my own expense, but it's true. Who would believe me? Amara? She'll never set foot in this house again.

Tobias reaches for the padlocked cabinet next to the sink. Everything's behind lock and key now. There are so many secrets inside this house. He pulls out a leatherbound book, thin and brittle. "This is Silas's notebook. His *real* notebook. All his recipes are right here."

Even in death, Silas is still leading poor Tobias around. I recognize Silas's handwriting. I notice a hand-drawn image of a man with what looks like toadstools sprouting from his shoulders. A halo wraps around his head, like a medieval painting of Christ. A mushroom cap of light.

". . . And you took it from him?"

"I didn't *take* it. We were working on this together. Prepping for phase two."

"Phase *two.*"

"Time to tell our ghost story to the world. Let it spread even further."

"You wanna franchise."

"Why not? We'll become the stuff of legends!"

"Your own Bloody Mary?"

Tobias laughs. He's still in good spirits. "Sure. Pop a pill and say my name five times in the mirror." He might be kidding, but I can tell he doesn't think it's a bad idea. "Seriously, though, look at what we're doing. You've got to see the value of this, right? The service we're providing? Fuck closure. You never have to let go of your loved ones. Death isn't the end. Not anymore, thanks to us. Thanks to Ghost. Don't you want to be a part of that? With me?"

"Can I see the book?"

Tobias thinks about it before holding the book out to me. Even now, he want to impress me with his cool toys. The blistered binding

of the book feels like it might rip as I run my finger over the spine.
There's a soft, rawhide quality to it. Not quite like leather. It's spongy.

"The cover feels *weird*."

"That's because it's skin."

I throw the book at him. Tobias catches it. "Careful! That's the
only copy!"

"That's disgusting!"

Tobias's laughter fills the kitchen. "Oh, man, you should see the
look on your face! I'm just messing with you . . . It's actually mushroom leather. *Phellinus ellipsoideus* is a parasitic fungus that's as tough
as animal hide when it dries. Aborigines used it for binding their
books." He puts Silas's notebook back in the cabinet and locks it up
again. "This is just the beginning, Erin. Before long, anyone—*everyone*—will see ghosts. And it'll all be because of us."

He plucks a pill from the dispenser and holds it up. My eyes have
a hard time latching onto it, shifting in and out of focus, eventually
settling on the glistening gelcap.

"What do you say? The first dose from a new batch is always the
strongest."

I should say no. I need to say no.

Tobias doesn't wait for me to answer. "Come on. Don't you want
to see Silas?"

I do. I really, really do. "I'm okay right now, thanks."

"Go ahead," Tobias prods, bringing the pill closer to me. "Tell him
the good news."

"What news?"

"That you're helping spread the word. It'll mean the world to
him."

Who am I kidding? Of course I'll take it. Tobias knows that. He's
always known.

"Adam took a bite out of the apple." He sighs. "He was gifted
with knowledge. *He now sees* . . . But what if the Bible got it all
wrong? What if it wasn't an apple? What if it was *this*?"

I reach for the pill.

Tobias yanks his hand back. My fingers remain open, ready to receive. "But you . . ."

Tobias turns his cheek toward me.

I feel my temperature rise along my neck. The familiar itch—the need to get haunted—spreads across my skin. That simmering itch becomes an ache becomes a fever becomes a fire.

"What if Silas sees us?"

"We're all friends here, right? I won't tell if you won't. Just a peck between friends."

I lean forward and press my lips against his cheek. His skin is dry. Flaky. The bristles on his cheek prickle. When I pull back, there's a fine grit on my lips.

"That wasn't so bad, was it?"

I hold out my hand. Palm up. "Can I have my Ghost now?"

"Say *please.*" Tobias turns his other cheek. He taps the pill against his skin.

I don't waste any time. I just want to get this over with. I press my mouth to the side of his face, approximating a peck, then pull back just as quickly. "*Please.*"

"Open wide." Tobias slips the pill between his teeth. The capsule is delicately perched between his incisors. I see his tongue hiding behind it, a snake waiting to spring out and strike.

I lean in, tilting my neck *just so.* I close my eyes. Hold my breath. I open my mouth and receive his sacrament.

I can't do this alone. Can't stop Tobias on my own. Maybe Silas will listen.

spirit writing

The faint blue lines lace the blank page like veins across pale skin. I don't know how long I've been staring at the open notebook, waiting for the Ghost to kick in, but the paper remains stubbornly bare. I brought Silas's empty composition book upstairs, the one he used to reach out to me before.

Where the hell are you, Silas? Tobias isn't the only one who can perform a séance in this house. He's acting like some kind of supernatural drug czar, but he's just some dumbass wannabe who couldn't get a date back in college.

Now look at him. Look at the power he holds over these people. The absolute sway.

Silas will know what to do. Tobias always listens to Silas. He just has to show up.

"Silas?" No answer.

Marcia's still asleep in the master bedroom, so that leaves the—

nursery

—second bedroom down the hall. My tag is still scribbled on the closet wall.

ERIN IS HERE

Is, not *was*, thank god, only now the black ink has seeped deeper into the plaster. The letters appear fuzzier than before, almost as if the words are spreading, growing on their own.

"Silas, can you hear me?" He should be here by now, shouldn't he?

I worry my tolerance for Ghost is getting too high. When you take any drug over time, your body chemistry readjusts. How much will I need to take to achieve the same haunting?

Where are you where are you where are you where are—

Maybe I need to take more? Up my dosage?

—you where are you where are you—

The blue veins on the page start to pulse.

Finally. Here we go. I stole a grease pencil the contractors left behind. Closing my eyes, I press the stub against the page and start drawing circles. There's no need to see. I simply grip the notebook in one hand and let the pencil glide over the blank page in a steady stream of spirals.

I need to shut off my mind and let Silas's spirit enter. The page quickly fills with a kudzu of loops. When I sense one page is covered, I flip to the next and begin all over again.

Three pages. Now four.

"Take my hand, Silas . . . Speak to me." I don't have Tobias's new-found eloquence, but I still have my connection to Silas. In college, we would all cram into his dorm room, smoking way too much and mouthing off about *Infinite Jest* or *Gravity's Rainbow*. We'd read our own work. Silas could command the cramped space, his words drifting through the smoke-choked air. He lived within his writing, existing inside his work in a way I never did. He'd call in the dead of night to share a poem, eager for feedback, not even realizing it was two in the morning.

Those moments felt precious; the privilege of listening to something new. I became his editor. Maybe editor is going too far—transcriber? Agent? Benefactor? I typed up his poems and submitted them to publishers. They rejected everything. Rejected him. So I flipped for photocopying expenses, self-publishing a chapbook of his work. We agreed I'd get the money back after he sold out his stock, but Silas ended up giving away most copies to people he met at the bar. I never saw a penny back, but his words were spreading, weren't they? Isn't that what actually mattered? Isn't that what I wanted for him?

I flip to a fifth page, picking the pencil up from the paper long enough to turn to a clean sheet, a record needle skipping through a groove on some vintage vinyl, barely missing a beat.

My wrist locks. I can feel the muscles in my hand contract. I'm no longer on autopilot—someone else is moving my arm.

Silas.

I let him take my hand. The pencil digs deeper into the paper, no longer loopy spirals but tight, jagged strokes. Silas's voice flows through me now. I can hear him whispering his words into my ear, which I dutifully transcribe onto the page. It feels like we're writing together. Is this what he wants? To bring his words back to life?

My wrist aches but I can't stop. If I pull back now, our connection might—

Crack! The pencil snaps in half in my hand.

My eyes fly open as if I've just woken up. I flip back through the notebook. A rough cursive spreads across the pages, every lacerated letter connecting to the last in a continuous stream. Slowly piecing the words together, I read his message out loud:

THERE IS A LIFE WAITING FOR US HERE

INSIDE THESE WALLS

JUST GIVE YOURSELF OVER TO OUR HOME

TO ME

LET GO ERIN

That's when I see something on the wall.

ERIN IS HERE SILAS IS HERE

I gasp as the words materialize like black mold, creeping out from the closet and across the wall.

ERIN IS HERE SILAS IS HERE ERIN IS HERE
SILAS IS HERE ERIN IS HERE SILAS IS HERE

I can't stop myself from laughing. I clap my hands against my mouth, unable to stop. Silas's correspondence turns the corner, into the hallway. I leap up to my feet and chase after it.

HOME ERIN HOME NOW

He won't stop writing. I feel giddy as I keep reading, racing after him. He's using our home to speak to me. His words flow from one room to the next. On the plaster. The wood.

They're everywhere. *He's* everywhere.

I chase him through the house, following his sentences as they scrawl across the hall and slip into the neighboring room, then scale the ceiling and wrap around empty light fixtures.

Who needs a notebook anymore? We have a whole house to write our masterpiece on.

Our home.

STAY WITH ME STAY ERIN STAY

Crying. Why am I crying? I can't stop myself from crying and laughing all at once, the tears flowing along with the joy, the absolute glee of it all. I've never felt so happy in all my life.

I'm running faster now. Faster. Room to room. I can't stop myself can't stop from—

"Erin!"

I spin around at the sound of my name. It startles me, hearing it out loud. Who said it?

"What're you *doing* up there? Sounds like you're running a marathon." Now I recognize that voice. Of course I know who it is, but I can't bring myself to say it out loud—say his name.

". . . Erin? Helloooo?"

I tiptoe to the top of the stairs, taking each step slowly, straining to hear. How long has it been since we last spoke? It's been days, hasn't it? His voice draws me in, tugging at my skin.

"What's taking you so long?" It's him, his words, faint but alive. "Dinner bell's ringing!"

I swear I hear him humming. *What song is that?* It's on the tip of my tongue.

"*Is that all there is . . .*"

I take each step slowly, the floorboards creaking beneath my feet.

"*If that's all there is, my friend* . . . Dinner's growing cold, Erin! Don't make me eat alone."

The closer I get, closing in on his voice, as if the song itself is luring me in, the harder I can feel my heartbeat against my chest. I can't tell if I'm excited or terrified or both. I'm intensely aware of my pulse, feeling it thrum with every step, until I reach the dining room.

"*Then let's keep . . .*"

Candles are lit. The walls are painted a powder pink. I recognize it. I've seen it before, but I can't remember where. A chandelier hangs from the ceiling, pendeloques shimmering. If I look for too long at the crystals, a dizzy spell washes over me. The dining room shouldn't look like this. None of this furniture was here a minute ago.

"There she is." A silhouette stands on the other side of a mahogany dinner table. Their face is obscured by the chandelier, but when I step into the dining room, I finally find—

Silas

—at the head of the table. "I was just about to send out the search party."

He fills a glass of red wine and hands it to me before pouring his own. I don't know what to do with myself, simply standing there. Staring. Silas holds up his glass. "To domestic bliss."

"Domestic bliss," I echo.

"Eye contact," he says. "Don't want bad luck."

I look into his eyes—his hazel eyes—and lose myself as he taps his glass against mine.

Clink.

"Cheers." The table is set for two. I take in the meal before me: steak, rosemary-scented roast potatoes, asparagus bundles. "I wanted to surprise you. Our first proper meal in our home."

This doesn't feel right. Something about this domestic spread feels . . . *off*. I push back, rejecting this on some subconscious level. Is this actually the kind of life I want? With Silas? It seems so, I don't know, *unlike* him. So unlike *me*. And yet . . . Here we are. The perfect night at home, just the two of us, in our dining room. Who wouldn't want this life? Who could—

just say no

—turn him down?

"You okay?" Silas asks, sensing my apprehension.

I don't want him to think I'm ungrateful. All this effort—he's never done anything like this for me before. Shouldn't I be happy? Appreciative? I put on a cotillion-trained smile. There's something I wanted to ask him. Didn't I need Silas's help? What was it for? For the life of me, I can't remember. Staring deep into the candle, the pulse of light, I lose sight of myself. The room wobbles by a fraction. It tilts—or is it me? I'm losing my balance. I need to—

"*Sit.*" Silas reads my mind. He pulls out a chair for me. "Here. Take a load off."

"Thanks," I manage to say. It does feel better to sit down. The room settles. "I . . . I don't know what happened. Dizzy spell, I guess. I haven't eaten anything in—"

Hours? Days? How long have I been here?

"Don't worry." Silas takes his seat and holds out his hand to me. "Shall we say grace?"

"*Seriously*?" I almost laugh but cut myself short as soon as Silas bows his head. This totally throws me. When did he find religion?

"Bless this oracle so that it may see," Silas says slightly above a whisper. "Bless this sacrament so that we may summon forth, bless our katabasis so that we may cross over—"

I stare at Silas, listening to him repeat this bewildering prayer. He's intoning words that leave the English lexicon—and me—behind. He opens his eyes and finds me staring back.

The smile he offers should provide some comfort, but I feel cold. He picks up his knife with his free hand. "Want me to serve you? Hold still."

Silas turns my wrist until my palm faces upwards. Before I know what's happening, he slips the knife's blade across my exposed skin. I hiss at the sting.

"Sorry," he says, still gripping my wrist. "Mr. Butterfingers over here."

Blood weeps from the cut in the center of my palm. It seeps through our knuckles and onto my plate. I try to yank my hand away but he won't let me go. "Silas, you're hurting me—"

"Almost done." He holds my hand over my plate. I hear the *pitter-pat* of my blood as it strikes the fine china. "Just a little more."

Once I've bled enough for him, he bandages my hand with my own satin napkin. I worry we won't be able to wash the stains out, but I don't want to ruin Silas's magical night any more than I already have. He's trying so hard to be romantic, even if this is completely unlike him.

Who is this? What the hell's going on here?

"So Marcia invited us over this weekend," he says as if nothing's happened. "I know you've been wanting to tackle the garden, but this is the third time she's asked and I couldn't come up with an excuse. I'll take the bullet for the both of us, if you don't want to go."

"That's okay. I'll go." *What am I even saying?*

"Really? You'll be my wingman? We don't have to lose our whole afternoon. One, two hours tops, I promise. I figure that'll give me enough time to finally lay down those planters."

"Planters?"

"You still want them, don't you? What should we grow?"

"What about . . ." *I can't think straight. I'm blanking on my veg-etables.* "Sugar snap peas?"

"Wrong season. Don't worry, we'll figure something out." Silas slices through his steak with ease and places a portion on my plate.

The pain radiating from my hand fades to a dull throb. I'm barely aware of it anymore. I glance at my palm and can't find the cut. It's *gone*. No blood. Just a napkin in my hand.

Silas lifts his glass and toasts. *Clink.* I feel the sound in my teeth. "I'll hop down to the hardware store and pick up some topsoil. I need a few more things to build the planters. Let me know if you need anything and I'll pick them up."

Leaving the house doesn't appeal to me. There's a knot in my stomach and it twists when I think about stepping outside. Not a knot—an octopus. Its tentacles reach up my esophagus and I feel like I—

"Hey." Silas takes my hand. "It's okay. Have another sip."

Silas says eat of my body.

Silas says drink of my blood.

Silas says . . . "Feel better?"

The nausea passes. The wave washes over and is now gone, just as quickly as it came.

"I was thinking," Silas says between bites, "maybe, once we finish painting the rest of the place, we can finally throw our own little house party. Nothing big, just friends and fam."

". . . Here?"

"Yeah, why not? We're finally settling in. Don't you think it's time we share?"

This isn't Silas. *Who is this person?* Since when did he start wanting to slip on an apron and grill on the barbecue? This isn't like him at all. This feels so strange. So—unreal.

"We can invite your friends over," he says. "Finally show them the house. Give them the grand tour. Spread the love. Doesn't that sound nice? Who could you invite, Erin?"

"Well . . ." I'm drawing a blank. Who even are my friends anymore? "Amara, I guess."

"Who else? Think, Erin. Who in your life is hurting? Who should we welcome home?"

"I . . . I don't know."

"What about your parents? They'd love it. I want to share our little slice of heaven. Don't you think we should share, Erin?" His voice keeps pushing its way into my mind, as if he's forcing my own thoughts away, until I can no longer think for myself.

"I guess we could . . . could invite . . ."

"Who? *Who*, Erin? Think hard. Who do we know who's lost someone?"

"What about . . ." A name materializes in my mind. ". . . Callie?"

"Yes! Yes, that's a *great* idea." I don't understand why Silas can't reach out to his own sister, if he wants her here so badly. Why does he need me? "I didn't overcook it, did I?"

He's talking about dinner. I haven't touched my food.

"Just can't find my appetite." I can't remember the last meal I had. I'm never hungry anymore. But I need to show Silas how *devoted* I am. How *faithful* I can be.

I spear the meat with my fork and bring it to my mouth. The

tines scrape against my teeth. This doesn't taste like steak at all. The texture is different—spongy. It doesn't have the marbled fattiness of beef. I work my tongue over the morsel and I swear I feel gills, delicate and lacelike. A fuzzy numbness fills my mouth. I take a heavy gulp of wine to wash it down, but I'm still stuck with this peppery aftertaste. I need to spit it out. I need to—

"Erin?" Silas reaches his hand across the table and takes mine. "You okay?"

I manage to swallow, clearing my throat. "Something just went down the wrong pipe."

Silas is off and chatting again, as if nothing is out of the ordinary, as if this conversation is completely normal and I'm just trying to keep up. "So someone *finally* moved in next door."

". . . Here? Who?" None of the houses here are finished. How could anyone live here?

"Young couple. Younger than us. Stephanie and Adriano. No kids . . . *yet*." Silas wipes his lips with his napkin. The cloth is the same color as the walls, an off-pink creaminess that glows and undulates slightly in the candlelight. "You ever think about trying again? You and me?"

"Try for what?"

"You know . . ." Silas takes my hand and squeezes my fingers. "One of our own."

ring and run

"How about this color?" Silas's voice pulls me through the fog. I blink back to consciousness, slowly coming to, only to find myself sprawled across the couch.

Weren't we just in the dining room? How long have I been lying here? Did I fall asleep?

What's happening to me?

Silas looms over me with paint sample cards in hand, pressing one against the wall. "What about this shade? Not bad, right? Pretty easy on the eyes. This one gets my vote."

"It's . . . bright," I manage to say, miles away, wincing at the pink hue. It practically shouts at me. I have to bring my hand up to my eyes to shield them from the color.

I keep losing time. I can't tell if it's night or day.

How long have I been in this house?

"You don't like it." Silas is losing his patience. There's a heft to his words that wasn't there before, almost as if his voice has changed. He sounds different to me. I can barely make out his silhouette against the blinding pink. I can't get off the couch. I'm rooted, unable to move a muscle. The cushions carry a vague mildew aroma, as if they had been left out in the rain.

"No, I like it. It just—hurts my eyes."

His face prunes. "I think it lightens up the room, don't you?"

"What color is it?"

"It's . . ." Silas glances at the swatch. "*Sarcophyllum*."

I feel like I'm fast-forwarding through my memories of moving in. I remember setting up the kitchen, our bedroom . . . That leaves the living room. Silas has been a good sport about letting me pick the color scheme. Our house has begun to feel more like home already.

This is what I always wanted, isn't it? A home? A family?

A life?

The furniture is covered in plastic drop cloths to protect them from splatter. The floor is shielded, too. Whenever Silas takes a step, the faint crinkle of plastic fills the room.

"Are you gonna make me paint all by myself?"

"Looks like you've got it covered."

Silas carefully pours the paint into the paint tray, *glug-glug-glug*, mixing in some white. I have this vague recollection of chilled soup. I remember my dad's birthday party and I find myself fighting off another abrupt wave of nausea. I feel like I'm—

Like I'm about to—

"You okay?" Silas asks. "You want some water?"

The seasickness passes. I breathe in deeply. "I'm okay. Just the paint fumes."

Silas takes a brush and swipes it haphazardly across the far wall. I lose myself in the serpentine strokes. He's not going up and down—his zigzagging forms a pattern. A symbol.

"What's that?" I hear myself ask. I've seen it before, haven't I? But where?

"What's what?" Silas asks, turning to me.

"*That.*" I prop myself up on one elbow and point. I try to focus on the bleeding icon. I know it's there, even if Silas is pretending like it isn't. The brushstrokes waver against the wall. The paint is practically pulsing. I notice the pan on the floor is of a darker hue, no longer the vivid pink from before. Now it's red.

The room suddenly feels crowded. From the corner of my eye, I see the plastic-draped recliner shift, turning to take me in. A woman's face is pressed against the clear sheet. There are more eyes on us—on me—leering out from the shadows. The plastic drop cloths move on their own, as if the furniture underneath were closing in. It's not furniture at all—I'm not alone.

I need to leave. The overwhelming urge to escape this house takes hold of me—*Run! Get out!* I try to pick myself up from the couch, but as soon as I sit, the room tilts.

"What do you want from me?"

Silas huffs. "To figure out what color you want for our living room."

"I can see the—"

Nothing's there. The paint is just paint. Vertical pink brushstrokes cover the wall.

"It was just there." It was blood, wasn't it?

"You're looking a little green in the gills, hon. Why don't you go upstairs and take a—"

Silas falls silent. He hears something—we both do.

Voices. I swear I hear children right outside the house.

"Do you hear that?" I ask. I don't trust my own senses anymore.

But Silas is gone.

". . . Silas?" I turn and take in the rest of the room. I'm alone. The light shifts—it's no longer cast in that seething pink glow. The plastic tarps lose their translucence, like melted fat coagulating into thick tallow, as everything within the living room returns to shadow.

"It's all boarded up," I hear a boy whisper. "Can't see inside."

"Over here."

They're coming closer. I peel myself off the couch and slip to the floor. It takes more effort to move than it should, the dull ache in my bones weighing my body down. The plastic crinkles beneath my hands and knees as I crawl across the tarp toward the closest window.

"See anything?"

"*Ssh!* Keep it down. Think I heard someone . . ."

The fog dissipates in my head and suddenly I'm struck with a strong need to cry for help. I try, but my voice is too hoarse. It aches. I'm croaking, as if I haven't spoken out loud in days—

Has it been days? That makes no sense. I was just speaking to—

Silas

—but he's gone now, pulling another vanishing act on me, and I'm here wallowing on the floor, feeling the creak in my joints, as if my body has withered into a desiccated husk.

The boys keep whispering, eager for a peek, daring each other to step up to the window.

I'm right here, boys, I want to say. *Come closer. Just a little bit closer. Don't be afraid . . .*

"Think we can get in?"

"I'm not going in there!"

"*Bwok-bwok-bwok . . .*"

Three nimble silhouettes hover by the bay window, obscured by plywood, save for the lower corner where there's still a few inches of exposed tarp. Each boy takes a turn peering in.

If I can just make it to the window, I think, if I can just let them see me, they'll get help. *Save me from this house*, I want to say. But the words are sand in my mouth. *Save me, please—*

"What if someone's in there?"

"Like what? A *ghost*? *Woohoooooooo.*"

"Shut up." Where did they come from? The nearest neighborhood is so far away. These boys must have biked for miles. They have no idea I'm right here, a ragdoll on the floor. I hold my breath as I crawl to the wall, reaching for the window frame. *Help me, save me, help me—*

"I've seen people go inside . . . but they never come out."

"Yeah, right . . ."

"I'm telling you, this house *eats* people."

Word is spreading about our home. One boy hears about a haunted house: he tells his friends and they tell theirs, until the house gains a potency it didn't have before, resonates with an energy that will continue to grow the more people whisper about it. These boys are just the first wave. More will come. Maybe that's what this house wants. More guests. More ghosts.

"Hold up. I see something."

"What?"

"*Sssh!* Something just moved."

"Where? *Where?*"

"Let me see! Move over. *Move.*"

"Stop hogging the view! I wanna look . . ."

I see him. A fresh-faced child, all of ten years old. He and his friends have no idea I'm staring back. The tarp obscures their view, blurring everything beyond into greasy shadows.

"Holy shit! I see someone!"

"You're lying . . ."

"I'm serious! Look over there. In the corner. It's a woman, I think."

"Where? Where is she? Let me see, *let me see!*"

"I don't see any—"

I manage to lift myself up to the window, directly in front of their faces. "*Help . . .*"

The boy screams. His entire body repels itself from the window as if I had just blown him over with my breath. He slams into his friends, all three falling onto their backs.

"Run! RUN!" Each boy clambers onto his feet and races across the lawn. Their bikes are waiting in the cul-de-sac. I watch them grab their handlebars and launch themselves onto their seats in an adrenaline-fueled frenzy. They keep shouting as they pedal off, voices fading:

Did you see that! Holy shit, what was that? Did you see her? What was that!

Then they're gone. And I'm still stranded.

My back slides down the drywall until I'm on the floor, chest heaving. I didn't realize I was laughing. This is laughter, isn't it? I can't stop cackling. It's funny, right? They thought I was a ghost! A ghost! My lungs are dry, throat raw. My laughter has a rasp to it. A death rattle.

I'm never leaving this house, I think as I keep laughing. *I'm going to die here, aren't I?*

Those kids will never come back. I wipe the tears with the back of my hand, looking up—

My laughter catches in my lungs.

Someone else is in the room. A woman stands still in the far corner, where the shadows gather. How long has she been standing there?

"Have you seen my son?" *Marcia.* I almost don't recognize her—her prim composure has eroded. Her yellow spandex outfit bunches loosely around her skeletal frame. Her eyes sink into the depths of her skull, her tan faded to a parchment gray. "I can't seem to . . . to find Sean. He's hiding from me."

How long have we been here?

Marcia turns and heads down the hall. I follow her into the kitchen. She opens the unlocked cabinet under the sink and peers in. Empty. When she notices me, she absentmindedly asks once more, "Have you seen my son?"

"Maybe he's in here." I point to the padlocked cabinet. I jostle the knob but it won't budge. It's not even wood, just cheap particleboard. "Wanna see?"

Marcia nods eagerly. We run our fingers along the cabinet door until we each find enough leverage to pull. There's a newfound determination in Marcia, an electricity sparking in her eyes. We keep pulling and pulling.

"Put your back into it." I feel guilty for getting her hopes up like this, but a few hard tugs and—*shnk*—the screws yank free from the hinges. The padlock remains secured around the handle while the door itself dangles freely, no longer mounted to the cabinet.

"Nope . . . No boys hiding in here."

But Silas's notebook is. His sickening grimoire. The binding has puckered since the last time I saw it. I push the thought of mushroom skin out of my mind as I head upstairs to my—

nursery

—bedroom. I've made a nest for myself, plucking the pink insulation from the closet wall and padding the floor with it. The bedding is soft. I curl up in my nest and flip through the book.

What am I looking for? There's none of his poetry. No short stories. No diary entries that offer access to his mind. It's Silas's handwriting, but I can barely read his scribbled litanies and recipes. Spells. Several of the symbols he sketched are now painted across the walls of the house. This is not the notebook of a healthy person. These are the rantings of a lunatic. An addict.

The crack in the closet wall is wide enough for me to reach in and deposit the notebook. I feel it's wiser to hide it from Tobias. Nobody will know I've tucked it behind the—

I hear a faint scrape against the plaster.

Something is in the walls.

It must be a mouse. But this sounds larger. A squirrel? It sounds like something heavier dragging itself against the Sheetrock. Is it stuck?

If I lift my arm through the crack in the wall and pluck out a few more tufts of insulation, I could probably see it. I tear a fluffy swath out, exposing a wooden beam.

The scraping is louder now. The insulation pulses. Something is pushing against it. It's right there, whatever it is, just on the other side. I stretch my arm all the way inside the wall, blindly searching for that last tuft of insulation.

I feel it brush against my fingertips. *Got it.* My fingers pinch the insulation and with one swift tug, I pull it out. Just as I do, something slips and falls onto my hand. I scream as I feel it—whatever it is—scramble against my knuckles and struggle to climb back up into the crawlspace to hide. It's soft—fleshy—doughy, almost. No fur. It almost feels like a . . . doll's foot?

I yank my arm back, but I can't let it get away. Gripping the edge of the drywall, I pull back until the plaster crumbles in my hand, widening the hole. I force my head through and peer up as quickly as I can. *Don't let it get away, don't let it go.* Bits of plaster shower down onto my face. I wince as dust scrapes my corneas, but for a split second, within the shadowy crawlspace just a few feet away from where I'm lying, I swear I see the pale leg of a baby—*a baby*—just above my head. Just as it slips deeper into the darkness of the wall, it turns.

A child with no eyes. No nose. Its lipless mouth opens, not as a mouth with a jaw might—there are no bones, no mandibles—but as a muscled sphincter loosens, exposing a hollow grotto at the center of its featureless face. The baby barks at me, flecks of creamy spittle showering down, then turns and crawls back into the blackness of the house's inner cavities.

peekaboo

Tobias took my lighter away after I set Silas's notebook on fire. I figured if I'm seeing faceless babies crawling through the walls, it's probably high fucking time that I cut this shit out of my life. I made a bonfire in the middle of the—

nursery

—using tufts of insulation. The pink cotton went up too fast—I worried it might flare out before it could burn the book, but the flames embraced its mushroom leather hide. The spongy flesh bubbled and cracked across the cover, blistering and peeling away. The smoke smelled of scorched cork.

I swear I'll never eat another portabella for as long as I live. However long that is.

Tobias burst through the door with Adriano and they started stomping on the flames straightaway. "What the fuck," Tobias shouted as soon as he realized what was on fire.

There wasn't much of Silas's notebook left. The spine survived, still holding a few shriveled strips of its fungal binding. The burnt edges curled over backward, its pages chewed through with flame.

"What were you thinking?" Tobias stamped down the fire's dying embers, sending a last gasp of ash into the air. "You could've burned the whole house down!"

"Try cooking up your drug now."

"Do you honestly think I still need the book? *I am the book.*"
Tobias snatched Silas's REHAB IS FOR QUITTERS lighter out of my
hand. "I'll take away your toys if you can't act—"

I spat in his face.

Tobias kept his eyes closed long enough to wipe his cheek. "Fine.
No more Ghost."

Anxiety flooded my chest. "I—I'm sorry. I didn't mean it."

Tobias turned to leave, Adriano following right behind him. He
wasn't listening to me anymore. "Just, please, I need to see—" The
door slammed shut before I could say *Silas.*

Typical Erin. Sent to my room without any dinner.

I could still feel the tremor in my hand, that familiar itch reaching
through my bones. I fucked up. No Ghost means no more Silas . . .
What's a haunted house without its ghosts? It's just an empty shell. I
suddenly feel hollow. Dispirited.

Skrch-skrch. The scraping came from behind the walls.

I wasn't alone.

The baby peered blindly from the cracked drywall, its features
sanded down like a cemetery cherub with its granite face all but
erased. Was this Sean? Marcia's son? Had she begun to imagine him,
only to slip into a nightmare halfway through? What *was* this thing?

"You can come out now. I'm not going to hurt you."

It took some coaxing, but the faceless baby slowly slipped out
from the wall. Before I could stop it, it scurried into my lap. The soft
thing nestled into the space between my legs like a hairless cat and I
had to fight against my instincts of self-preservation—of sanity—not
to fling it against the wall and run for my life.

It purred. Its pudgy, spongey limbs branched out from its plump
torso like tuberous roots and hugged my left thigh. It rubbed its
cheek against my hip. The thing somehow smiled. I couldn't explain
the feeling that swept over me. Maybe it approximated parental love,
but I don't know what that is. All I knew was I wasn't afraid. Not anymore. Who could be afraid of this little bundle? It rolled on its back,

exposing its navel-less belly. Was I supposed to scratch its tummy?

"Coochie coo." I tickled its belly. "Coochie-coochie-coooo."

It giggled with delight. Something about its voice convinced me it was a spirited boy.

A *he*. "What'll we call you, huh?"

———

I know he's not ours—what had been mine. That was just a cluster of cells.

This is a housewarming gift. The nucleus of our new family. The child that will help me and Silas lay down roots. I never wanted this life, never imagined having a family, especially with Silas. We were never going to have a house, 2.5 kids, a dog, a nine-to-five job. That life was never in the cards for us. But Ghost is giving me hope, showing me that there is another life beyond this one, a better rendition of this existence waiting for me on the other side of the veil.

Look at what we have here—look at what this house has given me.

Silas with open arms.

Our son.

We name him Lonnie. Well—I name him Lonnie. He just *feels* like a Lonnie. He follows me around the house wherever I go, scurrying behind the drywall. I haven't told anyone else about him. Not Tobias, and certainly not Marcia. I don't want to hurt her feelings, thinking I'm trying to steal her own baby from her. No, Lonnie is our little secret. Just between me and Silas.

What's your ghost story? I hear Tobias's voice slip out from the living room.

Our ghost story is spreading on its own now. There's always a knock at the door—*Wanna get haunted?*—while Tobias performs his *halluséances* around the clock. People bring their own ghosts—BYOG—letting them loose in our home, haunting every last inch of it. It's getting difficult to tell whose ghosts are whose in this house anymore.

We carry the ghosts that haunt us wherever we go, I hear Tobias say from the living room at the beginning of every session, his voice reaching through the halls. *I can reconnect you.*

I hear him even when I'm not there. The sound of his voice fills every room. *You just need to open the door in your mind . . . open yourself up to getting haunted . . .* There are times when I can't tell if Tobias is really talking, or if I'm simply hearing things. *Just let your ghosts in . . . with this. One dose. Ghost acts as an incantation. Possession in a pill. A séance inside your mind.*

Whenever the urge to run away rises, right on cue, almost as if the house can read my mind, Lonnie comes crawling through the ceiling, spying on me from the other side of the Sheetrock. I sense him peering down, eyeless yet leering all the same. I pretend not to notice, playing along. The two of us have made a game out of it, even.

"Has anyone seen a baby boy around here?" I ask the empty room, turning this way and that, well aware that he's crammed in the crawlspace above me. I can hear his slippery giggling.

"*Hmm.* I wonder where he could be . . ."

Lonnie watches with his gilled rictus opening and closing. I tiptoe to the closet.

"Could he be . . ." I lean into the emptiness. ". . . *in here?*"

Nothing but shadows. This game of ours helps pass the time. I see less of Silas now that I have Lonnie to look after. Or maybe he's looking after me.

"Where in the world is that boy?" I announce in mock exasperation. "I just don't know!"

Lonnie mewls with excitement.

"Maybe he's in another room. Let's go see!"

I tiptoe toward the door, slowly lifting my feet high into the air so that it's obvious that I'm sneaking around. Sure enough, I hear the soft padding of Lonnie's hands and feet scrape against the other side of the drywall.

"Is he . . . *in here?*"

I make the mistake of opening the bathroom door, assaulted by the smell. A swarm of flies scatters. I feel the buzz of their wings in my teeth. On the wall, written in shit, it says:

BOO

I hear a slight gurgling rise up from the clogged toilet bowl. The softest murmur mewls from within the cistern. It's not the plumbing. Lonnie giggles up from the hollow pipes, only for this persistent thought to resurface: *I need to get out of here.* Don't I? Shouldn't I be looking for a way to escape? It should be as easy as walking through the front door. But the house doesn't want to let me go. It's keeping me here. It eavesdrops on my thoughts. Someone—Silas?—is listening to what I'm thinking. How else can I explain what's happening to me?

"I'm gonna find you . . ."

Lonnie scurries for the hall, shimmying his soft bulk through the wall.

"I'm gonna find you . . ."

There's a crack in the ceiling above the doorway to the living room, the plaster fracturing just enough to peer inside. I wait for him to catch up to me before—

"Peekaboo!" I spin around and catch him in the fissure. "I see you!"

Lonnie lets out a wet, phlegmy shriek. I reach out to grab him, but he's too quick for me. He forces out a determined grunt before scurrying back into the walls, vanishing from sight.

I have no choice, there's no other option here, we have to keep playing and playing, endlessly running, as if we'll chase each other for an eternity through these rooms.

"Peekaboo!" I catch Lonnie in the kitchen—or maybe he catches me.

"Peekaboo!" I catch Lonnie in the closet. We're running out of rooms.

The front door. I can go through the front door, can't I? *Just pretend like you're playing, Erin. Don't let them know what you're thinking. Don't let on that you're going to—*

Open the door.

"Peeka—"

Sunlight stings my eyes. Lonnie isn't there. In his place, I find a woman standing on the porch. She's familiar. I know this woman. She looks just as startled as I am.

". . . Erin?" She knows my name. Her mouth hangs open, unable to say more.

Callie.

Oh god, it's Silas's sister. It's hard to say who's more alarmed in this moment.

"Erin . . . What's going on?"

A cold rush of shame surges through me. I don't want her to see me like this. She shouldn't be here. She shouldn't know about this place.

"What are you doing here?" I ask.

"You invited me. You said . . ." There's a stone in her throat. "You said Silas was here."

". . . When?" I have no memory of reaching out. I haven't even seen my cell phone in—I don't know how long. Tobias took all our toys away. I have no memory of calling her.

The warmth of the sun makes my skin itch. Already I can feel the persistent tug in my chest, as if an invisible thread connecting me to the house is pulling me back inside.

". . . Is he?"

"What?"

"In there." Her voice sounds so small. I can hear the slightest splinter of hope. Even though she must know it's not true, that it's not possible—she was there at his funeral, for Christ's sake—she can't stop herself from wanting it, *needing it*, to be real. That Silas is here.

I could offer her that solace, that connection to her brother. I can say those simple words—*Do you want to get haunted?*—and then all she has to do is walk inside and become a part of our home. Our family. She'd be reunited with Silas forever and—

No. I can't. Not to Callie. Not to anyone.

"You can't be here."

"But you . . ."

"Get out. *Now.*"

Callie shrinks back at my words. She's confused, but I have to push her away, push her out of here as hard as I can before she walks in and can't escape.

"Erin, what's going on—"

"GO." I step out of the house, breaking the protective shell of our home for the first time in an eternity and push Callie off the porch. She stumbles down the steps and I follow.

"You told me to come—"

"Don't come back. *Don't ever come back.*"

I push her again. I can only imagine what I must look like to her. I've seen the same look on all the other houseguests here: wild eyes, hollow sockets, taut, waxy skin. Greasy hair clinging to my sweaty neck. I'm a shambling corpse, hissing at her. "GET OUT *GETOUT-GETOUT!*"

I don't care if Tobias hears me. I don't care if I'm sent to my room and my haunting privileges are taken away. Not Callie. She runs all the way back to her car. I stand on the lawn, chest heaving as I watch her pull away. It's the smallest of victories—I saved her, didn't I?

I'm not alone in the street. A dozen lost souls cram shoulder to shoulder in the cul-de-sac. One revenant turns toward me, then another, as if my mere presence outside the house is enough to draw their attention.

I've broken the seal. I've exposed myself. Their eyes are like oysters in half shells, nearly oozing out of their sockets. Their mouths open and shut, open and shut, lips syncopated with one another, a dozen greedy newborns reaching for the teat. They lick their lips with sandpaper tongues. One takes a hesitant step toward me, reaching out. Others follow.

I step back through the doorway. The symbol is still there, rusted flakes of dried blood—*of course it's blood, but whose*—crumbling off. I check my hand to see if I can still see the slice running through my skin. *Is that my blood? Is it me painting the house red?* Once I close the door, hiding behind the crimson emblem, the revenants stop, set adrift once more. Whatever magnetic pull drew them toward me is severed, cutting these lost souls loose in the cul-de-sac.

I hear the sound of feet scrambling through the walls. Something scurries over my head. Lonnie is waiting. He grunts impatiently.

I'm trapped. I can't escape this house—and even if I could, I'm so addicted to my ghosts, I don't know if I could stay away forever. Isn't that what haunting a house is, after all? You can never leave. I need to accept that this is where I live now. Where I haunt. Home sweet home.

"*Hmmm,*" I announce to our home. "Where oh where could my little Lonnie be?"

My little ghostlet. My baby boy . . .

rent-a-cop

"You're on kitchen duty," Adriano informs me. He's clearly not a fan of mine since I see right through his gutter punk posturing. He's just another trust fund kid who hit the streets after his mom and dad cut off his allowance. He can go back home whenever he wants to.

"I thought I was grounded."

"As long as you stop trying to set the house on fire . . . and scaring away our houseguests."

"Why doesn't Tobias tell me himself?"

"He's busy."

I'm dosing two or three times a day to maintain my haunting. There's taking Ghost and there's everything else. The next fix is never enough. Ghost isn't a way of life anymore.

It's a way of death.

But Tobias doesn't want us haunted while we work. I'll get my next dose after kitchen detail: *Chores first, then you get your allowance.* Time to slip on my latex gloves and disposable face mask decorated with the same symbol that's painted on the front door.

I'm working with Melissa and Stephanie. We form a three-woman assembly line: Melissa scoops the off-white powder and I disperse the dust into the capsule distributor, then Stephanie places the pills in Tupperware containers. We use plastic shovels from a kid's beach kit, as if we're building sandcastles out of pulverized mushrooms.

"Ever fucked on Ghost before?" Melissa asks like we're besties. But I don't want friends. Not anymore. I want to get haunted, not hang with the living.

"It's a hundred times better when you're haunted," she singsongs. "It's almost like a . . . like a religious experience, you know? An orgy with the angels. When it's me and Tobias—"

Gross. Not an image I want occupying my headspace right now.

"—and our ghosts, it just feels like . . . like there are all these hands on me, touching me all over." Melissa is on Ghost right now, I can tell. Big no–no. She has that empty-eyed gaze, like a ventriloquist's doll. She pulls her mask down and wipes her nose and I can see her apple cheeks have all but shriveled, revealing sharp cheekbones that threaten to pierce her skin.

We're prepping for our housewarming party. That's what Tobias calls it. Our ghost story isn't spreading fast enough for his taste. We need to invite people into our house. Friends. Family. Anyone we can share this experience with. Let them get haunted just like us. It's not enough to take the drug ourselves. We need to share. Let it spread. Until everyone is haunted.

I hear bare feet shuffle into the kitchen and turn to find Marcia wandering aimlessly around. She opens the cabinet beneath the sink, peering in. Empty. "Have you seen my son?"

"Sorry." I still haven't had the heart to tell her about Lonnie. I know she'd be jealous, so I don't mention he's hiding in the recesses of the wall just above her head, observing us.

"Have you seen my son?"

"Nope." Stephanie glances at Melissa, the two of them silently snickering. Poor Marcia. Her bare feet shuffle through the hall, fading further into the house.

Melissa starts nattering away again, but I lose myself in the motes of dust swirling around the kitchen. A helix pattern of particles rotates in the air, captured by a stray beam of sunlight reaching through the boarded-up window. It has a copper tincture, darker than dust.

Not dust, I realize—*spores*. Mushroom spores set adrift through-out the house. The kitchen is thick with it, a miasma of mushrooms floating through the air. Even with the face mask on, I can taste it at the back of my throat. *How long have we been breathing this junk?*

"Tobias said he's going to give me my own house," Melissa says.

"What did you just say?"

Melissa gives me this half grin that exposes her gray gumline—*tee-hee*—pleased to be Tobias's favorite now. "He says I can take my pick. Whichever house on the block I want."

"Don't worry, Erin," Stephanie says. "I'm sure he'll give you a house, too, if you *ask nicely*."

Both start giggling. Fucking witches. "I don't want another house. This is my—"

"*What the hell?*"

An unfamiliar voice breaks through the kitchen, startling all three of us. Melissa turns. I see her panicked expression, those dead Betty Boop eyes bulging at whatever's behind me.

I turn to see a man sweating in an ill-fitting uniform in the door-way. A yellow emblem is sewn on his chest—just a flimsy patch made to look authoritative enough to strike terror into the hearts of tres-passing teens. But there's nothing official about him.

"What's going on here?"

A rent-a-cop. Just some middle-aged heel hired by a security company to intermittently patrol the housing development, mak-ing sure no one vandalizes these empty homes. His paunch presses against his black uniform. He's sweating, wet shadows seeping from his armpits. I glance at his belt to see if there's a gun holster. Noth-ing—just a key chain dangling from his hip.

"You—you can't be in here." There's nothing in his tone for us to be afraid of. He looks genuinely perplexed. Of all the things to walk in on, this clearly isn't what he expected to find.

Melissa bolts for the kitchen door like a spastic spider, thin limbs waving through the air. The rent-a-cop performs a sloppy side step, too late to obstruct her. Her body collides with the doorjamb before slipping off into the hall. "Hey! Come back—"

Stephanie doesn't wait around, either. She pushes against the man, thrusting him back and rushing out of the kitchen to hide somewhere else in the house.

"STOP!"

I haven't moved. It never occurred to me to run and now I'm trapped.

"Okay," he says. "Okay, just—"

I step to my right.

The guard's arms shoot up to shoulder height, a sweating vulture ready to take flight. "Don't! Just—just stay right where you are, okay?" He pulls out his cell phone. He doesn't even have a walkie-talkie. It takes a few swipes with his slippery fingers to unlock it, his attention shifting. He's no longer looking at me. This is my chance to run.

Before I can even take a step, I notice movement behind him. Shadows gather just behind his shoulders, solidifying, becoming something, *someone*. My first thought is *Silas is here!*

But it's not him. Tobias's eyes sparkle in the darkness.

"Don't!" I shout. Not at the rent-a-cop. To Tobias.

Too late—the guard's shoulders jerk up to his ears. His chin juts out, and the rest of his head tilts backward. His eyes go wide. He bites his own tongue and a sliver of spit shoots across the kitchen. The motion of his jaw snapping at his tongue creates a sickening "*Hyulp.*"

The cell phone slips from the guard's hand. It hits his shoe before clattering across the floor. His knees soften as his body collapses to the floor, revealing a slender block of wood adhered to his skull. I spot the nail head sticking out of his cranium.

Tobias stares at the guard, his sunken chest heaving so fast it looks like his rib cage is about to sprout branches. He leans over and grabs the two-by-four as the man's body convulses. He tugs, but the block of wood won't pull free, the nail so deeply embedded in the man's skull. He has to plant a foot on the guard's shoulder for leverage, really putting his weight into it, and yank back *hard*. As he works, I notice fresh lacerations carved into Tobias's arms. Blood seeps through his shirt. The flesh above his chest is branded with the same symbol I've seen in the house.

The nail finally loosens. It only takes another couple of pumps— *left, right, splck*—before he drops the two-by-four on the floor, sending an arc of blood through the air.

The rent-a-cop stops convulsing and his body goes limp, one arm under his chest, the other flung over his back.

"Help me," I hear Tobias say from somewhere far off, but I can't move. My attention is on the fresh blood weeping from the sigils etched into his flesh.

"Silas," I hear myself moan. "Silas, please . . . make this stop . . ."

"*Erin.*"

"Silas . . . Where are you?"

"Shut up and open the basement door!"

Tobias clambers over the body and flosses his arms through the rent-a-cop's, cradling him.

"The door." Tobias grunts as he reaches out for me. In his hand is a key. The basement—he wants me to unlock the basement door. All I have to do is move, one foot in front of the other, make my way across the kitchen, and slip the key—

"*Hurry.*"

The padlock unlatches with a single tug. Cool air brushes against my cheeks as soon as I open the door, but it's the smell that stops me in my tracks. The rotten milk aroma has only grown stronger since the last time I stood here, staring down into the abyss. The basement now has a fetid cheese stench. Something is fermenting below. I gag at the smell of it. I think I'm going to be sick—

"Stand back." Tobias does his best to drag the rent-a-cop over, leaving long streaks of blood on the linoleum.

I move away from the door. I have to press my palm against my mouth to keep from retching as Tobias drags the guard closer. He clumsily maneuvers around the man's bulk, stepping into the basement to align the limp body with the doorway.

It's stuck—the guard's limb catches on something. One of his sleeves must've snagged.

"His arm," Tobias says. "Free his arm."

I lean over and rip the fabric of his sleeve free but when I pull back, I can see his eyes are open.

I scream, falling backward and landing on the floor. I try to stand up but I slip on his warm blood. As I scramble away from the cop, my hand hits hard plastic.

The cell phone.

Tobias grabs the guard's shoulders, yanks him back in a single fluid motion, and sends him toppling down the basement steps. I hear a sickening crack as his body hits the basement floor.

Tobias is hyperventilating. "Fuck. *Fuck.* What the hell happened?"

"He—" I start. "He just came in—"

Tobias catches his breath, leaning against the doorway. He peers down into the darkness. "Stay there. I'll deal with this. Don't come down!"

His footsteps echo down the stairs.

". . . Tobias?"

No answer.

"Toby?"

Now's my chance—I grab the rent-a-cop's phone. Still unlocked, thank god. My fingers are soaked in blood and I'm fingerpainting the screen red as I try dialing a number, any number.

Amara. I can dial her number from memory.

I force myself to steady my breathing as it rings. I can't stop my wrists from shaking. She's not going to pick up. She won't recognize the number.

Please pick up pick up pick up—

If it goes to voicemail, I'm dead.

Pick up pick up pick—

"Hello?" Amara's voice reaches out from the other end of the line and I can't keep myself from crying, the sudden lifeline of her words sending me into sobs of relief.

"Amara?! Amara, it's me, it's Erin, please, please help—"

"Erin? Slow down. Where are you?"

"Amara, *please*, I need you—"

I suddenly hear metal rattling, like the chains on a cartoon ghost.

Keys, not chains—it's the security guard's keys, rattling in the basement. Tobias storms up the steps, taking them two at a time. He grabs the phone from my hand and throws it against the floor. He brings his foot down once, twice, shattering the screen beneath his heel.

"*What're you doing?!*" Tobias seizes my shoulders and shakes me so hard, I feel like my neck might snap. "Who are you talking to?"

"Nobody . . . I didn't . . ."

Tobias's eyes bore into me. "Do you ever want to see Silas again? *Do you?*"

"*Yes!*"

"Take these." Tobias drops the ring of keys into my hand. They're so wet. So red.

"Erin? *Erin.* Are you listening?"

I nod, slowly, unable to say a word, as I stare at my hands. My hands covered in blood.

"Get into his car and drive it away."

"Where?"

"*Anywhere*. Just away from here. Do you understand?"

He wants me to step outside the house. Into the open. With *them*. "I—I can't."

"*Erin*. You *need* to do this. The police will come looking for him and we can't have that. We control the guest list in this house. They can't know he was here. Do you understand?"

I'm barely holding on to the words. They sound so far away.

"Erin. *Erin*. If you want to see Silas, you'll do this. But if you run away or try contacting someone else, you'll never—*ever*—see him again. Do you understand? *Do you understand?*"

I must nod, because Tobias grabs the basement door and slams it shut so hard a current of air rushes against my cheeks.

I'm alone in the kitchen. My hands tremble so much, the keys start jingling again, chains rattling all around. I hear the scraping of tiny fingers from the other side of the drywall. There's a breach in the plaster and I spot a flash of pale skin. A face with no eyes: just a mouth, wailing. Sweet little Lonnie is disappointed in me. Now I know how my mother must've felt all these years.

The first revenant I spot in the yard is carrying a baby. The two are adrift on our lawn, vacantly staring, as if they're waiting for the rapture to whisk them away. The baby never cries. Not once.

The number of lost souls clustering in the cul-de-sac has only grown. I can't bring myself to count them all. There are bound to be thirty, maybe more. Tobias thinks he can pluck whichever spirit he wants from the other side of the veil—depending on who's buying—while forcing the rest of these revenants to stay outside, as if the bloody velvet rope painted across the door is enough to keep these ghosts from crashing our house party. Sorry, invited ghosts only. But they'll find a way. I know they will.

I glance at the sigil smeared over the front door. Someone freshened it up—it's wet now. Whose blood is it? How long will it hold?

Get in the car. That's it, that's all I have to do. Simple. Anyone could do it. It's just a matter of making my way across the lawn and trying not to draw their attention.

The rent-a-cop's Subaru Impreza is parked on the street in front of the house. The same emblem from his uniform is emblazoned on the passenger side door: TOMPKINS SECURITY.

Several revenants have gathered around the boxy car, blocking the driver's side. There's no way to reach the door without pushing through them.

This is my chance to escape—the keys are right here in my hand!

I'm almost free. Finally free of—

our home

—this house. All I have to do is make a break for it. I take a deep breath, gathering as much air as I can and holding it in my lungs. Stepping off the porch, I feel the sun hit my skin. I wince at the light and shiver, hot and cold all at once.

Nothing moves. The revenants remain frozen in place, as if they're chess pieces scattered haplessly around the board, waiting for me to make a move.

Take it slow, Erin, I think. *One step at a time. Just keep your eyes—*

A revenant to my left turns. A Black man. His head tilts at a severe angle, his ear to his shoulder, as if he's questioning me. My presence wakes him. He sniffs at the air. I watch him as I pick up my pace. I should keep my attention on the car, but I'm not looking where I'm going. I can't help but stare at the lost soul as the look of desperation on his face grows—

I collide into the mother and child. The impact sends her arms fanning out, and for a moment it looks as if this woman is offering me her own newborn.

The baby slips from her hands and falls to the ground. When it hits, the infant still won't cry. It merely gazes up at me, mouth opening and closing, opening and closing, opening—

A scream escapes my throat.

All at once, the surrounding revenants turn. Their gray eyes ignite with a dull glimmer. Their mouths gum at the air like newborns hungry for a suckle. All they want is a taste of what haunts me, haunts all of us. They're hungry for life. They want to see it, experience it once more.

I'm running now, racing for the car. They're following, reaching for me. The desperate need on their faces is too much. I can't look. There's too many—they're all around me.

I push away the lost soul standing in front of the driver's side door, my hand connecting with what feels like a slab of beef.

My wrists shake so much, I can't find the right key.

They're gathering around me—surrounding the car. So many. Too many. I hear them closing in, but I will myself not to look. *Don't look don't look don't look*—

I try one key. The tip of it scrapes the door before I can force it into the lock. It doesn't fit, so I scramble for the next. *Too many keys,* I shout in my head, *too many keys, too many*—

The hairs on the back of my neck stand up, like so many radio towers receiving an electric signal. Someone's standing right behind me.

The next key doesn't fit, either. I feel the sandpaper rasp of a cold tongue scrape at the back of my neck. *Don't look don't look don't look don't look don't*—

The third key slides into the door's lock. I twist my wrist. The lock pops and I fling the door wide, leaping in and slamming it shut. *Don't look don't look don't look*—

I lean forward, my chest pressing against the steering wheel and accidentally honking the horn—*fuck fuck fuck*—as I plunge the key into the ignition.

Fists hammer against the driver's side window, pounding right at my ear. Someone tumbles onto the hood. Feet scramble up the windshield, scuffing the glass. I don't look, forcing myself to focus on my trembling hand. I can barely steady my grip long enough to perform the simple task of starting the car.

Start the car, start the car, START THE FUCKING CAR—

They're everywhere. Banging their fists against the hood, slapping their hands on the windows. Eyes wider than I've ever seen before, filled with the same hungry look, begging to be let in. They slip their fingers inside the cracked window and try to pry open the door. They're licking at the window, running their gray tongues against the glass. They want a taste of me.

I can't see out the windshield anymore. The sun has been eclipsed by spirits, each and every one banging on the hood, the roof, the windows.

Among the mass of bodies, I see the woman's baby, its face smushed against the glass. I scream as I force all my strength into my wrist and twist the key, turning the engine over once, twice, grinding until it finally shrieks into existence.

My foot presses on the accelerator, the car still in park, the engine heaving under the strain, roaring all around. I slip the car into drive and speed out, parting through the sea of revenants. Their pale bodies grow smaller in the rearview mirror until there's nothing left of them to see, their gauzy silhouettes swallowed by the horizon.

I'm free. Free of that house. Finally fucking free of Tobias.

Silas is still there, I think. Still at home. *Our home.* I want to blame him for abandoning me in that house—but it wasn't his fault, was it? It was the drug. It was Ghost. He lost himself to his addiction. I understand that now because the same thing nearly happened to me.

But I'm free now, aren't I? I got out of there. I escaped our haunted house.

I'm free, I keep repeating to myself. *Fucking free!*

I laugh so hard that tears stream down my face.

overdose

I put a few miles between me and home when I sense a pressure against my chest that only grows heavier the farther I drive. No matter how fast I go, *pedal to the fucking metal*, my flesh begins to feel like it's getting yanked in the opposite direction, as if the gravitational pull of the house will skin me alive. Home's calling me back.

There's no escaping your own haunted house. It reels you in whenever you try to run.

There's a Shell station on the side of the road and I pull in, parking haphazardly next to the pumps and abandoning the car. *Pay phone*, I think. I need a pay phone. I borrow a quarter from the man behind the counter. He doesn't want any trouble so he simply gives it to me. I think I thank him but I'm not sure he hears me.

It takes a moment to remember my parents' number, struggling to keep my hands from trembling. I dial the wrong number and have to start all over. Gripping the phone in both hands, I try to hold myself together as it rings. And rings.

Mom finally answers. "Hello?"

"Mom! Mommy, can you hear me?"

"*Erin?*" I hear the slightest gasp escape my mother's mouth from the other end of the line. "Is that you? Good god, honey, where *are* you? Whose phone is this?"

"Mom, please, I—I need you to listen."

She doesn't. "You haven't answered *any* of my calls. We were worried half to death about you—"

Only half? "Mom. Just—*stop*. I need you—I need you to help me—"

"What? What's wrong? Do you need money?"

Of course she'd think this is about money. "I don't want your fucking money!"

A chill slips through the receiver. She's finally silent.

". . . Mom? Mom, are you still there? Mom?"

She's already retreating into her protective shell, muttering under her breath as she passes the phone. ". . . *sounds like she's on something.*"

"Erin?" Dad's taken the phone. His voice has a soft edge to it. "Is everything all right?"

"*Daddy!* Daddy, it's me! I—I need help. Please. I don't know where I am. Somewhere in Hopewell, I think. I need you to find me, Daddy. I need you to—"

"Are you high right now?"

Not high, Daddy.

Haunted.

"Erin, listen to me very clearly." The sharpness in my father's voice cuts right through the receiver. "I don't know what you've gotten yourself into—"

"You don't understand, I—"

"—but your mother and I will not tolerate this type of behavior."

"But . . . but Daddy . . ." I can't keep the tremble out of my voice. I feel so small. He's treating me more like one of his clients than his own flesh and blood. His own daughter.

"Whatever you've gotten yourself mixed up in, it ends now."

Oh god, he's cutting me off . . .

"Are we clear? We'll have none of this."

He's cutting me out . . .

"When you're ready to come home . . ."

Cut, cut, cut . . .

"We'll get you the proper care you nee—"

I hammer the receiver against the pay phone. I know I'm crying but I can't feel it. My parents are perfectly content to throw money at me, if they think it'll fix the problem. Or at least make the problem go away. But they refuse to get their hands dirty, even if it's their own daughter asking for help.

Where am I supposed to go now?

What should've taken thirty minutes takes two hours as I get lost on back roads, the sun quickly sinking below the horizon. It's dusk when I find my way back to my apartment building. I can't enter without getting buzzed in. Once I slip through and slowly navigate the stairwell, finally reaching my door, I find someone inside my apartment. Someone else has moved in.

"What are you doing here?" I hear myself ask but whatever answer the woman gives doesn't reach my ears. She's looking at me like I'm sick. Like she doesn't want to touch me.

I want to apologize for writing my name on the bedroom wall. I offer to paint over it, since Erin is no longer here, but she won't let me in. Her lips move but I can't make out the words. Something about *calling the police. I'm dialing 911.*

I've got nowhere to go. Nowhere else but home again.

Home again—

—jiggety jig.

Nobody seems to notice I was gone.

Or care.

I head upstairs to my nest in the nursery. I need to be alone for what comes next.

I reach into the crack in the closet and pull out the Ziploc bag where I've been stashing pills. I've been double-dipping into the reserve whenever I'm on kitchen duty, stockpiling my spirits for a special occasion.

I've never ingested more than a couple caps at once.

This time I take five.

I know he's testing me. His absence lately is just his way of trying to prove my love.

But we can be together forever now.

I just have to cross over.

"Silas? I'm here . . . I'm on my way." Maybe he can't hear me. His words are still scrawled on the wall, but the letters have lost their sharpness. Black mold rotting.

I've built up too high a tolerance. I have to push through—tear the veil away and dive into the afterlife. So I swallow another pill. And another. I lose count of how many caps I've taken.

"Silas, I'm coming . . ." I need to let go of this body. Peel my spirit away from this skin.

I haven't eaten anything for I don't know how long. All I ingest are ghosts now.

"I'm ready, Silas. Please. Take me. Take me away."

My stomach pinches. The cramps reach in deep.

"Silas—"

I retch. Nothing but liquid spills out. Something keeps pushing, working its way up. My tongue swells, pressing against my jaw until I gag. A slender stalk of pulsating pink pushes past my lips. Tears well in my eyes but all I can do is watch the cap expand in a fleshy umbrella, gills rippling in a halo just over my head.

The spirit turns to me—*sees* me. It has eyes, a slit that mimics a mouth.

Hey there, Li'l Deb, it whispers.

I try to bite down on the stem, but my teeth keep slipping.

The spirit unspools. Its tapering tail of ectoplasm slips from my lips with a wet flick, releasing me. My body drops, hits the floor. *Slap.* I can breathe again but every inhale burns. My throat is raw, like a cord of rope has been flossed through my insides and out my mouth.

Spots of mold dance before my eyes. I'm about to black out. *Please don't pass out.* I can feel the darkness coming from all around. *Please don't pass out don't pass out please—*

"Erin?"

Someone is shaking me. My head rolls over the floor. There's a pair of hands gripping my shoulders, lifting me up and dragging me back from the shadows.

"Erin—wake up!"

It takes a moment for my eyes to peel open, as if they're crusted shut. I focus on the face hovering above me as it comes into view.

"Erin—can you hear me?"

Amara to the rescue. There's the vaguest halo around her head and I want to believe she's real, *need* to believe she's actually here, but I can't trust the touch of anything anymore.

"Is it you?" Please let her be real. Please let it really be her.

"It's me, I'm here."

"I thought I saw a . . ."

ghost

It's really her. *Amara.* I can't stop crying. I never thought I'd see her again. I have to touch her, feel her face. I wrap my arms around her, pressing against her so hard. It's her.

"You stopped answering your phone . . . Nobody's seen you for over a month."

"This is my home." The words hurt my throat.

"I'm taking you to the hospital." Amara's voice strains as she lifts me to my feet. My legs buckle, but Amara props me up, draping my arm over her shoulder so I won't fall.

My feet feel weighed down with concrete. My muscles ache so much. "I can't . . . leave . . ."

"Yes, you can." Amara does most of the walking for both of us. I'm nothing but dead weight. How many times have we propped each other up after a night out? Just like old times.

"You got this," she says. "Come on, Erin. Baby steps. One foot in front of the other."

From the corner of my eye, I spot the black mold following us along the walls. Silas is reaching for me—calling me.

"Silas is here."

"No, he's *not*. He's not even in his fucking grave anymore—" Amara cuts herself off.

". . . What?" The words don't compute for me.

"Someone . . . someone dug him up."

What does she mean? His coffin?

"Whatever's going on here, it's . . . not good, Erin. You need to get out of this place *now*."

My attention drifts. Amara keeps talking, pleading with me, but her words fade. I'm no longer focusing on her, but behind her—in the far corner. Where the dark gathers.

A shadow takes shape. The spirit I just expelled is collecting itself—I see it now.

"There he is."

Amara turns to look behind her. "I don't see any—"

"Silas?"

Amara looks again, losing her patience. Her eyes never land on the right spot. Is she being stubborn and just pretending not to see it? "Erin. *Stop*. We don't have time for this."

She doesn't see it. See him. "He's coming closer."

"Erin, goddamn it—"

"Silas is right behind you."

"Erin, no one's there—"

"He's reaching out."

"Nothing's—"

Amara chokes. Something has grabbed her by the back of her neck, like a kitten caught by the scruff. Her feet lift off the floor. I simply watch as her spine arcs backward, arms cutting through the air. She reaches behind her, but she can't grab hold of—

Silas

—whatever is holding her aloft. I can barely make out the hazy outline of his silhouette rippling in black mold. He's there one second, gone the next, raising Amara up.

"Erin . . . ?" She's about to say more, but before she can give the words voice, Amara's arm snaps back at the elbow. The hollow *pop* reverberates through the nursery.

I flinch at the sight of her forearm dangling loose.

Amara screams. I've never heard her—heard anyone—scream like that before. She's thrown across the room. Her shriek is cut short the moment her face makes impact with the far wall, sending a crack through the Sheetrock. A crooked fissure erupts across the plaster, smeared with her blood. Her body slides to the floor in a soft pile.

"Amara?" I push myself onto my knees. The room wobbles. I try to find my balance and stand on my own two feet, but I can't.

"Amara?" She isn't moving. Her eyes remain fixed on one spot, looking at nothing.

She isn't answering me. Isn't blinking.

"Amara, please . . ."

Silas draws closer. His body won't take shape, won't clarify itself. His silhouette is there but he remains persistently in shadow, in fluctuating mold, rippling black.

"Why—Why did you . . . Amara's *your friend*. She—she was—"

A cold thought enters my mind. It's faint at first, but once the notion takes root, it grows and grows, until there's no taking it back. "Who are you?"

The silhouette vacillates, stubbornly refusing to come into focus.

"You're not Silas . . . are you?"

The shadow shakes its head—*No*. I can't tell if it says it out loud or if I simply hear its gravelly voice in my mind, but the word rushes through my brain, blossoming with such force.

NO.

When was the last time I connected to Silas? What if . . . What if

I've been haunted by . . .

What if it pretended to be . . .

What if it never was . . .

My head reels. My eyes drift around the nursery and now I can see black mold swelling from every corner. The rot moves on its own. There are letters. Names forming on the wall and then sliding across the floor, toward me.

GENEVIEVE IS HERE JOHN IS HERE CORRINE IS HERE REBECCA IS HERE MATTHEW IS HERE ANA IS HERE CRAIG IS HERE NOAH IS HERE HANNA IS HERE WALLACE IS HERE DEB IS HERE MATTEAS IS HERE VANESSA IS HERE IVY IS HERE JOSHUA IS HERE MAC IS HERE DANIEL IS HERE LUNA IS HERE CHEYENNE IS HERE PIKO IS HERE SHAUN IS HERE CALEB IS HERE KENDRA IS HERE MARCUS IS HERE WINSTON IS HERE MARGARITE IS HERE . . .

The black mold expands over my hand. First my fingers, then my wrist. The words work their way up my arm, my chest. They wrap around my neck. I try to scream but nothing comes. There's no sound beyond the hiss of the words as they release their spores into the air. The black mold grows over my eyes and everything goes dark.

So this is what death feels like.

Waves of black. An endless ocean of shadows. The water reaches as far as the horizon, met by gray clouds. The sky is ash. The dull glow of what could be the sun barely penetrates the ozone.

There is no land in sight. Nothing but ink. The cold water boils over and forces up massive summits of waves that crest and crash into one another before collapsing.

I can barely stay afloat. The water is so cold, I can't feel my limbs. I try to swim, forcing my legs to kick, but they are so numb, I don't know if they're even there anymore. My head slips below the surface and the black water works its way down my throat.

I push with all my might until my head breaks through, gasping for air. I can't do this for much longer. Already my muscles ache, weak with fatigue.

Something silvery shimmies before my face. It drifts across the water's surface before plunging back into the sea. It's long and slender. An eel. No—not an eel. Larger.

I feel something brush against my leg. It startles me. More water slips past my lips. It doesn't taste salty like the ocean should, but of charcoal. The lining in my throat feels as if it's covered in wet ash, clumps forming along my esophagus.

There it is again. That flash of silver. Not a fish or an eel—an arm. A back, the nodules of a spine. Long black hair, like kelp. It's a woman. Was a woman. Her glistening gray body circles around me like a shark closing in on its prey. The next time she brushes against my hip, I kick, struggling to force her away while keeping my head above water.

Another body breaks through the surface. There are more of them. The woman lifts her head above the water and stares back. Her eyes are nothing but black. She lets out a hiss. Her gums have gone gray, barely holding her crooked teeth in place. She licks her lips, gliding that maggot of a tongue across her jagged teeth, then plunges her head back into the water. She swims toward me. This time I kick her straight on, lifting my knee and making impact with her skull. It's soft. Her cranium collapses under the force of my kick, sending a cloud of ink across the surface of the water. Rings of iridescent color pour from the woman's fractured skull, shimmering on the surface of the water like an oil spill.

Others thrash at the woman's body, pecking at her flesh. They're eating her, devouring her in a frenzy. They tear through her in seconds as their limbs kick up a froth of gray, summoning more. The water all around us is alive. There have to be hundreds—thousands.

One grabs my ankle and pulls me under. I kick free and find the surface again, but there's another hand grabbing at my leg, my waist, my arms. They're pulling me under the surface. Into the black. I barely take a breath before I'm dragged below. The darkness of the water makes it impossible to see anything beyond the vague gray shape of bodies churning in the water, thousands of silverfish swarming the sea. Whatever air is in my lungs burns as I'm pulled deeper down. I feel myself plummet into the endless depths, until there's no light from above.

Nothing in my lungs. No feeling anymore. There's nothing left of me at all.

"Hold up." Someone's voice pierces through the darkness. There's a grit to it, like crumbling plaster. "*Shit*, she's still *alive*. How the hell is she still alive?"

"You said she was dead." Their voice is faint at first, gaining depth. Luring me back.

"I couldn't find a pulse. She wasn't breathing a second ago, I swear."

"Won't be alive much longer." I feel their hands now. All their reaching hands, grabbing me. Pulling me in separate directions, wolves fighting over carrion. "What happened to her?"

"ODed. Look. She took, like, ten doses all at once. What the fuck was she thinking?"

"What about the other one?"

"Bring her down to the basement." That voice. I know that voice. Tobias—but not Tobias. The intonation is off somehow. "I can still use her."

"What about the car? It's still out front. Do you think the cops—"

"Would you shut up and let me think?" Tobias leans forward. I can feel his breath spread across my face. "I want her out of my house. *Now*. Grab her legs."

The disembodied voices surround me. I keep my eyes closed. I don't want to see. Their hands, so many hands, fingers wriggling over my body, like maggots. *The worms crawl in, the worms crawl out, the worms play pinochle on your snout . . .*

"On the count of three," Tobias says. "One . . . two. . . *three*."

My body lifts in the air.

"Where are we going?" That's Adriano's voice. I recognize it now.

"Over there. Careful."

I throw up. I can't stop myself, can't control the muscles in my stomach as they pump out all the charcoaled water I swallowed. "Jesus!" Adriano shouts as he lets go of my leg.

"Don't drop her!"

I feel myself listing, about to slip from their hands and hit the floor.

"The hell is this shit . . ."

When they lay me down, I hear the sharp crinkle of plastic at my back.

A clear plastic tarp.

"Roll her up."

Hands grab my shoulder and flip me onto my stomach. The sheet follows my rotations, spinning with me until I'm mummified in plastic. I'm a present, gift wrapped and ready to go.

I crack open my eyes. Their faces are blurred through the other side of the sheeting. I can't see their features anymore. Their skin is gray, sallow. Their heads spiral around me.

I feel my body being lifted again.

Light as a feather—

I am in the air, hovering.

—stiff as a board.

They're taking me away. My breath mists over, clinging to the clear plastic.

"Watch the steps," Tobias warns.

"Stop pushing," a woman—Melissa, probably—says.

"I'm not pushing!"

"Do you want to trade places? Slow the fuck down."

I hear a door open. We must be leaving the house. The light changes. The air feels cooler. My spirit is flying much faster now. Where are they taking me? Where are we going?

"Hurry . . ."

I hear the squeal of a door opening—no, not a door. Something else.

Gravity finds me. I fall, landing inside a cramped, confined space. There's no room to move. My shoulders press against the walls. A coffin. *Oh god, they put me inside a coffin . . .*

"Pick a house," Tobias says. "Just put her in the basement and I'll deal with her later, then get rid of the car. It can't be anywhere near here, okay? This can't come back to us."

"We should just dump her, man," Adriano says. "She doesn't deserve to ———"

"I wouldn't be here if it wasn't for her!" Tobias shouts. "Just do as I say and hurry back."

I can smell the reek of rubber. My head must be pressed up against a spare tire. They've stuffed me inside the trunk of a car. Not a coffin—*it's Amara's car.*

"Goodbye, Li'l Deb," Tobias says as he slams the trunk. "See you on the other side . . ."

giving up
the ghost

rock bottom

I wake up with a mouth full of plastic. The harder I breathe, the more I suffocate in my cocoon of polyethylene.

My fingers can't find a loose corner. The tarp is endless. I try tearing through, but my nails can't dig in deep enough; my hands simply slip over the surface. My body feels as if it's been shrink-wrapped. I can't find my way out. Can't take the plastic off. Can't live like this.

I can't breathe—

Just keep still, I think. Very, very still. The more I panic, the more I struggle, the more the tarp seems to tighten, cinching all around me and sealing me in. The plastic constricts against my skin like a python swallowing a mouse.

Don't panic, Erin.

I feel the softness of soil beneath me. The rush of passing traffic sends loose dirt and gravel skittering across the tarp.

I'm in a ditch.

My lungs strain but I focus. My hands are stuck by my sides and there's not much room to maneuver, but I have no choice but to try. I rub the nails of my index fingers against the sides of the tarp until I feel them puncture the first layer of plastic. I force two fingers into each hole, then three, slipping both hands through the polyethylene. I feel around for the next layer of plastic and begin again. My head is spinning, my vision blurring as my breath fogs up the tarp. But I don't need to see. I just need to keep scratching.

My nails break through the next layer. I slip my fingers through again and feel another layer of plastic. Jesus, how many fucking layers are there?

I feel the chill of the cold night air as my fingers break through. Working quickly, I begin to tear at the layers, panicking again now that I'm so close, my body convulsing from lack of oxygen.

The cool rush of fresh air spills over my skin like water.

I suck in as much oxygen as my lungs will allow. I lie there gasping for a moment and then slowly tear the rest of the plastic away until I can crawl out of the tarp.

I'd heard Tobias tell Adriano to put me in a basement but Adriano clearly didn't follow instructions. He decided to dump me on the side of I-95 like I was nothing but a piece of trash.

I wrap the tarp around me for warmth.

Baby steps, Amara's voice echoes in my head. *One foot in front of the other.*

I do what she tells me to.

I can't stop shivering. The tarp isn't keeping me warm. The cold has already seeped into my bones. I glance at my hand and notice my skin is turning blue.

One foot in front of the other.

I spot a lost soul wandering along the center lane of the interstate. She was a child when she passed, probably no older than ten. Just a girl. Where did she die? How long has she been wandering aimlessly? Does she even know where she is anymore? She ambles across the highway with no regard for the traffic.

I'm a lost soul now, too, I think. I can join their listless pilgrimage. I simply drift along with the rest, with the soldiers and slaves, the Indigenous families and settlers. The revenants see me as one of them now, all of us hitchhiking to oblivion.

A squad car sounds its siren behind me. Gravel crumbles under its tires as the car pulls onto the shoulder, but I don't pay it any mind.

I hear a car door open and slam shut, but I don't turn to look. "Ma'am?" It's a woman's voice. It has a soft authoritative quality to it, bored and stern all at once. "How're we doing?"

How can she see me? Doesn't she know I'm dead? I can't waste my time with the living anymore, I need to go—

"Home." My throat is nothing but sandpaper. "Need to get home."

"Are you injured? Let's take a minute, okay? Can you stop walking for me, please?"

My feet aren't touching the ground anymore. I'm floating. Drifting with the undertow . . .

"Can you tell me your name, ma'am? Do you have any ID on you?"

A hand grips my shoulder but I pull away from it. "Need to go *home*."

"You're bleeding, ma'am. Where are you hurt? Are—"

"*Home!*" I'm shouting it now, matching the volume of the passing traffic. I feel the officer's hands on me, pulling me back toward the squad car, but I need to go *this* way. *This* is the way *home*. "Let me go let me go I need to go home I need to go home I need to—"

———

I'm barely coherent when the paramedics bring me into the ER. These sterile rooms are filled with so many spirits. I scream each time I spot one, but the nurses never follow my eyes, never look over their shoulders. I give up trying to convince anyone to see what's standing *right behind them*. They strap my wrists to the rails of my bed and increase the dosage of my sedative until I slip off.

The doctors say I suffered from multiple organ failure. My kidneys and liver nearly stopped working. I'm on a ventilator for acute respiratory failure.

But the real headline is that I have a fungal infection—*Psilocybe cubensis*, I overhear one of the doctors say. Mushrooms are growing in my blood.

The mere thought of all that rot spreading through my veins terrifies me. I can't compartmentalize it. They're inside me, even now. *Growing.* I can't stop repeating it: *There are mushrooms growing inside my body.* How does someone—*how can anyone*—survive that?

Along with a bevy of antibiotics and antifungal drugs, the doctors try to handle my "hallucinations" with Haloperidol. Keep me sedate with Lorazepam. Benzodiazepine.

But the ghosts never go away. Drugs won't stop them—I know this already. The dead are always in the room.

So I look away. It's all I can do. I try to pretend they're not there, staring back.

Reaching out for me.

Touching me.

This forced detox feels like an exorcism. They keep me bound to my bed and all I want is to break free, but they won't let me go until I'm clean.

Clean. Now there's a joke for you. How will I ever feel clean again? Even now, I can feel the fungus growing just beneath the surface of my skin. It's there, always there, just waiting to break through my flesh and sprout across my body.

The nurse on call leaves after her routine check-in, making sure my restraints are on nice and tight. I have the room all to myself.

Just me and my ghosts. Six spirits linger in the room. They sniff at the air, aware of a scent that has them all licking their lips. Their robin's-egg paleness matches the linoleum. They must've been patients who passed in this very hospital. Now they blindly tiptoe toward me—tentative steps. I start moaning low as they make their way to the edge of my bed. I yank at my restraints, but my wrists are still cinched to the handrails. I can't sit up. Can't escape. I'm forced to lie here as the spirits surround me, picking up my scent. They must smell the Ghost still flowing through my blood. They want a taste.

One spirit crawls onto the bed, slowly edging her way up my chest until her face is inches from mine. We stare at each other. She's young. She must have been my age when she died. There's very little difference between us; she is a mirror of what I've become. I see the track marks pocking her arms and I realize she must have overdosed. Her stringy hair rakes over my face as she leans in. She breathes in through her nose, then slides her gray tongue across my chin. Her eyes roll up into her head in ecstasy. She can taste the Ghost oozing out from my skin.

I'm going to sweat this drug out of my pores and she's going to lick every last drop and I'm reminded of something Silas once told me: how maggots are used to clean deep wounds by devouring the dead tissue. They eat away the necrotic cells, debriding the injury of its infection and I suddenly wonder if these lost souls will debride me of my own addiction. Can they lick the last of the drug out of me? Lap at the Ghost until it's all gone? *Oh god, they're licking me clean.* All six of them wrestle against one another just to get a taste of me, pushing and shoving as they lean down, shoulder to shoulder, lapping at my neck, my ears, my arms. Any inch of exposed skin is up for grabs and there's nothing I can do to stop them. I can only lie there, losing my mind as they lick and lick and lick any lingering hint of this haunted drug and I just stare at the ceiling and pray for this to all be over soon, *please end this,* praying that I'll flush the Ghost from my system fast and they'll leave me alone before I snap. Even when I close my eyes, I can still feel the sandpaper scrape of their tongues against my body. I'm a mother pig, a desiccated sow getting devoured by her own litter. The spirits lean in, rutting for their spot to suckle and I think, *if I die here, I'll never leave this room again . . .*

I don't want to die.

I actually say it out loud, "I don't want to die." You can say it a hundred times over and never mean it. Not until you hit rock bottom. It's then and only then, in the blackness of the abyss, when you truly hear the sound of your own voice, echoing all around as you cry out—*Please don't let me die.*

I change my mind. I take it all back. Please, don't let it be too late.

I don't want to die. I keep repeating it as these spirits lick at my skin, licking me clean, a litany for survival: *I don't want to die, I don't want to die, I don't want to die.*

I want to live.

homewrecker

I stopped paying attention to the revenants. They can tag along, if they want. I pick up a handful of stragglers as I wander past the NO TRESPASSING sign at the entrance to Shady Acres, letting them follow me through the tangle of streets. The more, the merrier, I say.

A funeral procession back to Hopewell.

I was a model patient, saying *please* and *thank you* and *I'm feeling much, much better now*, speaking only when spoken to, biding my time. Eventually my arm restraints were taken off. I had achieved a level of trust with the staff because I'd been such *a good little girl* and now they could unfasten my bruised wrists.

The first moment I was alone, I pulled the IV from my arm and slipped on my job interview dress turned memorial dress turned dinner party dress turned going away party dress turned getaway dress and walked right through the sliding glass doors of the main entrance. Nobody stopped me. No one noticed.

I take in the vacant houses with fresh eyes. It's not just one house anymore—the phantasmal cancer has spread down Shoreham Drive. Every house is decorated with its own sigil, and I can't help but wonder whose blood was used to paint them. I notice a few new neighbors peering out from the plastic tarps on their window, living skeletons taking in the sight of me as I wander down the road. I wonder who they could've been before they came here.

Tobias sure has been a busy boy. While I was strung out in the hospital, he expanded his spiritualist empire through the cul-de-sac. Before long, he'll have an entire neighborhood of haunted houses filled with addicted phantoms.

The police questioned me in the hospital once I was coherent enough to talk. They wanted to know about Amara. She'd gone missing. I vaguely remember mumbling my answers from bed—our family attorney present, hovering over my shoulder like a Brooks Brothers vulture. *I haven't seen her since her going-away party.*

What am I supposed to tell them? That her—

ghost

—body is still in Tobias's house in Hopewell somewhere?

They wouldn't believe me even if I told the truth. And if I did, who knows what the spirits would do to them once they arrived. I already saw what they did to Amara.

No. I have to be the one to go back. I have to find her, to save her from that house.

I owe her that. I owe her my life.

Mom visited me in the hospital a few times. I have the haziest memory of her sobbing in silence. *I hope you know*, she whispered, *everything we've ever done for you was out of love . . .*

She might've held my hand, but I couldn't feel it. Dad never came.

The crowd grows denser the closer I get to home. I force my way through the horde of spirits. There have to be hundreds now, pressed shoulder to shoulder, the biggest block party I've ever seen. Our home, the supernatural pull of it, won't let these lost souls go. All those séances, every last dose, has lured the homeless ghosts to our house. Tobias keeps calling out, drawing them in, only to slam the door in their faces. I know because he's calling for me, too. I can hear him. I can feel the dull ache in my bones. I'm sweating before I even reach our lawn. The withdrawal hurts the closer I get. My body knows how close I am. My muscles burn before freezing before burning again and all it would take to make the hurt go away is one pill.

But I'm here to find Amara, I keep telling myself, repeating it in my head.

You can bring her back, Silas whispers. *Bring her home.*

Quitting Ghost means choosing life over death. That simple decision—*I want to live*—seems so obvious, but the real challenge is what comes next. Detox just won't do. You have to give up your ghosts. The hospital might have flushed the drug out of my system, but when you're haunted, *truly haunted*, you never let go of your phantoms. They follow you. I feel them on my back even now, pressing against my neck. The only way to escape my addiction is an exorcism.

A home starts from a place of love. But I look at this house—our home—and I realize, it was never loved. It was abandoned by its builders before it even had a chance to live. This neglected phantom will never know what love is. Only pain. Our pain.

No one's on door duty. It's unlocked, so I let myself in.

There's no light. The windows remain sealed with plywood sheets. The air is musty, thick with a miasma that only grows stronger the deeper I walk down the hallway. I almost gag.

The wood warps and sags. Water damage spreads throughout the drywall, black mold overwhelming the ceiling. Rust-colored runes are scrawled everywhere, like a page ripped out of Silas's archaic cookbook.

Lonnie is sitting on the hallway floor, facing away from me, his legs spread out. He's smearing sigils made from his own fecal matter across the wall.

My little artist, I think.

He looks up from his scribbling with his eyeless face and grins. The hollow *O* at the center of his face expands, vermillion gills rippling. I hear him purr. He's happy to see me. He knew I couldn't stay away forever.

"You're not mine." I give him a swift kick in the tummy. The punt sends him skidding down the hall, limbs spiraling at his sides like a whirling dervish. He hisses at me once he comes to a stop, white flecks of saliva sputtering from his mouth-hole before he scurries up the wall. He scales the ceiling, disappearing into a fresh fracture above. I can hear the soft pad of Lonnie's hands and knees through the walls as I make my way to the living room. He's following me, keeping tabs on me like always. The little fucking spy.

Nobody seems to notice me—or care—as I walk in. None of the bodies on the floor move. Are they even breathing? I count at least a dozen users—maybe twenty. Every shadow hides more bodies. They nestle into one another like a litter of puppies. They seem content to stare vacantly into space, suspended in their own sickness. Each user has the same haunted look on their face—a mass-produced Halloween mask—hollow eyes, waxen skin, a rash of acne cropping along their cheeks and chin. These people brought their trauma into this house. They dragged in their past, the phantoms on their backs, in their bellies. They brought their pain. All their hurt, their loss. Their rage. They brought it in and planted the seed of what haunts them the most inside our home. Now all those seeds are blooming.

Our ghosts. So many ghosts.

I spot Marcia in the heap. She's still wearing the same yoga outfit she wore the day I met her. A whole lifetime ago. Now the spandex is full of holes, as if it's been chewed through by moths. Sweat stains sprawl from her armpits, the vibrant yellow faded to a bone white.

"Have you seen my son?" Her brittle voice cracks. The very words crumble in her mouth. Dust in the wind. She lifts her head, the faintest shimmer of hope flickering in her eyes.

I don't answer. I don't think Marcia would be able to hear me even if I did. Her head eases back to the floor once more, eyes staring off at some unknown spot in the ether.

I head to the kitchen. Tobias toils away like some whacked-out Julia Child. He's so preoccupied with his cooking, he barely turns to look. One dull-eyed glance is all I get.

"You're alive." He's bleeding all over now. His arms lacerated in weeping red symbols. The back of his neck has the same sigil from the door sliced into it.

"Sure. If you call this living."

"Adriano was supposed to give you a new house," he says over his shoulder. "I wanted you to have a home you could haunt all on your own. I figured I owed you that much."

"Should I say thanks?"

"You might not believe me, Erin, but for what it's worth, I was trying to protect you. You deserved a house for yourself. This place . . . This place was just getting too crowded."

"Yeah, well, Adriano tossed me in a ditch."

"If you want something done right . . ." Tobias sighs. "You look good. Healthier."

"I'm clean."

That makes Tobias laugh. "Congrats. How about we celebrate?"

Yes, my body aches, *god yes*. "This has to stop."

"Says who?"

"I'm saying it," I say, "as your friend."

"Friend," he repeats flatly. The word holds no meaning for him.

"I still am." Even I can hear the lie of it, the outright emptiness of the words.

"You've still got some Ghost rattling around your bloodstream right now. I can hear the chains from all the way over here. That shit never leaves your body."

"I'm clean," I repeat, less certain of myself.

"Your ghosts are never through with you, Erin. They never leave. You'll always be haunted, whether you dose or not. I thought you would've figured that out by now."

I spot Silas's lighter on the counter. REHAB IS FOR QUITTERS. I hope Tobias doesn't notice me reach for it. I try distracting him. "Will you at least tell me how Silas found it?"

"We didn't find it. It found *us*. That's how a ghost story always starts."

"And it killed him. Silas died here, didn't he? In the house? Is that why you dug him up and brought his body back?"

Tobias finally turns back, intrigued. If he's surprised I know about Silas's missing corpse, he certainly doesn't show it. But now he wants to chat. "Death isn't the end, you know."

"Was that always the plan? Start your own empire?"

"Yeah, sure. Kingpins of the kingdom of the dead. Tobias was too timid to follow through, so I took over. *I* found all the right books, *I* recited all the spells. *Me*."

He must notice the confusion on my face. He breaks out into a grin that leaves him looking like the cat who ate the canary.

I've never seen Tobias smile like that before. I've only ever seen that look on—

". . . Silas?"

"Our plan was to show you that first weekend, when it was just the three of you. If we could prove to you that Ghost worked, then we knew you'd come on board. Tobias just couldn't bring me back on his own. He needed you, Erin. Your voice was stronger than his. But then you and Amara bailed and Tobias had to think fast. He let me use his body . . . Which is funny, if you think about it. Tobias always wanted to be me—so win-win."

"For how long?"

"As long as I keep dosing," Tobias—no, not Tobias, it's Silas—says. "Death really isn't all it's cracked up to be, trust me. I had to find that one out the hard way. You don't know the loneliness . . . the outright emptiness. It's an ocean of ash. I can't go back, Erin. I just can't."

I don't say anything, but I know exactly what he's talking about. I've seen it for myself.

"Tobias trusted you. How could you do this to him?"

"He offered himself to me. He wanted it just as much as I did. Trust me, it's better for both of us."

I feel a flicker of fear. "Where's Toby now?"

"He's not coming back."

"You mean he's *dead*."

"Just under new management."

Once Silas was in Toby's body, he must've carved the sigils into his own skin as binding spells. Now the homewrecker will never leave.

"He . . ." I start. What is there left to say? "He was your friend."

"Still is. We're closer now than ever. We were actually wondering if we could all be together. You know, the three of us . . . Sex is so much better when you're haunted."

"You're disgusting."

"What, has your sense of humor left you? Amara was always better with the comebacks. She'd probably call you the spiritualist village bicycle."

"*Fuck you.*"

"I'm teasing! Jesus, lighten up! I'm a better Tobias than he ever was. And he's who he always wanted to be."

"A puppet."

"I don't know how much longer I can stay inside him. Itches like a son of a bitch. I was actually wondering if you might want to connect. Been a while since we got haunted together."

"Every time I reached out to you, every time I thought it was you . . . who was it?"

"Me. Most of the time."

"How many other ghosts were there?"

"Why keep count? Erin—don't tie yourself up in knots about this! You've got such a powerful voice. You cut through the din. We all heard you calling. You brought us here."

My voice. My need for him. My addiction. Silas used me. Used my love for him. He knew I would do anything for him, just like some lovesick junkie, and he exploited it until I nearly died. I *had* died, even if it was just for a few minutes.

"Erin." Tobias—*no, it's Silas*—brings his hands to my face, cupping my chin. "You're an astronaut, you know that? A pioneer! You took my hand and dove in. I'm so proud of you."

I'm crying. I know I'm crying, even if I can't feel it.

Used me, I keep thinking. *Silas used me.*

"Look at this." Silas gestures to the kitchen. The gangrenous house. Its ghosts. "Look at what we've achieved! Think about how much further we can go. We've only gotten started. I want you to be a part of this—with me. We can finally be together. This can all be yours, too."

"You got me to invite your own sister."

"Our ghost story deserves to be heard, don't you think? Everybody's haunted by somebody . . . This is our chance to reconnect. We can all be haunted together."

"You can't do this forever . . ."

"Why not? Did you see the people in the living room? They came to me 'cause they're looking for something to fill their lives back up again. Ghost gives them that. I give them that. Our ghost stories are spreading. It won't matter what happens to this house or the house next door or any of the other houses in the neighborhood. Ghost will be *everywhere* soon. This city—the South—is steeped in it, but nobody fucking *looks*. We've been taught to avoid death at all costs. To look the other way. But Ghost erases that barrier, doesn't it? We're ready to rip that veil away once and for all. You never have to be alone again, Erin."

His voice lowers and I can hear him, actually hear Silas's voice slithering across Tobias's tongue. "Isn't that what you always wanted? We can be together forever now. You and me. Two spirits. One body. Isn't that beautiful?"

He used me. Silas used me. "People are dying."

"People die all the time! What does it matter when we have Ghost?"

"*Amara's dead!*" I shout. "I saw you kill her—"

"Erin, that—" Silas stops, takes a measured breath before laughing, actually busting out laughing, as if this is the funniest goddamn thing he's ever heard. "That was *you.*"

He's lying. "I saw someone . . . in the room."

"That was all you, Erin. Talk about brutal. Remind me not to get on your bad side."

"That's not true . . ." I slowly shake my head. There's no way I could have done that to her. It's not possible. I saw her body lift off the floor. I saw her get thrown across the room.

I saw her die.

"We all heard screaming," Silas says. "I ran upstairs and when I came into the room—"

"Stop it." The sound of her neck breaking still echoes through my head. There's no possible way I could have done that to Amara. She's my best friend. The only friend I had left.

"When I came into the room, I found Amara on the floor and you were *smiling*—"

"STOP IT!"

My bones grow heavy. All I want is to lay my body down and let the ghosts take over.

"I didn't. I couldn't . . . I . . ."

"You shouldn't have called her, Erin. That's on you. You brought her here. If you didn't want her to die, you shouldn't have reached out to her in the first place—"

"That wasn't me . . ." I say.

"Why don't we ask her?" I see Tobias step forward and I instinctively step back. "Come on. All it'll take is one quick hit and we can call her up."

"No!"

"Let's reach out to Amara now. She'll set the story straight. I'll bet you a buck it was—"

"NO!"

Silas backs away, hands held up, a smile on his lips. "Fine, it wasn't you, it was the Ghost. Some bad spirit made you do it. Nobody'll blame you for what happens when you dose."

He offers a consoling hand, palm up.

I spot the gelcap. It shimmers. "No," I moan. "Please, don't . . ."

"Come on, Erin . . . Don't make me beg."

"I want to live."

"Then live forever. With me." Tobias looks deep into my eyes and I see Silas lingering within, his eyes staring back at me, settled into the sunken sockets of his spineless friend.

"You were my original vessel, Erin," he says. "My first. I always knew you could do it. You proved Ghost could work for anyone. Jesus, just look at you . . . Your vapid life. Your willingness to do whatever I told you to. You were perfect. You've always been so *empty*."

I try to keep myself together, not wanting to believe him. But of course he's right.

I am an empty vessel. I always have been.

calling all spirits

"Let us begin," Silas intones as if this is a church service. Even if it's Tobias's body sitting on the living room floor, I know it's Silas who's speaking. It's always been Silas. He is an emissary for Ghost, spreading his addictive religion, pleased as punch to be its messenger. Or dealer. *A mushroom by any other name . . .*

"This will unlock our ghosts," he says. "Whoever haunts you the most."

His followers crawl out from their corners of the living room, reviving themselves long enough to circle around. The wood warps under their hands and knees. It's like they can smell the Ghost, revived by its scent. Their glassy eyes reflect the candlelight. The flames pulse under the duress of everyone's breath, dancing with each fetid exhale. I see the same starved sneer on everyone's lips. Their eyes sink into their sockets, the flesh so taut they have no eyelids at all. They came here to reconnect with someone they lost, only to succumb to this addictive existence, losing hold of their lives, no longer alive or dead but caught somewhere in between.

I'm just like them. Even now I can feel the undertow of our home.

The house is calling for me.

"Everybody grab a cap." Silas passes a Tupperware container. It makes its way around the room. "Take two! We have a special houseguest. Everybody say, 'Welcome home, Erin.'"

And they do. Good god, they all turn to look at me with eyes that are no longer eyes, smiling with lips that no longer look like lips, echoing Silas: "Welcome home, Erin . . ."

"We're ripping the door to the other world right off its hinges today, folks, so let's get ready to open our minds as wide as they'll go . . ."

Each member receives their sacrament. I watch the container move around the room until the skeleton next to me turns, her smile a withered rictus.

"Melissa?" I barely recognize her. All that's left is a skull draped in an ill-fitting husk of dried parchment. An outcropping of white-heads sprouts all across her cheeks, threatening to burst. She holds out a gelcap for me. "Here you go . . ."

I feel the sweat seep out from my pores. Here's the craving again, the slumbering worm tightening around my intestines, desperate for a fix. *Don't.* I'm dizzy within my addiction's grip.

Even now I'm trapped. My ghosts won't let me go. This isn't life. It's death.

There's nothing beyond our world. The dead know this. *Silas knows this.* That's why they're clamoring to crawl back in. This drug isn't a door for us—it's for *them.* To come home.

"No," I say.

"Come on, Erin," Silas says. "Don't make us force you . . ."

"I won't."

Silas barely nods and all at once, his followers swarm me. They grab my wrists, my legs, my head. I can't pull free. Their bony claws sink into my cheeks as they pry my lips apart.

"Here comes the choo-choo . . ." Melissa brings up the gelcap and presses it against my tongue. I bite her fingers but the skin is so brittle and loose that the top layer of dried baklava flesh simply sloughs off between my teeth. She tugs her fingers out and presses her palm over my mouth, pinching my nose until I have no choice but to—

"*Swallow*," she says. I feel the pill plummet down my throat, practically hear the hollow tumble down, down, all the way down the well and crashing into the pit of my empty stomach.

They let me go and I slip to the floor. I couldn't do it. Couldn't escape. *God help me I'm home.*

"Everyone hold hands," Silas instructs. "Let's get haunted."

There are two circles, an inner and outer ring, to accommodate every member of the family. Tobias's body sits in the center. The others sit in silence. Already their bodies sway.

Silas takes a deep breath and recites, "*Exsurgent mortui et ad me veniunt.*"

Both circles sway in a steady pulse, gaining speed. The faster they go, the more their bodies blur, until they're no longer individual bodies but a single band of color. Their faces slip by so quickly, their open mouths blending together.

At any moment, I fear the floor at the center of the circle will bottom out, like a carnival ride, plunging Silas all the way through the earth. I sense the house buckling under the weight of so many users and their ghosts, clamoring for a chance to slip inside.

"*Exsurgent mortui,*" he repeats.

There is safety in a contained séance. Just a small group of people, no more than five or six at a time, all sitting around a table, lights dimmed, save for a single candle.

"*Exsurgent mortui . . .*"

Speaking to spirits in someone's parlor is more manageable, more controlled, but there's an overwhelming presence in the living room now, a density of specters.

"Rise. Come through to us. Speak to us."

"Rise," his users breathlessly echo, repeating his evocation. "Speak to us."

Tobias warned us about breaking the barrier. I can feel the gravitational pull in my bones, my very skeleton wanting to take root in the house like a sapling, as I exit the living room and stumble down the hall, my hands skidding across the wall as I head toward the front door.

If Silas taught me anything, it's that Ghost opens the user's perception to the other side—but there's no controlling what spirit you connect to. No telling who's on the other end.

So let's reach out and touch someone.

I fling the front door open.

The lost souls clustered in the cul-de-sac haven't moved since I entered the house. It's not long before a revenant senses something has stirred; a fresh scent.

"Hey!" I wave my arms through the air. "Over here!"

One, then two, turn toward the house. "Here! Over here!"

The door is open. The sigil is broken. The vessel beckons.

In a breath, all the lost souls sense my presence. A hundred ashen spirits crammed in the cul-de-sac turn to face me, staring with their milked-over eyes. I now have an audience.

"Come on," I shout as loud as my lungs allow. "Come to me!"

I am a beacon, a bright guiding light tempting them to enter. I'm the invitation they've been waiting for. One revenant takes a first step. His body is covered in trenches of scar tissue. He's almost hesitant, as if he doesn't trust me. But I watch the pull of his desire take over.

"Come in," I call out, like I'm some supernatural realtor and this is my open house. I imagine staking a sign into the front lawn with my own soft-focused face emblazoned across it:

OPEN HOUSE. WALK-INS WELCOME. NO APPOINTMENT NECESSARY.

Others follow. I see the dull excitement in their eyes grow. They look like babies taking their first few steps, tentative at first, but their pace picks up, a herd of gray bodies.

"Come in," I keep shouting, my voice raw and cracking. "Come home!"

I step back inside the house, slowly walking backward, making sure the lost souls follow. I don't close the door, leaving the container wide open for any spirit willing to enter.

Silas said I had a strong voice, so why not use it? "That's it! This way! Keep coming . . ."

The first to peer through the doorway does so almost sheepishly, as if he's unsure what might happen. I'm inviting them in. I'm offering them four walls. A roof over their heads.

Finally, a home to call their own.

"Speak to us!" I hear Silas demand from the living room. "Speak!"

Pale bodies pour through the front door. Too many revenants try forcing their way in at once, their arms reaching through the doorway, and I can't help but picture ground meat funneling through a grinder. These lost souls are so desperate to enter, to feel the comfort of confinement.

"Speak to us . . ."

More revenants fill the hall, their naked bodies squirming. They run their hands over the drywall, plywood, and plaster. The energy from the séance draws them in. Their steps pick up until they're scrambling, bodies stumbling over each other as they surge into the living room.

"SPEAK—"The candles blow out. Darkness spreads over the living—

dead it's now a dead

—room. These users have no idea what hits them. A cold wave smashes across their bodies as every last revenant slips through their skin, inhabiting their fleshy vessels.

Two lost souls fight over the same body, three, even four or five cram their way inside a single user. I can't help but picture rabid customers rushing into a Walmart on Black Friday, fighting over the same flat-panel TV. Only these are bodies, *human bodies*, receptacles of skin and bone. How many spirits can possess one body at a time? How many is too many?

Ever watch a junkie take a bad fix? Their body jolts in revolt. These people know they've dosed on a bad ghost. It goes beyond cold. These are Freon phantoms. Their veins turn to ice. Their bones are no longer their own, bodies buckling, possessed, in the throes of an overdose.

Oh god . . . Look at them all.

The user in front of me—*Melissa, my god that's Melissa*—rakes her fingernails down her face. She moans, the very sound of it reaching up from some unknown depth. She keeps clawing, tearing through her neck now. Trenches of red are left in her fingers' wake. The skin comes away with little resistance as Melissa begins to eat her own flesh by the handful.

Silas can only stare, hiding behind Tobias's dumbstruck eyes. "What have you done?"

Too much. Too many ghosts. And they're all ODing.

Another user—*Adriano, that's Adriano!*—takes his forefinger and plunges it into his right eye socket and plucks it out. The eyeball slips free with a wet *spluuuch*. A quick yank snaps the connecting nerve, the broken thread retracting back into the socket like the pull string on a doll. Then he goes for his left eye.

"Stop." Silas can't muster any strength in Tobias's voice. "Stop!"

Adriano pops one eye in his mouth and swallows it with a smile. Then he gulps down the other. Blood seeps between his teeth and runs down his cheeks.

Silas can't stop them. There are too many lost souls in the house now, all of them punch-drunk on Ghost, their spirits slipping and sliding through these human vessels.

I watch as another user—*oh god that's Marcia, poor Marcia*—forces her hand into Stephanie's mouth. First her fingers disappear. Then her whole fist. Stephanie's lower jaw snaps back to accommodate Marcia's hand, lips wrapped around her wrist. When Marcia pulls her glistening fist back out, now painted red, she holds Stephanie's uprooted tongue—and eats it.

They're eating each other. The revenants greedily run their hosts' hands over each other's bodies, feeling for the nearest crevasse of flesh to peel away and devour. They all giggle like school children between swallows, lips glossed in blood. Their eyes roll up into their sockets—those who still have their eyes—leaving behind nothing but white in their wake. They don't need to see anymore. The veil is tearing open, two planes flooding into one another.

This is one really bad trip.

"Stop it! *Stop!*" Silas can't control his own séance, if he ever had control. Now they come for him. A cluster of lost souls filter through Tobias's body, revenant wrestling against revenant, three now four now five passing into his flesh like plunging into a pool of water. Tobias's body flings itself back and flops on the floor. He gasps like a fish desperate for water. Silas takes himself in, lost in his limbs, his own hands, as if he's never seen them before.

"I'm sorry, Toby," I say, even if I know he can't hear me. I pray he's already dead, that he's not trapped inside the prison of his own flesh to suffer through this, that Silas didn't push him into the deeper recesses of his consciousness. He doesn't deserve to die like this. None of them do.

I can't tell if it's Silas marveling at the sight of Tobias's skin, transfixed by his friend's flesh, or if it's any of the other ghosts now calling his body home. They're all trapped inside, bound by Toby's carved sigils. He runs a hand over one arm, then the other. His body has become a book, a grimoire bound in skin. Written in blood. Every layer of flesh is another page, revealing muscle tissue. Sinew. Tendons and blood.

The ghosts keep reading, page after page, flipping down, down, all the way down to the bone. It's best I leave them alone. Let them read in peace.

There's still one last room I need to visit.

/

harvest

The air is cool and dense below. The earthy smell only grows stronger as I descend the basement steps—an organic stench of decay that thickens, like rancid cheese. Every breath curdles in my lungs.

I wouldn't go down there if I were you, I can practically hear Silas whisper.

When you build a house, you begin with a grave. You dig a hole in the ground. Then the footings are formed and poured. The concrete foundation is cured. But it remains a grave, with or without a body, empty and waiting to accept. What do I expect to find down here? I'm not sure. I know I'm supposed to be here. Something is tugging me downstairs.

I take in the space—concrete walls, cold concrete floor. The only light comes from a ground-level hopper window, hinged at the bottom and open at the top for ventilation. The sun casts a tight rectangular beam across the floor, filled with swirling motes of dust. Not dust—something thicker, more granular. I taste cinnamon when I inhale. *Spores.* The air is thick with them. My eyes adjust to the dark and I see clusters drifting everywhere, forming constellations.

Exposed electrical wiring reaches out from the walls in coiled bouquets. This is where the washer-dryer unit would've gone. I spot several empty bags of topsoil, along with a rusted tin of paint thinner. Empty cans of spray paint, fluorescent pink and black. There's a milk crate full of cell phones. I consider fishing through them to find mine so I can call home, just to tell my mom I'm alive, I'm okay, but my family wants nothing to do with me now.

Besides . . . I'm too transfixed by the planters.

In the center of the basement are three freestanding raised garden beds. The wooden frames are six feet long and about a foot high. They're filled to the brim with thick, fertile earth, rich with peat moss and all kinds of nutrients to get your new garden growing.

The rent-a-cop's body rests in the closest planter.

I don't believe—can't fathom—what I'm seeing. *It can't be . . . It just can't.*

But it's true. He's resting within a fresh garden bed, stripped of his uniform so the soil surrounds the surface of his blue-tinged skin. His paunch rises up from the dirt like a hairy bubble about to pop. His head sinks back in the earth, eyes covered in grit. The earth slips past his lips, filling his hollowed-out mouth. He's up to his teeth in topsoil.

An outcropping of infinitesimal tumors spread along his stomach, threatening to burst at any moment. If I just pretend he's drifting along the surface of a pond—warm, soothing even, I can somehow navigate the absolute insanity of what I'm seeing. I don't want to believe this, *any of this*, is possible. *But it is.* Silas—with Tobias—planted this man's body in the basement.

How else would they grow their supply?

Silas said he wanted to give me my own home. My body was meant to be moved to another house on the block. How long before my ghost would've been planted in its basement?

Amara's body rests in the second garden bed. *No. Please, not Amara.* Her jaw has locked open to allow the fibrous stalk that was once her tongue to branch out and blossom. The fleshy veil lifts a few inches above her nose, its cap a blushing umbrella. A button peers out from her left nostril. More morels are about to sprout. It won't be long before her face is gone altogether, replaced by a fresh bed of fruiting bodies.

"Amara . . ."

This is your fault, I say to myself. *All your fault.*

"I'm so sorry . . ."

Amara blinks. Her eyes remain cognizant while the rest of her ruptures. I don't know how she can hear me, her ear canals clotted with yeasty cysts, but somehow she does. Both lobes are like honeycombed morchellas, spongy and yellow. They curl toward me.

A scream escapes from my mouth as I fall onto the floor. I scramble backward, unable to look away from Amara's planter, until I strike the garden bed directly behind me.

She's alive, I think. *Amara's still alive!* She came here to rescue me from this house, and this is what happened to her. This is my fault. All my fault. If I'd just taken her hand—

Something shifts at my shoulder.

I spin around, facing the edge of the third garden bed. This planter has been hidden in the far corner of the basement, pressed against the wall, where there's less light.

A fermented bouquet of mildew and stale sweat reaches into my nose. The curdled milk stench is at its strongest back here. The soil itself, from what I can see in the darkness, is an explosion of mycelium. An entire fungal colony sprawls out before me. And it's moving.

Silas.

The entirety of his flesh has erupted in mushroom caps. His skin ripples with pinheads. White buttons branch out from his fingertips. Patches of puffballs crop up from the crevices in his flesh, around his armpits and groin. Jelly ears fan out from his temples.

It can't be him. There's nothing left to recognize . . . But it's him. Of course it's him. This mass of branching hyphae was once Silas's body. He has been down here this whole time. I was supposed to plant his ghost, but it was Tobias who planted his body. *Just like a seed*, he told us. *You can plant a ghost in any empty vessel, letting your ghost grow.*

Silas found a mushroom. *Sarcophyllum*, was what Tobias called it.

As in *sarcophilous*. Fond of flesh. Silas performed a particular ritual and started this supernatural sequence, as if it were all some sort of psychedelic self-fulfilling prophesy. I see it now. The only way to grow more Ghost is to farm it from the corpses of its own addicts. It needs flesh. It's the life cycle of a fungus that feeds on its users: you die so that it can live. Once you start taking Ghost—*Have I been taking the drug or is the drug taking me?*—it changes you. We've all become fruiting bodies for more of the mushroom. Vessels, that's all we are. Receptacles. It needs our flesh to flourish. To proliferate.

That's how our ghost story spreads. That's how addictive this drug is. The mushroom consumes you from the inside out, your body a breeding ground for the next batch *and you don't even care.*

A gentle scraping sound of something soft—fleshy—fills the basement.

Silas's body slowly pulls free from its garden bed. Topsoil topples off his ruptured body as he sits upright. *I'm hallucinating,* I think. *None of this is real, this can't be happening . . .*

Silas is dead. It's not him. Not Silas. Not anymore.

Silas makes a sound. He wants to say something, but it's no longer his voice. No longer his mouth. His lips have fissured into gills. His cheeks mottle into yellow angel wings. The tip of his nose cauliflowers, the skin slowly boiling over. Threads of flesh lift into the air, a fungal colony of tawny-capped toadstools rising up from his exposed rib cage. The stems along his throat oscillate with every exhale, bending with what passes as breath.

All he wants is to flourish. Take root.

"Silas?"

The mushrooms along his body respond to the sound of his name. The toadstools find me first, turning toward me as if they have their own autonomous life independent of their host. The caps open and close, several dozen umbrellas vacillating—their colors pulsing in a dizzying, almost hypnotizing, rhythm. I don't want to look but I can't turn away, drawn in by the colors, all the stunning colors flexing along his body. His hulking frame rises up from the garden bed, onto his feet, mold-ridden muscles stretching. Soil cascades off his shoulders, spilling over.

"Silas," I say again, my voice firmer this time. "Can you hear me?"

I crawl away from the planter as Silas places one foot on the floor, then the other. I know it's not him. Not anymore. Just fungal flesh. Mold. And yet . . . maybe he's still there, somewhere.

He's in me. I'm the one haunted by him.

His body takes another awkward step forward. I stop crawling backward so Silas can catch up. He lumbers closer until his flourishing frame looms over me on the floor. I hear a leathery flex in his flesh as he leans forward, drawing near, the fetid smell of mildew drifting.

"I'm letting you go," I say.

Silas brings his hand down to my face and cups my jaw. The mushroom caps along his palms brush against my chin and I can feel them flexing and tensing, puckering up to me.

"*Li'l Deb . . .*"

Silas kisses me. I feel the gills rippling against my lips. He presses further. His face is too soft, the underlying skull spongier than any bone. When he pulls back, I see where my lips left the slightest dimple in his face, his skull sinking in for a few seconds before swelling back again.

The can of paint thinner is heavier than I expect. I nearly lose my grip. I struggle to keep my wrists from trembling as I unscrew the rusted cap, releasing a strong chemical scent into the basement that cuts through the reek of mildew. By the time I turn back to face Silas . . .

He's cradling our baby within the crook of his arm.

Lonnie nestles into Silas's chest, settling against his flesh. He fits so perfectly. I realize Lonnie is a part of him, this new body. Lonnie grew out from him, rooted in his skin, plucked free by his father when he was ripe to run freely through the house. To keep an eye on me.

Silas holds out his hand for me to take. So does Lonnie. They're offering me a choice.

We can still be a family.

This is my chance—it's not too late. The house, the family. *Our family.* Even now, Lonnie's mouth opens and flexes, as if he's hungry for my breast. He needs me. I sense a low-wattage ache in my chest, as if my body is yearning to feed this thing.

Then I see the others.

Their vermillion lips shimmer in the shadows, glistening. One baby leans forward, out from the dark, its face nearly identical to its mushroom brother. Or sister. Who can tell? They're identical in every way—and in that moment, it finally dawns on me: *There was never just one.*

The spongy offspring crawl out from the corners of the basement and climb up Silas's corpse, one now two now three, all finding their original spot within the nooks and crannies of his body. They complete him, somehow, pieces of a three-dimensional puzzle. He's whole now. All those mouths, opening and closing, reaching for me. Yearning for my body to feed them.

I splash Silas's body with paint thinner. Even then, the babies' mouths keep opening and closing, their sphincters widening and mewling for their mother *but I'm not their fucking mother I never was, it was all a lie to get me to stay to use me.*

I still have Silas's lighter. It always comes back to me. I glance at it in my hand—REHAB IS FOR QUITTERS—feeling the weight of it in my palm before tightening my grip and flicking the flint with my thumb.

"Goodbye, Silas."

His body goes up so quickly. There's no resistance, no scream. His offspring do all the shrieking for him. Each tiny mouth puckers and hisses as the fire sweeps over. His children curl all along his body, writhing within the flames. His steps are clumsy. He lunges forward, then back, collapsing on the planter he climbed out from. It looks like a cradle full of flaming babies.

I never want to have kids for as long as I fucking live.

I splash Amara next. A tail of flame connects the planters. I can't bring myself to look at her as the fire embraces her body, but for just a brief moment, I see—think I see—Amara reach for me. Her hand lifts up from the soil and something that was once her fingers branches out, twining together in the air and extending toward me, but I'm already racing up the stairs.

"Erin . . ." *It's not Amara*, I keep repeating to myself. *Not her anymore.* "Erin . . ."

Everyone in the living room is dead. Their bodies just don't know it yet. Those that are still moving are simply being puppeteered by the spirits possessing their fleshy vessels, gnawing on what skin they can still pull free. The Ghost must taste so good to these revenants. Good to the last drop. They dig into their own pulp for just another mouthful of that yummy substance.

None seem to notice the flames. Or care. The orange glow reflects within their blackened eyes as their bodies are quickly consumed by the mounting fire.

I'm on autopilot now. I have to bury my thoughts, *compartmentalize*, no matter how loud the screams in my head are. I can't dwell on what I'm doing—who these people were—going through the motions as I draw a trail of paint thinner from the living room into the hall, then up the stairs toward the second floor. The sharp chemical smell cuts through the hallway, eclipsing every other odor. I cough, breathing in fumes, but I keep climbing the steps.

I start with my nest in the nursery. I pour the paint thinner over the insulation and realize it's not the same pink padding as before. The insulation appears to have been replaced by a fleshy bedding of mycelium. Am I really seeing what I think I'm seeing? I have to be hallucinating this . . . It's not possible. The inner walls are padded with a fabric of filaments. I break off a chunk of drywall and realize the threads run through the house's inner cavities, branching out behind the plaster. A network of fungus consumes our home from the inside out.

The mycelium goes up fast. The flames chew through the soft tufts, like hair. It shrinks back, curls into itself, hissing and popping and sending spores into the air.

I don't want to think anymore. My body functions on its own, as though it knows what needs to be done, even if I'm not entirely sure. My mind ebbs into a catatonic state as the rest of me waltzes through the burning house and finds my way to the front door.

I need to finish this, before it goes—grows—any further. I need to cut it all down.

Cut it out. Cut it off.

Cut, cut, cut—

I stand in the cul-de-sac and watch the flames take hold of our house. There's a part of me that expects Tobias to stumble out, draped in fire, but he never does. He's home now.

I feel the heat radiate across my face and I can't remember the last time I felt this warm. A breeze blows through, whisking off a few lambent spores, embers so thin the cinders disintegrate as soon as they cool.

Once I'm certain there's no saving the bones of our home, no possible chance of salvaging its structure from the fire, I make my way down the street to the next haunted house.

And the next. *Trick or treat . . .*

I watch as the squatters leap from their windows, running from the flames.

That's right, I think. *Run. Run as fast as you can . . .*

I wonder what tales they'll tell about me. I've become my own ghost story. Move over, Bloody Mary. There's a new urban legend in town.

I'm able to burn most of the block down before the responding firefighters even reach Shady Acres. It's so easy. All these haunted houses, every last one, simply yearn to burn.

All of Silas's work goes up in smoke. All our ghosts, nothing but whispers now. And when it's all over, when the police finally drag me away, I can't help but say to myself . . .

Is that all there is to a fire?

EPILOGUE

recovery

The mural is of me. I don't know who the artist is or when it went up, but there's no doubt that's my face spray-painted across the building's broadside. My own sunken eyes stare down at me from their hollowed sockets. It's my skull up there, hair all aflame, towering along the eastern wall of the five-floor walk-up at the corner of Boulevard Avenue and Leigh Street.

I've worn that same haunted expression for nearly a year now. The artist wrapped my head in a halo, La Calavera Catrina on fire, an ecstatic living dead girl rising out from the very fire I started. The spirits of every last addict who died in the blaze drift through the surrounding smoke, dozens of gray wraiths curling around my shoulders.

If there was any doubt who the subject is, then the epitaph is a dead giveaway. In bright, vibrant colors, written in an urban gothic font, it reads:

> *Ever hear the tale of Erin Hill?*
> *She ground her lover into a pill.*
> *She lived in a house just down the lane,*
> *Until the day it went up in flames . . .*

When I first found myself looming over Leigh Street, I felt my knees nearly give out. The air in my lungs curdled, but I couldn't look away. Couldn't believe the sheer enormity of myself.

This is my legacy. I've become a part of this city's living history. When I die, I'll still be here—immortalized on this wall—forever.

I am here.

Do you want to get haunted?

I'll hear it whispered now and again when I walk down Grace Street, passing by faceless strangers, their hoodies pulled over their heads so they look like grim reapers.

"*Psst*," the dealers all sigh and murmur. "Wanna get haunted?"

What is a ghost? Is it a shadow of our past clinging to our present? I believe it's our addictions. The habits we form that end up consuming us if we allow them to take over.

You're here because you're haunted. This circle of foldout chairs is our campfire. This is where we share our ghost stories. Think of it as Apparitions Anonymous.

I'll go first:

Hi. My name is Erin and I am haunted. Here's my ghost story: I'm living proof that you can survive Ghost.

Living proof. That never sounds quite right, does it? The life I had before I started using is long gone. I'm not that person anymore. She is dead, for sure, so—when I say *survive*, I can't help but hear the hollowness in my own words.

I barely escaped my dependency on Ghost. The undertow, the supernatural pull of it, nearly killed me. Even now, I still find myself wanting to get haunted. I created a black hole within myself and I hurt the people who loved me the most. I lost everything. Everything that could've defined me is gone, good as ghosted.

I did more than just pull back the veil and peer through to the other side. I fell in: all the way to rock bottom. I should be dead. For a brief moment, I actually was.

I've seen what's on the other side. It's gray and cold and endless.

An ocean of ash.

There is no light at the end of the tunnel. No angels singing. No pearly gates. There is only this life. Once it's gone, our only hope for the afterlife is that our memories remain in the hearts of those still living. Those are the vessels we inhabit. I don't know if you can find comfort in that, but that's all I hold on to. That's the only truth there is, like Peggy Lee sang, so let's keep dancing.

My parting gift from my parents was access to the family lawyer. My father did this to keep his name out of the papers, but still. You want to talk about lawsuits? Imagine being the drug-addled subject of a massive arson trial. I'll forever be known as the addict who set a housing development on fire. Manslaughter was a miracle. Most of my charges were reduced as long as I agreed to enter a treatment program. White privilege in action.

Rehab saved my life. It allowed me to heal. I gave up Ghost. I made a choice: *I want to live.* That right there—that simple sentence—is the first step. Life can begin with those four words. But you have to believe.

Now I help others who are haunted. I started Richmond Revenants Recovery—RRR—a few months back. I wanted to reclaim *revenant*: someone who returns from the dead. If that's not spot-on for a person with addiction crawling out from the sinkhole of their haunting, I don't know what is.

As a recovering addict of Ghost myself, I feel like I can be a counselor to others who are just beginning the process of pulling free from their phantoms. We meet in church basements throughout the city: consecrated soil for people with substance use disorder. I pull out the foldout chairs and set them up in a circle, just like the ring we're sitting in now. This is our hallowed ground. We're safe here.

I start our meetings off by speaking about my own path to recovery. How I'm still on it. How I relapsed. How I came *this close* to haunting that house forever. I could've easily been just another phantom wandering its halls, drifting through its rooms, staring out its windows.

I've met so many wonderful people these last few months. People who lost so much. It's our task—my goal—to help these people rediscover something worth living for again. That takes time. I say, let it. As long as it takes.

We need to find a better way to live with our ghosts. Ignoring them gets you nowhere. After I cleaned myself up, I realized the best way—the only way, really—to keep living is to acknowledge the past. I have to try, at least. It's the only way to coexist now.

So I look. I acknowledge their pain the only way I can: I let them know they are seen. That they are not forgotten. I don't turn away anymore. I look at them head-on. In their eyes.

Ghost won't let us look away anymore. We have to learn to live with them. Our dead.

Ghost stories spread. They pass from one person to the next— *Hey, you heard about this new drug? Hey, you know where I can score some Ghost? Hey, you know where I can get haunted?*—until everybody's heard of it. This is something new and old all at once: a strung-out séance, a planchette in a pill. The media has caught on now, reporting harrowing tales of drug-addicted teens putting together "bake sales." This isn't stopping. There have already been reports of a dozen strange overdoses across the country—and those numbers are only climbing.

If anything, Ghost is just beginning.

I'm here to tell you—all of you—that you can beat this addiction. I'm living proof. I chose life. You can, too. All you have to say is four simple words: *I want to live.*

Being here is another step to getting your life back on track. There's more work to be done, believe me, tons more . . . but you've already made the hardest decision of all.

You chose life over death.

Now let's get living.

———————

The housing market is finally crawling out from its slump. Shady Acres had to be completely rebuilt from the ground up. Thirty people died that day. Some of those people were my friends.

The story I told the police, and eventually the barrage of lawyers, was a watered-down version of what actually happened. No Ghost. Just some junkies getting in over their head, how their brains were so fried they didn't even realize the house they were squatting in was on fire. Apparently that's an easier pill for these insurance companies to swallow. The initial developers sold the property to a new group of investors: a clean slate. The developers razed most of the properties in the development, tearing down the burnt skeletons to build new, sturdy houses.

I only return to Hopewell when I'm at my lowest. Sometimes I won't even realize I'm doing it until I'm turning onto the interstate. I'll find myself driving around the housing development—just to see. Any trace of what had happened here a year ago is long gone now.

They don't even call the neighborhood Shady Acres anymore, can you believe that? It's called Greenfield now. Like changing the name is all it takes to wipe its history clear. You can take the tombstones away, but that doesn't mean the graves aren't still buried below.

I thought about changing my name at one point, too, but I know I'll never be able to run away from who I am. I'll always be Erin Hill, just as Greenfield will always be Shady Acres to me. It's what takes root in the ground that I really worry about. The skin is just skin. But what about the roots that reach down deep, grabbing hold of the earth, lingering out of sight? Sometimes that shit grows back. Any person with addiction will tell you: the urge never truly goes away. It's always there, biding its time when you're at your weakest. Then it whispers into your ear—

You wanna get haunted?

I show up for Moving Day, which is the day all the new homeowners will move into Greenfield. Completely cornball. You have to see it to believe it.

I park my car further off from the development and walk the rest of the way. Green and white balloons are tethered to the main gate. They whip frantically about whenever a breeze blows through. Each mailbox has its own balloon, too. There's a welcoming committee, hired helpers wearing green T-shirts going door-to-door with fresh-ly baked brownies to give folks a feeling of entering a cozy, quaint neighborhood full of friends and family.

Anything to erase the taint of what had happened here. Do any of these families know? About me? *Erin Hill, popped a ghost in a pill, strung-out arsonist who liked to kill kill kill . . .*

There's enough going on that nobody seems to notice me, or care. I could be anyone. Hell—maybe I could even live here, in one of these houses. Can't I?

I make my way to the house. I'm saying *the* house—it's not ours, not anymore. I promise myself that I won't step onto the lawn. As much as I want to believe it could've been my life—my house, my family—it never was. Not really. But there's that ache, the low-watt-age throb, the itch in my skin. Even now, I can feel Silas.

There's a family unloading their belongings from a U-Haul, busy worker bees coming and going from the paved driveway into their home, then repeating it all over again.

I look up and spot a young girl in the window of her new bed-room. She's about six or seven, something of a tomboy from what I can see. She notices me in the street and I feel like I've been caught, so I wave to her. She waves back, all five fingers.

That had been Lonnie's room. The nursery.

That was never your future.

The corner of the girl's room fluctuates. I see it so clearly. A sil-houette. It looks like—

Amara

—but it's just a shadow, of course no one's there. Can this house still be haunted? I burned it down, scorched all its ghosts away. This house is brand-new. New bones. A clean slate.

So whose ghosts are inside now?

The lawn is a sumptuous, lush green, immaculately manicured. I don't think I've ever seen grass this vibrant before. It doesn't look natural; must be soaked in chemicals. They've planted a fully grown tree off to the side, a few yards from the street, pretending that it's been here all along. There's even a swing tied to one of its branches.

In the shade, beneath the swing, I notice a cluster of mushrooms forming a perfect circle.

What are you doing, Erin, what are you doing—

I step off the street, entering the lawn. I want a closer look. I need to see. To make sure.

Don't do this, Erin, please don't do this—

Just as my feet touch the grass, the toadstools turn toward me. Taking me in. Their fleshy stems flex, aware that I'm standing above them. Watching me. Bearing witness.

Erin you can stop Erin you can turn back turn away—

The past is never quite through with us, is it?

Don't look don't look don't—

The toadstools move in unison, following me. I take a step to the left, then the right, just to test them. Sure enough, the stalks lean in whichever direction I go. They sense me here, know who I am, and I know who they are. I almost say his name out loud, but I hold my tongue.

You're stronger than this, Erin. Just a look. What can it hurt? *Don't do it please don't—*

I lean over. The patterns across the mushroom's umbrellas fluctuate in unison, rippling rhythmically together in gentle waves of brown and yellow and orange and red.

Don't do this, Erin, don't don't DON'T—

I pluck a mushroom. Just one. Its stem snaps so easily.

ERIN

The cap looks like a tiny egg, pale ivory. I roll it around in my palm, then bring it to my nose. There's a meaty aroma to it. Already I can smell the earthiness, feel it seep into my skin.

Silas says take . . .

Silas says eat . . .

This is my body.

Silas doesn't say. So I slip the cap in my pocket before I second guess myself and ask—*what are you doing, Erin*—even though I know the answer already.

I'm taking him home.

Acknowledgments

To Andrew Mittman for planting the original seed of this story in my mind.

To everyone at Quirk Books: To my gurus Jhanteigh Kupihea and Rebecca Gyllenhaal. To Nicole De Jackmo, Gabrielle Bujak, Jen Murphy, Jaime-Lee Nardone, and Christina Tatulli. To Jane Morley, Mandy Sampson, John McGurk, and David Borgenicht. To Andie Reid for the amazing cover.

To Nick McCabe and everyone at The Gotham Group. To Eddie Gamarra. To Judith Karfiol.

To Chris Steib. To Estelle Olivia, Andrew Shaffer, Kyle Jarrow, and Nat Cassidy.

To Indrani. To the boys. Don't do drugs, guys . . .

To the friends I've lost. To the original Four.

Elements from previously published short stories "coatroom," "the battle of belle isle," "fairy ring," and "cyan, magenta, yellow and key" were used for this novel.

The following books proved invaluable to me during the writing of this novel: *Superstition* by David Ambrose, *Mushrooms and Mankind: The Impact of Mushrooms on Human Consciousness and Religion* by James Arthur, *Strange Frequencies: The Extraordinary Story of the Technological Quest for the Supernatural* by Peter Bebergal, *Bone Parish* by Cullen Bunn, *Junky* by William S. Burroughs, *Altered States* by Paddy Chayefsky, *Ghostland: An American History in Haunted Places* by Colin Dickey, "Dead Means Dead" by Steve Foxe and Michael Dialynas, *The Day of St. Anthony's Fire* by John G. Fuller, *Fungi* edited by Orrin Grey and Silvia Moreno-Garcia, *The Return* by Rachel Harrison, *Japanese Ghost Stories* by Lafcadio Hearn, *Magic Mushrooms in Religion and Alchemy* by Clark Heinrich, "The Voice in the Night" by William Hope Hodgson, *Night Parade of Dead Souls: Japanese Ghost Paintings* edited by Jack Hunter, *Pet Sematary* by Stephen King, "A Thousand Deaths" by Jack London, "From Beyond" by H. P. Lovecraft, *Fruiting Bodies and Other Fungi* by Brian Lumley, *In the Dream House* by Carmen Maria Machado, *Bright Lights, Big City* by Jay McInerney, *Mexican Gothic* by Silvia Moreno-Garcia, *Calling the Spirits: A History of Séances* by Lisa Morton, *Ghosts: A Haunted History* by Lisa Morton, "On the Haunted Lives of Girls and Women" by Rachel Eve Moulton, "The Facts in the Case of M. Valdemar" by Edgar Allan Poe, *Psilocybin and Mushrooms Cultivation* by Henry J. Powel, *Common Phantoms: An American History of Psychic Science* by Alicia Puglionesi, *Dark Archives: A Librarian's Investigation into the Science and History of Books Bound in Human Skin* by Megan Rosenbloom, *The Little Stranger* by Sarah Waters, and "Afterward" by Edith Wharton.

ABANDONED BOAT IN CHESAPEAKE CONNECTED TO UNSOLVED MISSING PERSONS CASE

BRANDYWINE, Va. The Virginia Coast Guard is searching throughout the Chesapeake Bay for a local fisherman after his boat was discovered abandoned on the southern shore of Gwynn's Island.

Henry McCabe, 35, is the owner of the 1974 Chesapeake *Deadrise*. The boat was discovered run aground by a passerby, who noted signs of recent occupancy, including food and children's clothes. Attempts to locate McCabe have been unsuccessful.

Spokesperson Sally Campbell said, "No distress calls were made to our current knowledge, and no hazardous weather was present. So far there are no signs of foul play."

The discovery of the abandoned boat deepens the mystery around McCabe, who was a person of interest in the disappearance of his 8-month-old son, Skyler, in 2018. No charges are being filed at this time.

Matthews County Fire, Poquoson Fire, and the Virginia Marine Resources Commission are aiding in the search.

Ghost Eaters Book Club Discussion Questions

1. At the beginning of the book, readers are introduced to college friends Silas, Erin, Amara, and Tobias in a cemetery. What were your first impressions of the group? And how does this introduction foreshadow future events?

2. After losing Silas to an overdose, Erin is dealing with both guilt and grief. Which emotion do you think drives her to take Ghost?

3. The pill-popping séance that Erin, Amara, and Tobias conduct occurs in an unfinished and abandoned housing development. Why do you think the author chose this setting?

4. Erin experiences unfathomable side effects under the influence of Ghost. Which side effect stuck with you the most? And why do you think she still kept going back for more despite the side effects?

5. Would you take a pill like Ghost in order to have the opportunity to be reunited with a loved one?

6. Addiction takes a horrifying turn at the end of the novel. Did you find the process of addiction up to that point realistic or relatable?

7. How do you think the use of the supernatural in this book captured the real-life horrors of addiction and America's sordid history?

8. What do you imagine happens to Erin after the book ends?